ISBN: 979-8-9929483-1-8
Library of Congress Control Number: 2025906151

PUBLISHING

Edited by Brilliant Cut Editing and Represent Publishing

Book Cover Design by 100Covers

SHADOWED SECRET

SHADOWED SECRET

A THRILLER

S.F. BAUMGARTNER

FB PUBLISHING

AUTHOR'S NOTE

To all readers, especially residents and those familiar with the state of Florida, I wish to clarify that the town of Marian and the Mirror Estate are purely fictional creations for this series.

All characters and events depicted in this novel are born from my imagination. Any resemblance to actual people, living or dead, or to real-life events is entirely coincidental.

RECAPS

BURIED SECRETS - WHERE IT ALL BEGINS, BOOK 1

Twenty-five-year-old Dylan Roche barely has time to mourn his mom before an attorney appears with an invitation to his long-lost maternal grandmother's opulent estate. Eager to learn about the family he believed dead, and armed with a mysterious key his mom gave him before her death, he's ready to uncover what he believes are buried family secrets.

After a lifetime of scraping by with his mom, he's shocked she grew up wealthy. But, while the estate is lavish, something's off, and he can't shake the haunting feeling that he's being watched. As he delves deeper, he unearths his family's dark history tied to organized crime. His focus, however, remains unshaken, latched onto what the mysterious key unlocks.

At last, he locates the buried box the key opens. Then, along with those buried secrets, he discovers that the ever-present, sinister aura he's been sensing is his mother's twin sister, believed to have died shortly after birth. Very much alive, this ghost is now a criminal mastermind out to kill him. Although he dodges her murder attempt, he's left questioning everything he thought he knew about family, trust, and his past.

LIVING SECRETS, BOOK 2

Twenty-two-year-old hotel worker Lily Tso has grown up in Hong Kong believing she's an orphan. Then her mother, Olivia, who's alive and working for the US government—possibly as a spy—entrusts Lily with a mission. Lily is to deliver an antidote for an experimental biological weapon to her father, US Senator Simon Roth.

FBI Special Agent Kyle Peters is assigned to get Lily safely to the US and to her father. Posing as her boyfriend, he works with Dylan Roche, a young tycoon asked to assist them. But the trio soon finds themselves pursued by mysterious assailants in a harrowing life-or-death chase.

Undercover Agent Olivia Tso, code-named Phoenix, has infiltrated the organization run by the Ghost (Dylan's aunt) and thinks she can stay in the background during this operation. But when Kyle's shot, Dylan injured, and Lily kidnapped, Olivia must join forces with Simon, her former lover and Lily's father, and an FBI task force led by Ron Peters, Kyle's father.

Symptoms of the bioweapon soon start to appear among the population. After multiple setbacks, the team locates Lily. They deliver the antidote and other critical information to Simon. While a few casualties occur due to the virus, global catastrophe is ultimately contained.

Now, Lily's reunited with her long-lost parents, but a new world of familial connections and covert operations awaits this fast-becoming tight-knit group.

FORGOTTEN SECRET, BOOK 3

In Forgotten Secret, Clara Khoury, a magazine writer who lost her memories two decades ago, faces a turning point when a TV news report about a grisly discovery triggers a fragment of her past. Married to Dr. Michael Khoury and mother to Faith and Jason, Clara's led a stable life until this moment.

Driven to investigate the murder for a magazine article, Clara embarks on a journey, but each step leads her closer to her forgotten history. As her investigation unearths troubling hints about her past, her persistence attracts attention, including attempts on her life.

Despite mounting evidence and suspicion, Clara refuses to believe her husband, who once saved her, could be involved. Then their daughter, Faith, is abducted. Concurrently, a criminal mastermind known as the Ghost seeks to live on Mirror Estate and, in exchange for the privilege, provides a lead to a man named Ray Ho.

Eva, operating undercover to uncover the truth about her aunt Clara, whom she believed was tracked, stumbles upon Faith instead. Unaware that Faith is her cousin, Eva rescues her with the help of a task force.

The climax reveals a harrowing past event: At a party, Clara witnessed her friend's ex-boyfriend assault and kill her. Then Ray Ho's men, called in to clean up, took both women. While Clara's friend's body was left in the building where her remains were eventually found, Clara was intended to be sold. However, Clara recognized Ray Ho from her part-time job at the foundation and became a liability. Unable to risk being exposed, Ray Ho shot Clara, leading to the traumatic amnesia that defined her life for the next two decades. This revelation ties Clara's fragmented past with the present, culminating in a dramatic and poignant conclusion.

TANGLED SECRETS, BOOK 4

Grace Benson, a young schoolteacher, lives a quiet life until a disturbing note shatters her sense of normalcy. Meanwhile, wedding planner Sheila Mitchell suspects her current husband,

Doug, of being a spy. Seeking help, she turns to her ex-husband, FBI agent Ron, and their son, Kyle. Initially, they dismiss Doug's behavior as infidelity, but their assumptions change dramatically when Sheila returns home to find Doug murdered. Sheila is knocked unconscious and awakens with the murder weapon in her hand, making her the prime suspect.

At the Marino Hotel, Lily takes charge of the Private Select Program and uncovers irregularities in an account, prompting her own investigation. Olivia, determined to root out a mole leaking classified information, faces growing danger. As Grace and Kyle become targets of a kill order, they are placed in protective custody. Lily's investigation leads to her mysterious disappearance, prompting Dylan to embark on a perilous search to find her.

Olivia eventually uncovers the mole, who meets an unexpected end. During the investigation into Doug's death, his secret double life is revealed. A SWAT team, led by Ana, successfully rescues Grace and Kyle from imminent danger. Meanwhile, Lily is taken into protective custody by an undercover spy, and Dylan is captured by a drug cartel during his search for her. In a dramatic turn of events, the undercover spy ultimately rescues Dylan, bringing the intense saga to a close.

HIDDEN SECRETS, BOOK 5

When Connor Murray spots a man from his past—his parents' killer—his fears resurface. Fr. Phil, who once sheltered him, warns that danger might be closer than Connor thinks.

Meanwhile, Olivia Tso, a covert operative, investigates Moneyman, a criminal financier tied to counterfeit currency and the Perez crime family. Dylan Roche, heir to the Marino empire, discovers that his family's estate may hold hidden treasures, but his aunt, the Ghost, isn't the only one searching for them. At the same time, young Sean Murray uncovers a hidden passageway, raising concerns about unseen threats.

Things escalate when Grace Benson is kidnapped, prompting her mother, FBI agent Ana Ruiz, and FBI agent Kyle Peters to track her captors. A mysterious ring at the scene hints at a deeper conspiracy. Simultaneously, Congressman Javier Jimenez is murdered, and his campaign manager, Nina Rodriguez, becomes a prime suspect—shocking Olivia and her fiancé, Simon Roth, who realize Javier had been hiding secrets before his death.

With FBI Task Force 629 racing to unravel these interwoven threats—spanning political assassinations, hidden fortunes, and criminal masterminds—the novel builds to a tense and unpredictable climax.

Relationship Chart

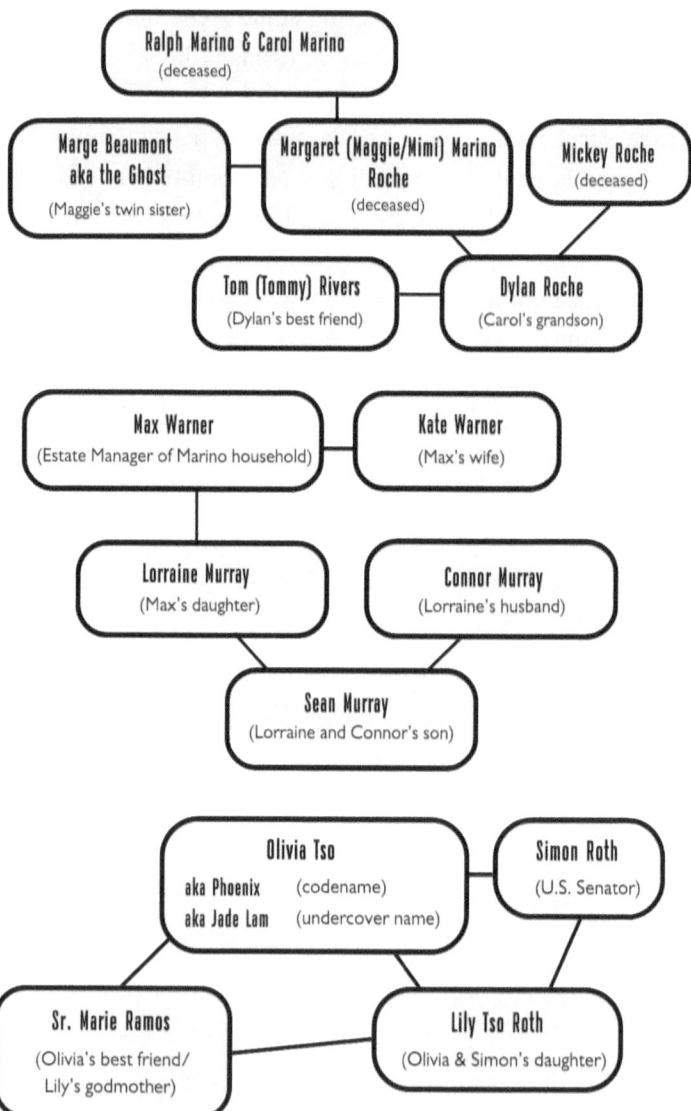

Ralph Marino & Carol Marino
(deceased)

Marge Beaumont aka the Ghost
(Maggie's twin sister)

Margaret (Maggie/Mimi) Marino Roche
(deceased)

Mickey Roche
(deceased)

Tom (Tommy) Rivers
(Dylan's best friend)

Dylan Roche
(Carol's grandson)

Max Warner
(Estate Manager of Marino household)

Kate Warner
(Max's wife)

Lorraine Murray
(Max's daughter)

Connor Murray
(Lorraine's husband)

Sean Murray
(Lorraine and Connor's son)

Olivia Tso
aka Phoenix (codename)
aka Jade Lam (undercover name)

Simon Roth
(U.S. Senator)

Sr. Marie Ramos
(Olivia's best friend/
Lily's godmother)

Lily Tso Roth
(Olivia & Simon's daughter)

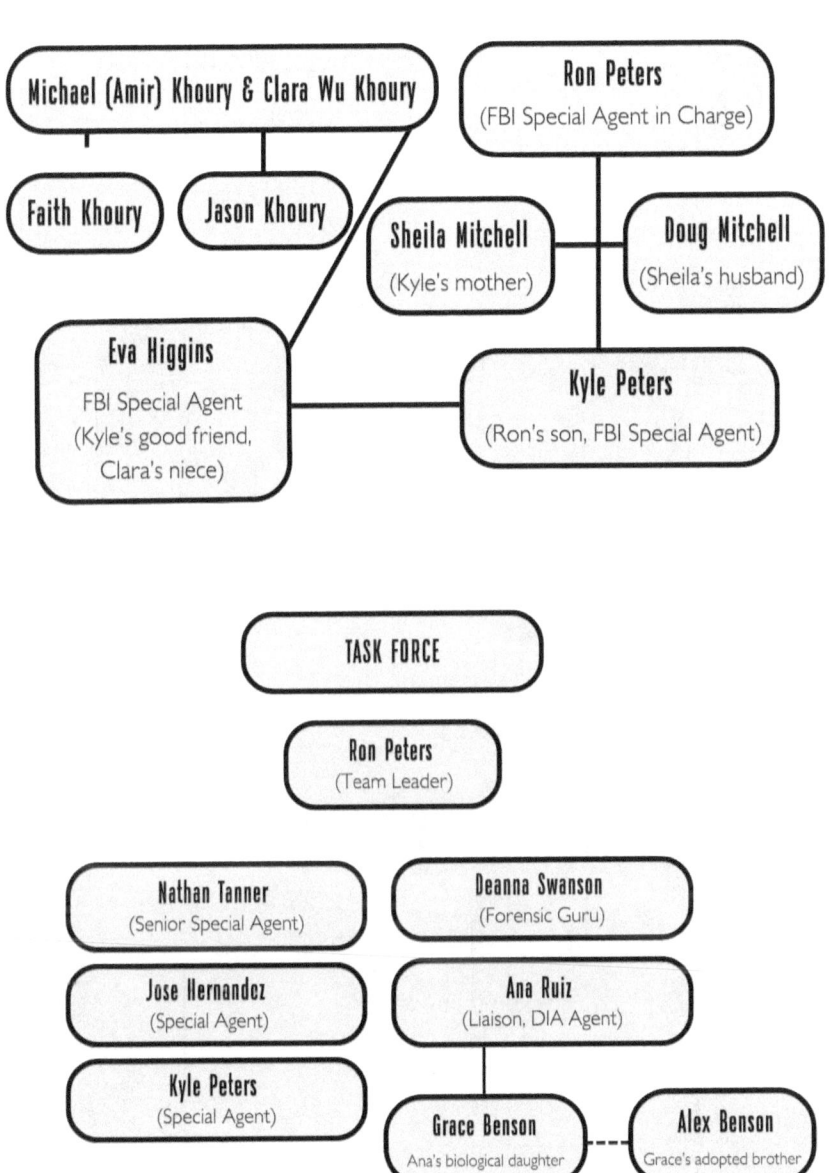

Michael (Amir) Khoury & Clara Wu Khoury

Faith Khoury

Jason Khoury

Ron Peters
(FBI Special Agent in Charge)

Sheila Mitchell
(Kyle's mother)

Doug Mitchell
(Sheila's husband)

Eva Higgins
FBI Special Agent
(Kyle's good friend,
Clara's niece)

Kyle Peters
(Ron's son, FBI Special Agent)

TASK FORCE

Ron Peters
(Team Leader)

Nathan Tanner
(Senior Special Agent)

Deanna Swanson
(Forensic Guru)

Jose Hernandez
(Special Agent)

Ana Ruiz
(Liaison, DIA Agent)

Kyle Peters
(Special Agent)

Grace Benson
Ana's biological daughter

Alex Benson
Grace's adopted brother

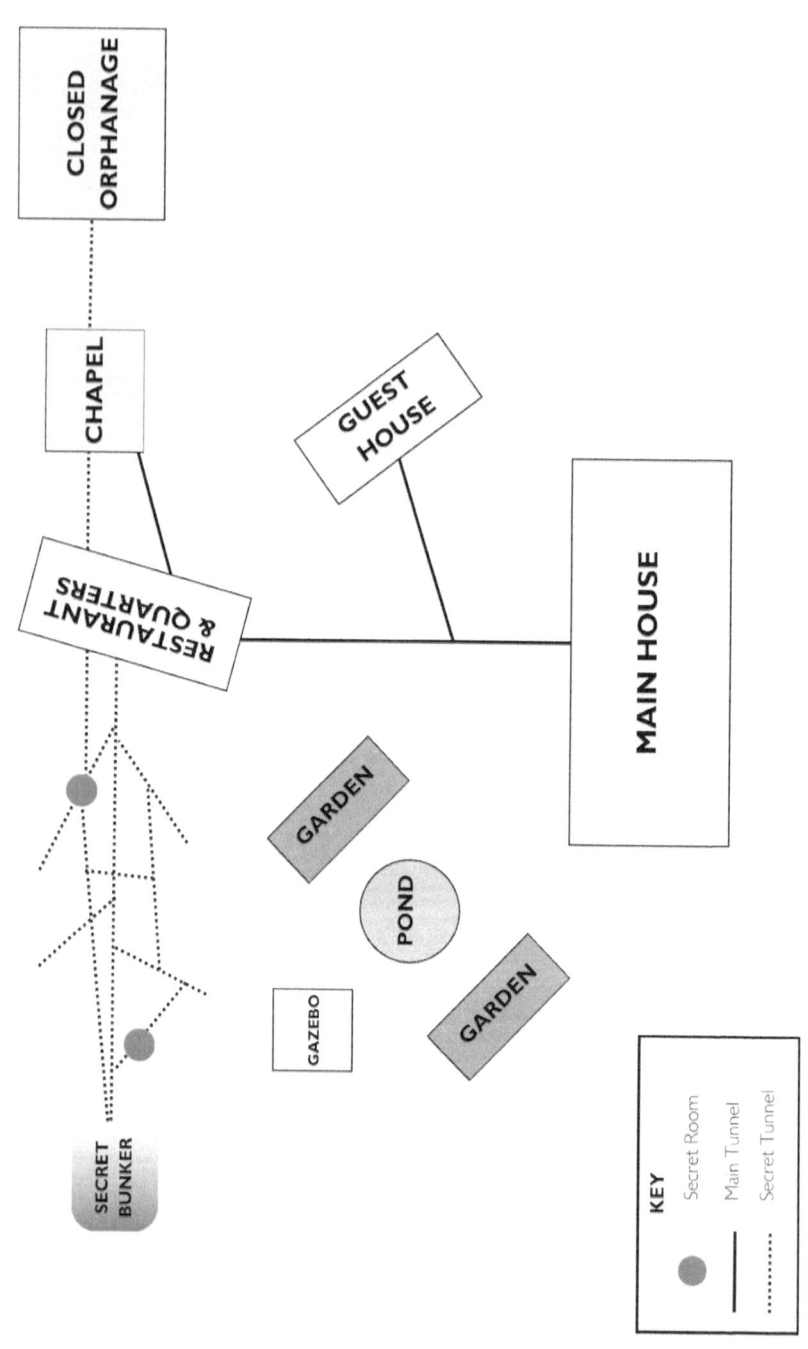

PRAISE FOR BURIED SECRETS - WHERE IT ALL BEGINS: BOOK 1

I felt that the author wove a story that had twists and turns with unexpected moments sprinkled here and there.

— DELPHIA, GOODREADS

They say that dynamite comes in small packages. This one was definitely loaded with plenty of information that will blow your mind.

— TAMMY, GOODREADS

What a great story! This had enough thrill and mystery to draw me in even though it was a short novella.

— MEGAN, GOODREADS

PRAISE FOR LIVING SECRETS: BOOK 2

A great crime novel! Loved that it picked up right where the prequel left off. Loved all the chasing of Lily and who was after her. Loved the cliffhanger and can't wait to read the next one!!

— KRYSTA, GOODREADS

The book is one you will not want to put down, and if you read it at night, you will jump at every noise and check the locks on your doors and windows. Highly recommend.

— BARBARA, GOODREADS

Edge of your seat reading that keeps you guessing until the end. Plenty of drama with twists and turns that keeps you going until the end. Great characters to follow along on this adventure. Good read.

— RHONDA, GOODREADS

PRAISE FOR FORGOTTEN SECRET: BOOK 3

PRAISE FOR TANGLED SECRETS: BOOK 4

These books are so addicting—I don't want to do anything else except for finishing the book! The suspense and anticipation was awesome. Getting reacquainted with all of the characters—Olivia, Dylan, Lilly, Ron, Grace, etc. were all great.

— LAURA, GOODREADS

The book has infinite layers, the plot is intriguing and secrets are way too deep. The world is dangerous. The book is filled with twists and turns. The ending shook me.

— RUDRASHREE, GOODREADS

This book had amazing characters, many with secrets that seem to connect them all together. The storyline is intriguing & mysterious. I was always wondering who the person was that had their hands in both sides of the game. The ending left me shocked and ready for the story to continue.

— LUNAWOLFWY, GOODREADS

PRAISE FOR HIDDEN SECRETS: BOOK 5

If there's one thing Baumgartner knows it's suspense. If you haven't already read the first three books of this series, I'd do that. There's a wrap-up/summary of the books at the beginning, which I appreciated, but you'll get a better look at the whole picture and story if you read all of the books in order. Another great story and I can't wait to see what comes next!

— LENA, GOODREADS

What a thrilling ride into this fourth book of the series. The twist and turns keep coming and the secrets keep being revealed. I can't wait to see what is going to happen next as I know there has to be more secrets!! if you enjoy fast paced, being on the edge of your seat reading you will enjoy this series.

— CAROLYN, GOODREADS

I love how fast paced this book is! Once I started it I couldn't put it down. I HAD to know what was going to happen! Between the kidnapping and murders everything was great about this book. There were twists everywhere!

— KRYSTA, GOODREADS

PRAISE FOR SHADOWED SECRET: BOOK 5

The characters, and there were many, are of amazing talent. There is intrigue, deception, betrayal, and lots of danger. The book is a page-turner with many twists and turns. The plot was intriguing and left me trying to guess its many secrets. Unlike other thrillers I've wanted to read, this one had moments of faith and was a clean read. The ending was haunting! Can't wait to read the next one.

— J.E. GRACE, GOODREADS

This is full of action suspense and intrigue so it's right up my alley! I was hooked instantly to this gripping conspiracy thriller! I found the book fast paced and I was on the edge of my seat. I love how all the characters in the book are connected in some way, and it truly has you wondering who is behind everything. It had an open ending so I am excited to see what happens in the next book.

— NIKKI, GOODREADS

The fifth book in one of my favorite series is the best yet. I couldn't put this one down. It has lots of intrigue, mystery, humor, and teamwork. Even though the author gives a brief outline of every book, you should read the previous books first to pick up the nuances. The chart that shows how everyone is interconnected is very helpful, as is the map of the estate. The way the author interweaves storylines is masterful.

— BETTE, GOODREADS

PROLOGUE

VATICAN

PHIL

The grand splendor of St. Peter's Basilica loomed behind them, its intricate façade bathed in golden afternoon light. The ceremony had been overwhelming—the Gregorian chants, the solemn laying on of hands, the lingering fragrance of sacred chrism oil. Now, standing outside in St. Peter's Square, Phil Shagley touched the diagonal white stole draped across his chest, the mark of his new role as a transitional deacon.

Around him, groups of newly ordained deacons and priests stood with their families, posing for photos, offering blessings. A murmur of conversation mixed with the footsteps echoing across the stone pavement. The peace he felt in those sacred moments inside was already fading. Maybe it was the memories of his SEAL days, the ones that always crept up when things got quiet.

"Deacon Phil." Fr. Michael Donovan, his mentor, approached with measured steps. Walking beside him was a tall younger man with a bright expression. Fr. Stanislaw Novak, a newly ordained priest from Poland.

Phil nodded his greeting, then addressed Fr. Donovan. "Thank you for being here, Father."

Fr. Donovan clasped Phil's hand. "Of course, Phil. I wouldn't miss this for the world." Warmth smoothed his voice, but beneath it lay something else, an unspoken weight. "I'm proud of you."

Fr. Novak shook Phil's hand. "Congratulations, Deacon Shagley."

They exchanged pleasantries, speaking of the beauty of the basilica, the solemnity of the ceremony, and the uncertainty of the road ahead. The square overflowed with jubilant commotion —clergy and seminarians congratulating one another, family members embracing their sons who had taken the next step toward the priesthood. Then Novak excused himself, moving toward a group of fellow priests and guests gathered near the basilica's steps.

Fr. Donovan's expression shifted. The warmth remained, but the lightheartedness faded. His gaze held something deeper, something that pulled Phil's attention like a long-forgotten instinct.

"I heard about Leon Roche," Fr. Donovan said. "I'm sorry, Phil."

Phil stiffened. He hadn't expected his mentor to bring up his stepfather's death, let alone know about it.

"You knew?" Phil whispered. At Donovan's nod, Phil exhaled. His gaze drifted across the square, past the towering columns framing St. Peter's Basilica. "They gave me leave for the funeral. Then I had to come straight back here."

During his pause, the din of the square intruded on the silence between them.

"I understand Mickey is at St. Ann's Orphanage now."

"St. Ann's?" Phil's head snapped up. "No, that can't be right. Mickey was supposed to be with an elderly aunt. That's where he went after the funeral."

"Well, 'elderly' is the operative word. My sources told me she had a stroke and is now in a care facility. She can't take care of a teenager. Mickey's been at St. Ann's for a couple of years now."

A hollowness carved itself way into his chest. They had never been too close, not with the twelve-year gap between them. And Mickey was still just a kid when Phil left for the service. "I didn't know. Why didn't he tell me?"

"Mickey's been through a lot. I imagine he didn't want to burden you while you were in formation. But he needs you, Phil. More than ever now."

"I should have been there for him. I should have—"

"You did what you had to do," Fr. Donovan interrupted. "Anyway, that's not why I'm telling you this."

Phil lifted his gaze, waiting.

His mentor edged closer. "I wanted to talk to you about an opportunity."

Phil tensed. He knew that tone.

"You've been here in Rome for a while now, and you must be thinking about what comes next," the priest continued. "I've spoken with some people, and there's a possibility for you to be placed somewhere closer to Mickey. Fr. Bob, the pastor at the chapel parish on Mirror Estate, is nearing retirement."

Phil narrowed his eyes. "Okay…?"

"The chapel parish is connected to St. Ann's Orphanage." Donovan let that sink in. "It would give you a chance to be close to Mickey, to keep an eye on him. But there's more to it."

"What do you mean?"

Fr. Donovan scanned the bustling square, then signaled him to follow.

As Phil trailed the priest, they approached a narrow stone passageway near the basilica, partially concealed by an ornate archway. A discreet but authoritative sign affixed to the wall beside it displayed lettering etched into aged brass: Accesso Riservato—Solo Personale Autorizzato.

Phil understood it meant "Restricted Access—Authorized Personnel Only." But his mentor barely spared it a glance as he pushed open the wooden door and led Phil into the dimly lit corridor. The hustle and murmur of St. Peter's Square faded behind them.

Only then did Fr. Donovan turn to him. "The Church has... certain needs in that area. People with your experience, both military and spiritual, are rare. I'm not asking you to pick up where you left off, but I am asking you to be aware. Vatican Intelligence has interests there and believes you'd be uniquely suited to assist them. Quietly."

Phil's pulse quickened. He left the SEALs for a reason. God called him to be a priest. And yet... he still maintained his training regimen as much as possible.

"What are you suggesting? For me to serve as a priest and... what? An operative?"

"Yes, in a way only you can."

He rubbed the back of his neck and dipped his head, his blood rushing. *Lord, is this what you want for me?* Even as the thought appeared, he was at peace. When he looked up again, he already knew his answer.

"When do I leave?"

Fr. Donovan gripped Phil's shoulder. "Relax. This is not an order. You'll be notified of your transitional deacon assignment like everyone else. And we'll be in touch."

Phil glanced at the basilica behind them.

Apparently, the life he thought he left behind wasn't done with him yet.

CHAPTER 1

CHAPEL, MIRROR ESTATE

PRESENT DAY

PHIL

Phil thudded closed his leather-bound notebook, marking the conclusion of the final meeting with Olivia Tso and Simon Roth before their nuptials. The years had etched subtle lines around their eyes—crow's feet framing Olivia's bright almond-shaped eyes and deeper creases marking Simon's distinguished face beneath his salt-and-pepper hair. Though both were in their middle years, Olivia's petite, athletic frame and Simon's trim, average-height figure spoke to their vitality.

"Well, that's it!" He clasped his hands. "You've made it through all the sessions. And you're still together."

Simon chuckled. "We are definitely getting married."

She smiled at her fiancé. "We'd better."

Phil got their attention back. "The rehearsal is the day before the wedding. I hope there's no last-minute changes."

She shook her head. "We're good. We'll be here. Hard to believe it's only two weeks away."

"Here's to new beginnings." Simon clasped her hand in an affectionate squeeze. "You should show him your medal."

"Right." She reached for the necklace and pulled out the medal hanging from it. "I'm sure you're familiar with this medal."

Phil took one look at the famous Medal of the Immaculate Conception and nodded. "The Miraculous Medal. It looks heavier than any I've seen."

"It is. My best friend, Marie—a nun, by the way—gave it to me years ago. She has one too. Her grandfather, after witnessing a bullet deflect off his friend's Miraculous Medal, had one crafted from repurposed military-grade steel. He believed it saved his life when it later deflected a bullet meant for him."

Phil smiled. "I've read countless similar testimonies, illnesses cured, accidents averted. Remember it's not the medal itself, but the power comes from God."

She slid her necklace back. "So, Father, how has the parish been lately? The holidays are always a whirlwind, but anything new as we enter the new year?"

He scratched his chin. "The same, for the most part. We had an enormous turnout for all the Christmas Masses, as always. It was good to see so many faces, even if some are what we call 'C&E folks,' only showing up at Christmas and Easter. But they're part of the flock too."

"Of course," Simon agreed. "It's wonderful that they have a place they can return to, even if it's not as frequently as you might like."

Phil inclined his head. "Well said. And, of course, Fr. Jeremy's been a blessing to have around. He took some time off to visit his family. Will be back any day now."

"Are you thinking about retiring?" Olivia glanced at the wall clock.

"I'm not quite at the mandatory retirement age yet, but it's on the horizon. It's good to have Fr. Jeremy around, so I can take a break now and then. And you? Still keeping busy at work?"

To most people, she was a consultant with an elite FBI task force, though he knew she was still an intelligence operative.

"You could say that. Nothing exciting. Mostly paperwork and consulting with other agencies these days. But I manage."

"We haven't had a lot of excitement since the Ghost's move. Come to think of it, she's been rather quiet." Simon drew his fiancée's hand into his lap. "She's still giving you names, isn't she?"

"Yeah, but nobody exciting."

Marge Beaumont, aka the Ghost, a notorious criminal, had made a perplexing deal with the government since her capture about a year and a half ago. She agreed to help an elite FBI task force apprehend those on the most wanted list. In return, she would stay on the Mirror Estate grounds instead of the supermax.

Phil remained quiet. At the beginning of last year, he visited the Ghost at the Federation Detention Center.

"Remember your promise?" he asked.

A pallor crept across her features, her breath catching as her eyes went wide, darkened by something only she could see. "Yes, of course."

He narrowed his eyes. "Not what I've been hearing."

She scoffed. "I have an image to maintain. Everything is going according to plan."

"I heard you gave the order to put Grace and Kyle on a hit list."

"Absolutely not!" Those darkened eyes flashed. "It was Rook's doing. I only wanted to find out who was responsible for Jade's death. As it turned out, their parents are."

He took a deep breath and muttered a silent prayer. Ah, secrets. So many secrets. He couldn't reveal to her Jade,

Olivia's legend, wasn't dead. "The agents had to do what they had to do, but their children had nothing to do with it. Most importantly, this is not the way to salvation."

Her defiant posture didn't waver, nor did she respond.

"Listen." He leaned forward. "Soon, you'll be living on the Mirror Estate grounds. Don't even think about escaping or reneging on your promise. Any funny business, I guarantee Vatican would hear about it, and then you know what would happen."

"Father!"

Olivia's voice brought him out of his reverie. He refocused on the couple before he stood up. "I should let you two go. If I don't see you before rehearsal, enjoy your week, both of you."

He led them to the door of the parish office. The warm afternoon air met him, heavy with Florida humidity and a lingering pine scent from the holiday season. They nearly collided with Jeremy, who hustled up the path, hands tucked into his coat pockets, head down.

The young priest beamed when he saw them. "Hey, Olivia, Simon, ready for your big day?"

Simon nodded while Olivia said, "Yes. How was your visit home?"

"Wonderful, thank you. It was nice to be with family. But I'm glad to be back."

They shared goodbyes, handshakes, and well-wishes before Olivia and Simon strolled down the path.

Jeremy waved them off with a grin, then stepped closer to Phil. "Anything I should know about?"

He shook his head. "Everything is good."

Phil's gaze drifted toward the chapel. A lone figure sat in one of the pews, head bowed, hands clasped. Something about the man seemed familiar, though Phil couldn't place him. The chapel's subdued lighting cast the man in shadow, but the briefest flash of white at his collar confirmed it—a clerical collar, like his own.

Odd. It wasn't unusual to see another priest visit the chapel, but something about this one made him pause. A vague, unsettled feeling prickled at the back of his neck.

He waved Jeremy on. "You go ahead. I'm going to check on something."

The young priest continued on his way, leaving Phil to edge closer to the chapel.

"Sorry, Father, are you going in?" Leo, the longtime custodian, stopped on the chapel door's other side, a toolbox in hand. "I can come back."

"Ah, yes, the loose hinge." Phil had reported that. He frowned. The man was gone. "No, go ahead. Thank you."

He walked toward his office, his mind racing through years of faces, names, encounters. Had he seen the man before, or was it his imagination? Or perhaps, something else?

CHAPTER 2

THE GHOST'S APARTMENT, MIRROR ESTATE

OLIVIA

Olivia Tso stepped into the Ghost's confined world, a secured apartment carved out of a defunct orphanage. Sparse but functional, it offered a bolted-down table and chairs, a narrow cot, and a kitchenette. No sharp objects. No potential weapons.

Her meals arrived through a secured hatch, eaten with plastic utensils. A hum from hidden surveillance enlivened the air, a constant reminder she was never alone.

The door locked behind Olivia. The Ghost sat waiting, composed but rigid. The usual icy detachment remained, but her eyes betrayed something else—urgency.

"What's so urgent?" Olivia pulled out the chair and sat across from the prisoner.

"Victor Marlowe."

Her brow furrowed. The name meant nothing to her. "Should I know who that is?"

The Ghost threw her a disdaining glance. "You might not, but

I'm sure your FBI Art Crime division or whatever they're called is well aware of him. Think of him as the Sotheby's of the underworld. As you probably know, the Nazis looted quite a bit of artwork. Though a lot have been recovered, many are still missing. Marlowe has auctioned a few of those, especially the masterpieces by the old masters, over the years."

Unlikely an art thief would warrant the task force's time and effort.

"I know what you're thinking. So, let me tell you. Marlowe is ruthless. If he gets a scent of something valuable and he wants it, he'll do anything to get it."

Olivia braced her elbows on her knees. "What can you tell me about him?"

A shrug. "I'm sure your FBI Art Crime folks have a thick file on him."

"You're gonna have to give me more."

The Ghost sighed. "There's gonna be an auction next week. That would be the best time to catch him since he'll be online more and will need to transfer whatever item he's auctioning to the winning party. Most importantly, he'll come out of his hiding and be in town for that. I hear he has something other than a painting this time."

Olivia frowned. Next week. And her wedding was in two weeks. "And what would that be?"

"That's for you and your FBI buddies to find out." Was that a hint of a smile on her otherwise expressionless face? "Oh, please ask my nephew to come by."

Dylan Roche, the Ghost's nephew and heir to the Marino empire, had been dating Lily, Olivia and Simon's daughter, for about a year now. He'd mentioned what the Ghost wanted— something about buried treasure. As far as Olivia knew, they'd made little progress, missing half a map and a cipher. The project had been relegated to the back burner.

"I'll let him know." Olivia stood up. She couldn't shake the feeling she was being sent on another of the Ghost's elaborate schemes.

What was it this time?

CHAPTER 3

MARIAN PINES GOLF CLUB

PHIL

The morning sun hung low in the sky, and cool golden light gleamed over the manicured greens of the Marian Pines Golf Club as Phil lined up his putt. The crisp air hinted at the promise of a beautiful day, and a semblance of peace stilled his soul.

The invitation had come from Tom, a longtime friend and golf enthusiast, who insisted Phil and Jeremy join him, along with the priests Mike and Frank, for a friendly round.

"Got a nice swing there, Phil." Tom clapped him on the back as Phil's ball rolled toward the hole. "I heard your parish was having a charity tournament in a couple of weeks. Are you participating?"

"Sure am. It's a fundraiser to reopen the school on Mirror Estate grounds. The former senator Simon Roth is running the foundation and spearheading the endeavor." The orphanage and the school had made an impact on Simon's life. And the former senator wanted other disadvantaged children to have the same opportunity.

"Sounds like a great cause."

The priests chatted as they strolled to the next hole, the relaxed camaraderie as much a part of the game as the swings and putts. The conversations bounced between their respective parishes' upcoming events and recaps of Friday night's football.

By the time they reached the ninth hole, Phil couldn't shake the feeling that he was being watched. And his watcher was pretending to be a fellow golfer. When his fellow golfing priests announced they were heading to the clubhouse for refreshments, he surreptitiously scanned the course.

Jeremy lingered by the golf cart, adjusting the side mirror. It reflected a man lining up a shot a short distance away, but something felt off. Muted polo, khaki slacks, golf cap. Perfectly normal, yet he wasn't playing like the others.

Jeremy nodded toward the mirror. "Something tells me he's not here for the birdies."

"Good observation." Phil checked the image without turning. "You still got it."

Phil had picked Jeremy for his military background. How satisfying that he hadn't lost his situational awareness.

Jeremy chuckled. "Since the tunnel excitement last year, I'm always ready." Then his expression hardened. "So, why is he watching us?"

"I don't know." Phil considered his golfing friends, their ages, positions, former professions. Then he glanced back at the reflection. Could he be the target?

RECTORY

After the game, Phil and Jeremy returned to the rectory. Jeremy went to his side. Back in the day when the nuns were living there, there were two wings, basically houses with a connecting entrance hall. Now, Phil lived in one wing, and Jeremy took the other. God willing, if those days returned, Jeremy and he would have to share the house.

He opened the door to…

"Buongiorno. Good game?" The priest who'd visited the chapel yesterday afternoon sat at the kitchen table, reading something on his phone. Now that he could see him clearly, Phil placed him. Although older now with lines around his eyes and topped by a bald crown, his face remained the same.

"Stan Novak, isn't it?"

"Good memory."

Phil muttered a silent prayer before saying, "Back in the day, I could have shot you."

"True." Novak lowered his phone. "*You* may have taken a hiatus—*I* haven't. Been in the game for thirty years."

Something tingled at the base of Phil's skull. He hadn't seen this man since his pilgrimage to the Vatican years ago. Why was he here? "And you couldn't just come to the parish office like normal people?"

The last time he had heard from him was soon after Marge's arrest, a year and a half ago. Why the Vatican Intelligence would work with Marge was beyond Phil. There was a reason the woman was a criminal mastermind. She was always ten steps ahead of everyone. If not for the leverage the intelligence had on her, he'd have wondered if they'd all been played.

Novak tapped his heart. "Mea culpa. But this is important. The book is missing."

Phil froze. It had been years since he heard about the book and the secrets along with it. *Act natural.* He went to the fridge and grabbed a water bottle. "Stolen? And you came all the way here to tell me this?"

"Yes, security footage was wiped for a few minutes, just enough time for someone to go in and take it. And no, I'm here to attend a conference with Cardinal Bernard."

The way Novak pressed his lips together before he spoke gave Phil pause. Could he be lying? But why? He downed a third of the bottle. "A pro, then."

"Looks that way. We'd like you to find it."

"Why me? Don't you have investigators for that? And I've been out of the game for ages."

"Rumor is the book contains names of covert operatives." So Novak wasn't going to answer his question.

"Who made that up?"

Novak shrugged. "Whoever stole it? Anyway, we need to find it."

"Again, why me? I have a parish here."

"Because you're here with the Beaumont woman. And you have an assistant pastor now."

"You think she has something to do with it?"

"Can't rule it out. Even though she claims she's playing ball, I never know if she can be trusted."

In the few times Phil had been to see her, he hadn't gotten the impression she would do this. But then again, she was devious. "She's been behaving. The last time I talked to her, she assured me things were going well."

"She went off script."

"That's an understatement. She claims she has an image to maintain." Phil sighed. "There's just one issue with her. She's intent on avenging a confidant's death."

A frown creased his visitor's forehead. "Who? She doesn't care for anyone, uh, almost anyone."

"I suppose it proves she's human, if nothing else."

Novak drummed his fingers on the table. "It's been over a year. She still hasn't delivered."

"She said things were moving according to plan."

"Has she given you any hint at all?"

Phil shook his head.

As soon as Novak left, Phil pulled his phone out, tapped out a text, and hit Send.

CHAPTER 4

MARINA

RON

Ron Peters leaned back in his boat. The waves' gentle rocking and the crisp morning air created the perfect Saturday escape. The calmer waters and cooler temperatures made it easy to lose track of time as the sunlight danced on the ripples. He was just settling into the moment when his cell phone's sharp ring shattered the tranquility. He muttered, freed it from his pocket, and checked the screen. Olivia. With a resigned sigh, he swiped to answer.

"Ron here."

"Hey, the Ghost gave us a marching order."

"Who is it?" Sheila, his ex-wife sitting next to him, whispered.

He mouthed, "Olivia." He set his can of beer in the cupholder, then turned his attention back to the phone. "Wait a minute. Why did you go see her on a Saturday?"

"That's because *Her Highness* summoned me. She claimed it was urgent."

"Well, is it?"

"It is time-sensitive. The target is Victor Marlowe. He's got something of value, not a painting, up on auction next week on the dark web. She claims the Art Crime folks would know who he is. According to her, the best time to nab him would be when he delivers the goods."

While she talked, his gaze landed on Sheila. He wasn't religious, but his ex-wife was. Was God giving them a second chance? They had reconnected since the violent death of her second husband. The recent shift in the task force mission gave rise to his new title, Special Agent in Charge. With it came a new set of responsibilities and less fieldwork or irregular hours, and in all of this, he learned to balance his life more. Kyle's transfer was a wake-up call.

"Dad, I'm requesting a transfer to FCU."

This was a surprise. "I thought you liked it here."

"I do. But Grace, uh, we, uh, kind of have this problem. Two abductions and then she saw the guy get shot dead, so she's kind of..." Kyle fidgeted.

"Worried you might meet the same fate. I understand. Your mom had the same concern."

"I'd have picked Cyber Squad if I had the skills. Almost zero risk of getting shot." A pause. "And she doesn't like the hours."

Ron chuckled. "Of course. Your mom's biggest complaint."

He sighed. Ana had been suspended pending investigation for failing to disclose pertinent information on her application. "Will you stay until Ana is back? Or until I find a suitable replacement?"

Olivia was speaking. "...I'm not sure if it's legit or if the Ghost is just yanking our chains, but I'm passing on the info."

Ron rubbed his chin. "Okay, let's—" His phone buzzed with another incoming message. Eva, an undercover agent.

Encrypted. He opened it, scanning the contents. Auction. He stood up.

"Olivia, I think we have a case."

"I'll conference in, if you need me." She disconnected.

He slipped the phone into his pocket, his mind still on the conversation. It wasn't until the boat lurched forward, the motor's steady rumble filling the air, that he realized Sheila had started it up and headed back to shore. Yep, there she was at the helm.

"I know, duty calls!" she called. "I'll save the bass."

After a few quick steps, he hugged her from behind. "Thank you."

"Should we tell Kyle we're going to the wedding together?"

"You're their wedding coordinator. Don't you need to be there earlier?" Answering a question with a question, he could spot his own stalling tactics.

"I do. But you'll still be my plus-one, and I'll be yours."

"You know, they got engaged on Thanksgiving the year before last. Wonder why they set the date this far out?" More stalling.

"I don't know. I have clients who have been engaged longer. So, should we?"

What a loaded question. Letting Kyle know seemed to signal something. Was Ron ready for that? "Er, let's do this after this case."

Her soft sigh escaped. "Sure. Now, go catch some bad guys!"

He let go of her, took his phone out again, and speed-dialed one. When his senior agent answered, he wasted no time. "Tanner, round up the troop and get them to the office ASAP."

"On it, boss."

CHAPTER 5

THE GHOST'S APARTMENT, MIRROR ESTATE

DYLAN

The crisp scent of fresh paint and industrial cleaner lingered as Dylan Roche stepped into the remodeled space. Sleek yet minimal, it felt controlled rather than confining. Recessed lighting softened the reinforced walls, and shatterproof windows let in the morning light.

By chance, he had stayed at the estate last night, and since he was in the area, he'd best see what his aunt wanted before heading back to town.

The Ghost was already seated at the sturdy table, her posture relaxed yet commanding. Even in her basic, state-issued clothing, she wore confidence like armor. The faintest smirk quirked her lips, her eyes sharp as they met his.

He pulled out the chair opposite her, the metal legs scraping against the wooden floor. "Olivia said you wanted to see me."

"Yes." She folded her hands. "Have you found anything?"

His jaw tightened. Straight to the point. No pleasantries, no pretense.

"I told you. No." He kept his voice even, measured. "If you

have any tips, now's the time to share. If there's some treasure buried out there, I don't know where it is or how to find it."

Which wasn't entirely true.

The half map, the key—everything he, Tommy, and Lily had discovered—he wouldn't let the Ghost know about. Not yet. Not until he understood what it all meant. After all, she might have the map's other half or at least know where it was. She always knew more than she let on.

Her fingers tapped the tabletop, a steady, deliberate rhythm. Not a fidget—the Ghost didn't fidget. A silent tell, something calculated. Something was off about her today.

"Do you even know what our ancestors buried?" she asked.

He frowned. "What's that supposed to mean?"

She inclined herself his way, a confidant cozying in. "During World War II, the Nazis looted a lot of valuables. Priceless artwork, gold, heirlooms."

Dylan stiffened. "Our ancestors were Italian, not German."

She smirked. "Not all Nazis were German."

His stomach churned. "Are you suggesting they were Nazi sympathizers? That they looted artwork?"

"No." She shook her head. "But they could have been benefi-ciaries of some ill-gotten valuables."

He let out a dry, humorless laugh. "That's rich, coming from you. Ill-gotten valuables. You've got plenty of those."

Her smirk faded, and her expression hardened. "This isn't about me."

"Isn't it?"

She ignored the jab. "Do some research. Look at the people our family was tied to. The businesses they ran."

He sat back. "Why don't you just spit it out? What are you trying to say?"

Her gaze didn't waver. "Check out the names Visconti and Moretti. Not just Marino."

His breath caught. The old photos, the grainy black-and-white images he'd found... Could some of those figures be Visconti and Moretti? "How are they connected to this allegedly buried treasure?"

"You'll figure it out." Her lips curled again. "You're smarter than you look."

He muttered a curse.

She wagged a finger. "Now, now, language."

His head knew this was his mother's identical twin, but sometimes his heart refused to accept it. Moments like these, when she played the role of a normal person, his heart wished his mother was still alive.

Snap out of it.

"What's your angle here? Why now? What's the rush?"

Her fingers stilled. "Because we aren't the only ones looking for it. And we need to find it before anyone else does."

His pulse quickened. "Who else is looking? Who else knows about it?"

She met his gaze, unblinking. "People you don't want to mess with." A pause. "Now, don't lose the key."

Lightheaded, he braced both hands on the table. She couldn't know about the key. The one he and Lily found a year ago. The one he told no one about, not even Olivia.

He swallowed hard. Did he just give something away?

The Ghost's smile widened, a slow, triumphant curve. "Child, you have so much to learn."

"We're done here." He pushed back his chair, stood, and strode toward the door, jaw tight.

"Dylan."

He stopped, his hand hovering over the door handle.

"Visconti. Moretti." Her voice was almost teasing now, deliberate. "And remember—you're not the only one with secrets."

CHAPTER 6

TASK FORCE OFFICE

RON

R on strode into the task force office. Nathan Tanner, José Hernandez, Deanna Swanson, and Charlie O'Rourke, a recent addition to the team, were already there, gathered around the big screen. Then Ana Ruiz walked in, tucking her phone into her pocket. Her curly bobbed hair had grown to her mid back, emphasizing how much time had passed.

As she dropped her bag by her old desk, empty in her absence, a welcome-back chorus rang out. The board had cleared her back in September. It took months for her to recover all her clearances. That was government bureaucracy at work.

"Are you sure you want to be back here?" Ron winked. "Not a nine-to-five position."

She chuckled. "I've had enough desk duty back in DC. Supporting field missions remotely isn't exciting. Besides, I get to be around Grace again here in Orlando."

He nodded. "Good to have you back. We missed you."

She thanked him and congratulated him on his promotion,

then focused on the lateral transfer, Charlie. "You must be the newbie."

He stepped toward her and extended his hand. "That's me, Charlie O'Rourke. Recently returned from overseas. And, please call me Charlie."

She shook his hand. "Nice to meet you." She proceeded to ask him about his last assignment.

"Just so you know, there's been a few changes, such as our expanded responsibilities." Tanner kept squeezing his stress ball.

"What?" She smirked. "Are we chasing deadbeat dads now?"

And that got a laugh.

Ron allowed them more catch-up. Then it was time to focus. He signaled Hernandez. "Let's conference in Olivia. You got Eva's message?"

"Yeah, boss." Hernandez tapped on his phone, bringing Olivia's face up on the large screen. Without preamble, she briefed them on Victor Marlowe.

"Eva mentioned an auction on the dark web." Arms across his chest, Ron braced against a table behind him. "Let's find out what Marlowe has to offer. Hernandez, Deanna, dig into the dark web. Find out all you can about this upcoming auction."

"On it."

"Yes, boss."

"Charlie, Ana, dig into this Marlowe character. Learn everything you can about him. And, Tanner—"

"I'll liaise with Art Crime and check for any connection to the Ghost."

After the briefing, Ana caught Ron in the hallway. "I don't know what you and Simon did, thank you."

He frowned. "What did I do?"

"Well, whatever you told the board got me reinstated."

"As far as I know, Simon and I didn't do it. Yes, we wrote recommendations for you. If I had to guess, Jorge made it happen. Don't ask me how or what he did."

"Oh." Her face fell. Jorge Perez, a crime boss and also her biological daughter's grandfather, had passed away from cancer months ago. He had turned himself in but hadn't lived long enough for the sentencing hearing. Then she exhaled. "I'll go find out about this Marlowe character."

CHAPTER 7

BOATHOUSE

OLIVIA

Olivia's footsteps echoed against the wooden floors as she made her final sweep of the boathouse. The familiar scent of varnish and salt water filled her nostrils. A sleek pleasure craft floated in the slip below, bobbing against its moorings. The boat itself was just for show, maintaining their cover as a private storage facility for wealthy boat owners.

She stepped up to the first floor, checking the living area that supposedly served as the facility manager's apartment. Beyond the windows, other boathouses dotted the marina, their weathered shingles and plain façades providing perfect camouflage. Behind a false wall panel, she found the cache of emergency supplies—sat phones, weapons, go-bags. All present and accounted for.

Before Jay's promotion to deputy director had taken him to Langley, they always met in his basement SCIF. Now, she met with him in the SCIF tucked away here.

The connection chimed, and his face appeared on the screen.

His Langley office, visible behind him, displayed the usual array of flags and commendations.

"Sorry to interrupt your weekend." He dispensed of any pleasantries. "We've got a situation. Adam O'Shea has missed three check-ins."

Olivia frowned, the name tugging at her memory. Ah, yes. About a year ago, they'd been hunting a mole in their ranks. The investigation led them to the Ghost's trusted lieutenant, Rook, who married an FBI deputy director and stole intel from her computer. Rook then used the name Adam O'Shea to gain access to the Ghost. But the deputy director had been onto him, and in the end, he'd been killed.

"Okay, so what about him?" Olivia tilted her head. "I thought you said the real Adam O'Shea was an agency asset."

"He's a covert operative, like you. But you didn't need to know then." Jay's image flickered as he shifted in his chair. "Anyway, his assignment was to retrieve intel from a trusted source. His handler last heard from him three days ago."

"Where was he?"

"Rome. I'll send you his most recent communication. The plan was for him to return here once he received the intel. He was confirming the details on his last call. Then he must have called an audible. For what reason, I don't know." He fiddled with something on the side, and a message notification pinged the screen. "By the way, he works as an in-house counsel at the local Morrison office." Most people understood that to mean Morrison and Associates, CPA, a large regional CPA firm.

Olivia clicked the video, downsizing Jay's window to the corner.

O'Shea's face filled the screen. Despite the secure transmission's grainy quality, she could see the forty-something man looked at ease, lounging in what appeared to be a hotel room. His dirty-blond hair was tousled as if he'd been running his hands through it.

"Package secured." He shifted, the bed creaking beneath him. "Everything's set for the transfer."

Then a slight furrow appeared between his brows. "Though I should mention…" He absently touched his shirt collar. "My contact acted a bit squirrely. Nothing concrete, just… off."

He shrugged and continued the recording. "Still, all systems go. I'll be at the exfil site as planned." A half smile lifted one corner of his mouth. "I'll check in when I'm heading home." He gave a casual salute before the video cut to black.

"I didn't notice any obvious signs of duress. Do you?" Jay's image filled the full screen again.

She shook her head. "No, except he described his contact as squirrely. Could it be a code for something I'm not aware of?"

"I don't think so. His handler didn't mention it. Find him."

CHAPTER 8

SUNSET NURSING HOME

PHIL

Faint grass clippings trailed Phil's golf shoes on Sunset Nursing Home's polished floors. He was cutting it close for the noon Mass. He did it on a weekly basis. As he walked the familiar path, his mind drifted to a night almost ten years ago, the night Fr. Donovan had him come to the Vatican Intelligence office during his pilgrimage to Italy.

"Phil, remember your training officer?" Fr. Donovan led the way to a private room.

"Of course. How's he doing?"

Jean-Claude Marchand was a legend in the spy world. If Phil remembered correctly, he mentioned Jean-Claude was obsessed with the Ghost and the Marino family. Jean-Claude was who uncovered Marge's secret—or rather, her weakness.

Fr. Donovan continued. "With our plan moving forward, we need to keep him safe. He has no shortage of enemies. So, I'm transferring him to a nursing home near you under the name Sam Rhodes—your uncle, who's suffering from early-

onset dementia. Everything is set. My source there can swap his medication for placebos."

As Phil began Mass in the interdenominational chapel, familiar faces filled the space, a few residents seated in their wheelchairs near the front while others clustered in the pews. Staff members stood toward the back, some attending out of devotion, others using the moment as a reprieve from their shifts.

The murmured prayers and soft strains of the closing hymn faded as he gave the final blessing. One by one, the residents returned to their routines, some lingering to speak with him before heading off.

He stepped into the hallway, greeted by the scrape of a walker against the floor.

"Watch your step, Padre!" Henry Janko, a younger resident, warned. "Some fool spilled coffee earlier. Though between you and me, I bet it was that new aide, Brian. Kid's got butterfingers."

Phil sidestepped the damp patch of carpet. "Thanks for the warning, Henry. How's the arthritis?"

"Terrible, as always." The retired postal worker grumbled before continuing his slow trek down the corridor.

Phil approached the community room entrance. Here, the lavender industrial cleaner he always associated with the place mingled with the lingering aroma of lunch—pot roast, if his nose was right. Sunlight filtered through gauzy curtains, casting a soft glow on residents' showcased artwork and seasonal paper crafts.

Margaret O'Malley waved him over to the card table, a mischievous twinkle in her eye. "Father, come be my partner. These sharks are taking all my quarters."

"Not today, Margaret." He smiled, his focus was already locked on his reason for being here.

Jean-Claude sat in his usual corner, a paperback thriller held at the right angle to observe the room while appearing absorbed in reading. Even after years of hiding in plain sight, the old spy hadn't lost his edge. How many of the man's former associates would laugh if they knew one of Europe's most famous operatives now lived out his days playing bingo and attending sing-alongs?

"Phil, you look troubled." The words came without Jean-Claude looking up from his book.

Phil pulled up a chair. Age spots mottled those deceptively fragile-looking hands, but no doubt, they could still inflict serious damage if necessary. Jean-Claude's brown eyes remained sharp as ever, missing nothing despite his pretense of frailty.

Phil positioned his chair close enough for private conversation. A quick sweep of the room showed the card players engrossed in their game by the windows, while two others dozed in front of the television. At a nearby table, the woman completing a jigsaw puzzle hummed to herself.

"Did you get my text?"

"Yes. Not to worry. Just remember I've set up a contingency, if anything untoward were to happen."

Phil crossed his legs and planted an elbow on the armrest. "What kind of contingency?"

"Why don't you concentrate on finding out who started the rumor?"

"Novak wanted me to find the book."

"The book, the real one, hasn't been in the archives for years. You think I'd come so far away without ensuring it's safe?"

Phil frowned. "I don't understand. So, what's missing if it's not the book?"

"Oh, I'm sure the guard or whoever fell for the rumor did steal a book. What it is, I don't know."

"So, there's a book missing, just not the one with secrets. But I can't report that to Novak. Besides, you're supposed to be dead. I can't tell him you said that."

"Bingo in five minutes!" called an enthusiastic voice from the hallway.

Several residents began gathering their belongings, heading toward the activity room.

"How are you, Sam?" Sally approached with a medication tray, her cheerful voice cutting through their tension.

The transformation was immediate and impressive. Jean-Claude's entire demeanor shifted as he jerked backward in his chair, his expression clouding with manufactured confusion. "Who is he?"

"Phil, your nephew. Here, take this." Sally held out the paper cup containing his medication, the only blue one. "Your special cup."

Jean-Claude began muttering, his words a jumbled mix of legal jargon. "The lawyer... the perp... need to review the evidence..."

Sally gave Phil a sympathetic smile and lowered her voice. "He's talking about the book he's reading. He's had good and bad times, like everyone here."

Phil smiled politely.

Once she walked away, Jean-Claude whispered, "Find the book. If they bothered to steal it, it's valuable. As for the one with secrets, you will have access to it when the time comes."

CHAPTER 9

TASK FORCE OFFICE

RON

R on came back from lunch hoping for some updates. His gaze narrowed as Tanner walked in, a Black woman in a pantsuit by his side. The sunlight streaming in from the windows caught the sleek badge clipped to her belt.

"This is Agent Berrigan from Art Crime," Tanner introduced. "And this is SAC Ron Peters."

He gave her a quick once-over, his instincts shifting into professional mode. "That was fast. Thank you for coming."

They shook hands.

"I understand this is about Victor Marlowe. My unit's been tracking him for years. I didn't want to wait if you've got news."

His lips quirked into the faintest of smiles as he nodded to Tanner. "I like her already."

That drew a smile from Agent Berrigan. Tanner led her to the bullpen. Ron followed.

Once all gathered around the screen, Ron waved to their visitor. "Would you like to start by briefing us on what you have on Marlowe?"

"Of course." She pulled a flash drive from her pocket. "Victor Marlowe has been one of the Art Crime Unit's top targets for the better part of a decade. He's orchestrated the theft and sale of priceless artifacts and high-value pieces—paintings, sculptures, manuscripts. His operation is vast and meticulous, designed to keep his hands clean."

She held her flash drive like a microphone, looking around.

"I'll take it." Hernandez extended his hand for the drive. Once she gave it to him, he inserted it into his laptop. Then he handed her the remote.

Berrigan clicked through the files until an image appeared on the screen. Victor Marlowe, sharp dark suit, styled hair, neutral expression. Ordinary in every way.

"Looks like a businessman." Tanner kept flexing his fingers.

Berrigan crossed her arms. "That's part of his charm. Marlowe never gets his hands dirty. He works through a network of middlemen, hires only the best, and keeps himself insulated from the crimes. Add to that, he's cautious—no social media, no public appearances. He doesn't even go anywhere without a bodyguard."

"You saved us a lot of trouble." Charlie pointed to Ana. "We were just getting started on his background."

The agent nodded. "As I said, we've been after him. So, we've got a head start."

"Charlie and I can look into his European connections, if he has any," Ana suggested.

"Do it." Ron remembered the auction. "We have intel that there'll be an auction on the dark web next week."

Berrigan's eyes widened. "We got the same intel. High-value item, exclusive auction, hidden identities."

He then shifted his gaze toward Hernandez. "What did you and Deanna find out?"

"Like you said, there's chatter about an auction on the dark web." Hernandez reclaimed the remote and clicked to a screenshot of the auction item. "From what we can tell, the item up for sale is a book. The description's vague, but the bidding pool looks... well, exclusive. If we want more details, we'll have to infiltrate the auction."

"Can we do that?" Ron frowned.

Deanna's charm bracelet jingled when she raised her hand. "Already on it, boss. We're working on setting up a fake account to get in. It's not going to be easy—they've got layers of authentication—but we'll get it done."

Tanner cleared his throat. "I've been reviewing the apartment's phone and visitor logs for any connections to Marlowe. So far, nothing jumps out, but I'm still going through it all."

Ron gave a short nod. "Keep at it."

"Excuse me, what apartment?" Agent Berrigan demanded. "Are you guys surveilling someone?"

All eyes were on him. The deal with the Ghost was classified. Ron didn't have the authority to read her in. "It's classified. We're just following all leads. Covering all our bases."

The woman narrowed her eyes. She definitely still had questions. At least, she decided not to pursue them.

"All right. Hernandez, Deanna, get into that auction and find out everything you can. Tanner, keep digging through the logs and liaise with Agent Berrigan. Once the auction details are confirmed, we'll need a plan. We're not letting him slip through our fingers."

Now that the Ghost was isolated in Mirror Estate, every single guard and personnel was highly vetted. How did she get her information? This was a mystery he wasn't sure he'd ever find out.

CHAPTER 10

MARINO HOTEL

TOMMY

Tommy Rivers shifted his weight from one foot to the other, boosted by the steady hum of voices and faint holiday tunes. He stood in the drink line behind Lily and Dylan, the two of them lost in animated conversation. Energy thrummed through the company holiday party, despite it being held in January—a decision Tommy appreciated. Less stress than during the actual holidays.

This was the second time he had attended the annual party. Already, he couldn't imagine what life would be like if the lawyer hadn't shown up in Seattle. His best friend, Dylan, had only found out about his maternal family roughly a year and a half ago. A real-life rags-to-riches story. Dylan then convinced Tommy to move to Florida with him and work for the family business. Since then, the young tycoon developed a penchant for getting into dangerous situations.

Now, Tommy was a corporate accounting manager while Dylan was in the upper echelon of the management team. Lily was saying something about her parents' wedding rehearsal.

"…then the rehearsal dinner. We need to be there." She shuffled forward, then nudged Tommy with her elbow. "You asked her yet?"

He blinked. "Asked who what?"

"Who else? Mia!" She rolled her eyes. "Is she your plus-one?"

Mia Granger, an outside auditor assigned to M&M Enterprises, worked out of the M&M office most of the time.

"Already done." He grinned. "We're grabbing a drink later. I can't wait to hear the bonus announcement. And speaking of…"

Gideon Walsh, the CEO, stepped up and began his usual speech to thank everyone, reflect on the last year, and outline what to look forward to this year. Tommy tuned out his speech until he announced the bonuses.

"Yay! Now I have the down payment for a house or a condo." He bumped fists with Dylan.

Lily swiveled and craned around.

The line moved. Tommy gestured her ahead. "Looking for something?"

"Mia. It's like she disappeared. She was here with us, got a phone call, and poof, gone."

"Here she comes."

Her navy-blue dress caught the light as she moved.

"Thanks for holding my spot." Her blue eyes intense, she swung her purse at her side, and her brown ponytail gleamed. "Sorry for the call. My boss wanted to remind me of this crucial contract. I left it at the office."

"Just go and get it." Lily smoothed back her hair while Dylan gave their drink orders. "You can access the office tower from here." The party was at the Marino Hotel owned by M&M Enterprises whose headquarters occupied several floors of the connected office tower.

"Oh no. I mean, it's at Morrison." Her fingers drummed against her purse as she shifted her weight from one heel to the other, stealing glances between Tommy and the exit. "I'm really sorry."

"No worries. We'll stop by your office on the way to Arlin's." He stepped off the line, then said goodbye to Dylan and Lily. "Let's go."

CHAPTER 11

MORRISON & ASSOCIATES

MARLOWE

Victor Marlowe sat in the SUV's back seat, the engine's faint hum blending with the muffled city sounds beyond the glass. The office building loomed across the street, its steel and glass façade reflecting slivers of stoplights and the restless glow of a distant neon sign. Inside, his men worked. Outside, he waited.

Luca, his bodyguard, sat in the driver's seat with his elbow propped against the door, fingers drumming a muted rhythm on the armrest. His eyes, sharp and assessing, swept over every shadow, every movement. A man lingering too long at the bus stop. A car creeping into the edge. Even the scrape of windblown leaves on asphalt couldn't escape his notice.

And now, Luca's phone beeped. He picked it up and read.

"What is it?" From Marlowe's angle, it looked like a magazine or newspaper article. "Not now! Not the time for news."

"Yes, of course." Luca locked the phone. "Uh, boss, what if this thing doesn't exist? This list. What if it's just another story?"

Marlowe didn't move, his gaze fixed on the side mirror displaying the nearby building. The glass distorted the lines, bending the structure into something warped and surreal. Fitting, for the game he was playing. He let the silence stretch before speaking.

"It exists." He gave a firm nod. "The guard didn't die for nothing. He stole something. Gave it to someone. That's not a story."

Luca shifted, his fingers pausing midtap. "And you're sure it's a list? Could be anything. Or nothing."

Marlowe turned his head just enough to meet Luca's gaze in the rearview mirror. The intensity in his eyes silenced further argument. "If there's smoke, there's fire. That guard handed over something worth killing for. Whatever it is, it's real. And it's valuable."

Luca nodded, though his tight-set jaw betrayed his doubts. "Rumor says it's a book, though. But the guy in Paris—"

"Didn't have it. Whatever he took, it's out there. Now that we put it on the auction block, we must find it."

The building's front doors swung open. Ringo stepped out, his broad shoulders cutting a silhouette against the glass door. He moved, the wind catching his coat and flaring behind him like the shadow of a predator.

Luca was out of the car before Ringo reached them. The door thudded shut behind him. They spoke in hushed tones, Ringo's words low and urgent, his expression tight. Luca's gaze flicked once toward the street, then to the building, before he opened the back door.

Ringo leaned in, his face illuminated by the interior lights. "Boss, he's not talking. Says he doesn't know anything."

Marlowe locked his gaze on Ringo. "And his office?"

Ringo hesitated long enough for the pause to feel heavy. "Clean, too clean. But..." He cleared his throat. "There's a name written on his desk blotter. A priest. Fr. Phil. And a chapel. Didn't get the full name before the guy started mouthing off again."

Marlowe's hand drifted to his breast pocket. He froze, fingers brushing his smooth leather jacket. The cigarettes weren't there —hadn't been for months—but the muscle memory refused to fade. He dropped his hand and sat back.

"A priest?" His gaze shifted past Ringo to the building. The windshield cast Marlowe's own image back at him, the sunlight reflecting in his eyes, twin pinpricks of cold fire. "What else?"

"Nothing, no files, no notes. Just that name."

His jaw tightened. The air in the car grew heavier, pressing against him. He exhaled, the sound sharp in the confined space.

"Keep working on him." His tone, softer now, was no less dangerous. "If he doesn't talk…" No need to finish. His meaning was clear.

Ringo strode back into the building, his coat snapping behind him. Luca climbed back into the driver's seat, his movements brisk, deliberate.

"You think the priest is connected?" Luca started the car. He gripped the wheel too tightly.

Marlowe didn't answer. His gaze lingered on the building, on the shadowed windows and the glowing lobby.

"I don't believe in coincidences." He straightened his jacket, smoothing the fabric over his chest. "If that name's on his desk, it's there for a reason. Find out everything about him. Where he lives. Who he talks to. What he knows. And if he knows too much…"

Luca pressed his lips into a thin line. "Understood."

As they drove away, a sedan veered into the lot. It stopped, then parked. A couple got out and entered the building.

"Alert Ringo." Marlowe settled back. "If they had anything to do with the lawyer, bring them to me."

"Yes, boss." Luca was already on his phone.

Marlowe cast one last glance at the building. The car rolled into the street. Behind them, the office building stood silent, but his mind churned. Loose ends had a way of unraveling everything. And he wasn't the kind of man who left anything undone.

CHAPTER 12

MORRISON & ASSOCIATES

TOMMY

Tommy parked by the sleek office building. With the streets almost deserted, the soft purr of his idling car intruded. The numbers 3:49 gleamed on his dash. They could walk around, grab an early dinner, then maybe a movie?

"This is it." Mia unbuckled her seat belt. "I'll just run in and snag the contract. It shouldn't take more than a couple minutes."

"Mind if I come with you? I'd love to see where you work."

"Sure, why not?"

He got out with her. After she punched in the code to unlock the door, they entered the building. The security guard's desk was unmanned, which struck him as odd, but he didn't mention it. They took the elevator to the fifth floor.

There, the office was dark, except for the dim emergency lights. Mia led him down the quiet hallway toward her office. Fluorescent lights hummed, and her fingers tightened around her purse.

"You all right?" He put his hand on her back.

"Yeah, it's just... something feels wrong." She shook her

head. "It's probably because I don't come here often and never on a weekend."

She quickened her steps to her desk, rolled out a drawer, and retrieved a folder. "Here it is. Let's—do you hear that?"

Her hand gripped his arm. He did hear some scraping noise, like a chair or something being dragged across the floor. He pointed to a room just left of the hallway entrance. "It's coming from there."

"There's no light. You think it's like a mouse or something?"

He hoped that wasn't the case. Surely, a nice building like this would have a cleaning service and pest control. "Let's take a peek when we walk by."

He followed her back toward the elevator. When she stopped and gasped, he almost walked into her. "What's wrong?"

Then his stomach dropped. The office was a mess—papers scattered across the floor, books and files strewn about, and drawers hung open as if someone had ransacked the place. And then he saw the body near the desk, unmoving. A man was face down, a dark pool of blood seeping out beneath him.

No, no, this is not happening. This is something Dylan and Lily would walk in on, not me.

A squeak from the frozen Mia brought Tommy back to his senses. "Call 911. Do you know who he is?"

"I think it's Adam O'Shea, our in-house counsel."

He took a breath, crossed the room, knelt, and pressed two fingers to O'Shea's neck. After the look of the body, the thready pulse surprised him. Then the man's hand shot out and gripped Tommy's wrist. He almost recoiled, but the man's fingers held him firm, his eyes opening slightly.

"Give...fee...X," the man rasped. When Tommy leaned closer, straining to hear more, O'Shea's hand slackened, and his grip fell away, lifeless.

Tommy called out, "Did you call 911?"

Mia uttered a cry and then—thud!

He turned his head and saw a figure. Maybe more than one.

There were running steps somewhere. But before he could decipher it, something jabbed the back of his neck. His vision blurred. He fought to stay steady on his feet, but he wobbled. There was a lot of commotion. He stumbled. Then all was black.

CHAPTER 13

MORRISON & ASSOCIATES

PHIL

S tillness shrouded the office, the kind of quiet that clung to the air like cobwebs. Almost quarter after four on the wall clock. Where was Adam O'Shea? The unlocked door downstairs should have warned him, but Phil assumed O'Shea unlocked it for him. After all, O'Shea's message suggested something for him at the office.

His footsteps echoed faintly as he edged through the disarray, his practiced gaze sweeping. Papers lay scattered across the floor, drawers gaped open like silent mouths, and the overturned chair near the desk hinted at a struggle. The metallic tang of blood met the sharp odor of sweat and fear, though the latter was long gone, leaving only a chilling reminder of what transpired.

Then he saw it—the body.

The man lay crumpled near the desk, one arm outstretched as if reaching for salvation that never came. Blood pooled beneath him, still warm and vivid against the sterile white tile. The sight hit with the force of a body blow, and time folded back on itself.

The humid air of Paitilla Airfield clung to his skin, thick with the scent of jet fuel and sweat. The mission was running smooth, the rehearsed operation ticking along like clockwork.

Then—

A blinding white light snapped on overhead.

"Ambush!" someone shouted.

Gunfire exploded.

"Move! Move!"

Mike was the first to go down, the sharp, wet crack of a bullet hitting home.

Carlos cursed, staggered. Blood bloomed across his chest as he dropped to the tarmac.

"Mike! Carlos!" Phil barely had time to register their bodies before Joey barreled past him, grabbing Chris under the arms.

"Come on, man. Stay with me—"

The roar of gunfire swallowed Joey's voice. Muzzle flashes lit up the night like a strobe, and then—

They were gone.

A searing pain punched through Phil's shoulder, a sledgehammer of fire and steel. His body jerked, spun like a puppet with its strings cut. The ground came up fast, cold against his cheek, his fingers scrabbling against the pavement.

More gunfire. More shouting.

His vision blurred, darkness creeping at the edges. Somewhere in the chaos, boots pounded the ground, voices barked commands, but it all faded beneath the blood rushing in his ears.

The mission had spiraled into disaster. Even now, the acrid smell of aviation fuel and the taste of blood on his tongue were as vivid as that day. Four dead. He lived. And some nights, in the silent void between waking and sleeping, he still didn't understand why.

He shook his head, banishing the ghosts. He wasn't in Panama. He was here. In Orlando. And he had work to do. He made the sign of the cross over the body and prayed for the deceased.

The man had left a message for him while he was busy with Novak and then with Jean-Claude. By the time Phil called back, Adam O'Shea never answered. Now, he replayed the cryptic message.

Father, it's been a while. Giles gave his best. I've brought back the candies you like. They're here for you when you visit. Hope to see you soon.

Phil had never met Adam O'Shea, never even heard of him. But one phrase caught his attention—"Giles gave his best."

"Giles" was a code within Vatican Intelligence, a stamp of authenticity. O'Shea was either an asset or someone entrusted with something valuable.

Candies.

His gaze swept the office. Candies could mean anything—a hiding place, a package, something small but significant.

Then he spotted it—a clear bowl of loose coins on the credenza behind O'Shea's desk. A bowl, not a drawer. Something in plain sight, yet easy to overlook.

His gut told him he was right.

He stepped forward, slipped a hand into the coins, and stirred.

Eureka.

A flash drive. He pocketed it, then stirred some more, just to be sure. A key. But were both items for him?

Better safe than sorry. He dropped the key in his pocket.

Now that he had his flashback in check, he scanned the room again, noting every detail with a soldier's precision. The disarray wasn't random. This was a calculated search, not a moment of panic. He crouched by the body, careful not to touch it, his gaze skimming the man's hands, his pockets, the faint smudges near his shoes.

"No. There was a struggle. Body's still warm," he muttered. "Just happened."

He stood and crossed to the desk. Did anything hint at the man's secrets? A smear on the desk edge caught his eye—a fingerprint, perhaps? He resisted the urge to examine it further. That wasn't his job. Not anymore.

Outside the office, he used his burner to call 911 and made an anonymous report about the dead body.

As he put his phone away, his thumb brushed against the drive.

He crossed back to the door, taking one last sweep of the room. His gaze lingered on the body. Was he ready to be pulled back into this world?

CHAPTER 14

TASK FORCE OFFICE

RON

A fresh coffee in hand, Ron headed back to his office, sat at his desk, and reviewed the stack of paperwork that never seemed to shrink. The team was out chasing leads or buried in research elsewhere. The promotion gave him better hours usually. Most of the time, it buried him in paperwork. Only in sensitive cases would he go out in the field now. This was one big factor for why Sheila was able to tolerate it. Or perhaps she knew better now what to expect.

"Knock, knock." Charlie leaned in the doorway, his frame filling the space. Something urgent flickered in his eyes.

"Come in." Ron waved him inside. He pushed the papers aside and leaned forward, elbows on his desk, attention on the newbie.

Charlie closed the door behind him, and his boots thudded against the linoleum. "Boss, I checked with my contacts overseas."

"Okay." Ron waved him on.

"Something big. A rumor is floating around about a list of

covert intelligence operatives. My contact in France said the chatter's off the charts. DGSE is aware, and... mobilizing."

He sat up straighter, his brow furrowing. The DGSE, the French Directorate-General for External Security, didn't move unless it was serious.

"You think this is what Marlowe's offering?"

"It only makes sense." Charlie gripped Ron's desk, bending over it. "The guy deals with the worst of the worst. If he's come across a list like that, he'd be all over it. It'd be the score of a lifetime for someone like him."

Ron tapped his pen against the desk, the tightness on his brow creeping down to his jaw now too. "If that's the case, how did he get it?"

"My contact didn't have those details." Charlie pushed himself up. Shrugged. "Could be stolen. Could be leaked. It could've been bought outright. You know how this game works."

A knock on the door, and this time, Ana poked her head in. "Hey, I checked with DIA. There's some kind of rumor about a list of covert operatives. Nobody knows if the rumor is true or not, but they aren't taking chances either. I wonder why Olivia hasn't mentioned it."

Ron's phone buzzed on the desk. The screen lit up with a name that ratcheted his tension up another notch. Olivia.

"It's her. Maybe she's telling me now." He picked up his phone.

The two agents walked out.

He swiped to answer the call. "What's up?"

"Hey, guess what?" It sounded like she was driving. "My friends from across the pond are chasing Marlowe."

"Oh?"

"Yup. Rumor has it someone put together a roster of covert intelligence operatives."

"You think it's legit?"

She didn't answer for a beat. Then a door slammed shut.

Possibly, she parked and got out. "Legit enough that two British covert operatives are here looking for it."

"Any chance your friends are open to working with us?"

A pause. "Thought you'd want that. I'll ask."

He was about to thank her when another call beeped. Before he could check, Olivia uttered, "Gotta go!"

The line went dead.

CHAPTER 15

ON THE ROAD

TOMMY

When he stirred, Tommy first noticed the unforgiving surface beneath him. His head throbbed, and oil and rust scented the air. He squinted his eyes, trying to focus. It was dim, and the realization hit him like a punch—he was in the cargo area of a van.

Cold metal ridges pressed against his back, and a faint hum vibrated through the vehicle as it sped along. He groaned as he remembered Mia. He turned his head. She was right there, just starting to stir.

Her eyelids fluttered open, and she gasped, her voice rising in panic. "Where are we?"

"Shh," he whispered. He couldn't see the driver through the solid wall separating the cargo space, but he couldn't take any chances. "I don't know. Inside a panel van."

The cursing from the front caught his attention. Was the radio on?

"...cops are responding now. We can't go back to clean up."

"I thought it was the weekend. Nobody was supposed to be there."

"That's what I was told. But you heard the scanner. Someone reported it."

Mia's touch brought him back to her. She blinked rapidly, her breathing uneven. "Why are we here? Weren't we in—" Her voice caught, and her eyes widened as her brain caught up. "Oh no. The body."

He gave a grim nod. "I think we've been taken by the bad guys."

She pressed her lips together, her knuckles white as she gripped the floor for balance. Her wide-eyed gaze darted around the space as if she could make sense of it.

He willed his heartbeat to settle, his brain to recall all the tidbits he'd picked up over the last year and a half. Hanging out with Dylan and Lily—and by extension, Olivia and the FBI—had made him the unwitting recipient of countless stories about abductions, chases, and close calls. He needed to stay calm, assess the situation, and figure out a way out of this mess.

"Okay." He kept his voice steady. "We need to stay calm. First, take a deep breath."

Mia complied, her chest rising and falling.

"Good. Now, are you hurt anywhere? Try moving your arms and legs."

She shifted, testing her limbs. "My foot's asleep, but yeah, I'm okay."

He nodded again. Talking things through helped ground them both, make it less terrifying. "All right. Let's look around."

The van was bare bones—no shelves, no tools, no supplies. Just a hollow metal box. Grime streaked the walls, and a suffocating metallic tang tinted the air. Dim light filtered through grimy windows, casting jittery shadows across the floor. The only real features were those windows on the back doors, their glass coated in dirt and old fingerprints.

Mia stirred, attempting to sit up, but he reached out and restrained her. "No. We don't want them to know we're awake. For whatever reason, they didn't tie us up. Let's give them a reason to regret it."

She whispered, "Does it feel like it's slowing down?"

He paused, listening. The vibrations were changing, the van decelerating. "Yeah. If it stops, let's pretend we're still unconscious. And if they open the door and walk away, that's our chance."

It sounded good. More wishful thinking than anything, it gave them a plan.

The van jerked to a halt, the hum fading into silence.

He forced his body to go still, his breathing shallow and even.

Muffled voices came from outside, then one said, "Check them."

The doors creaked open, and he fought the urge to flinch as cold air rushed in.

"They're still out cold. What do we do with them?"

"Let's find out."

The doors slammed shut again, but he didn't hear the lock engage. His pulse quickened. Had they forgotten to latch it?

The voices faded as their captors moved away, footsteps crunching on gravel. This was their chance.

He whispered, "Let's go."

She bolted upright, her tense expression giving way to determination.

Tommy crawled to the back of the van. He reached for the door handle, testing it. It opened with a faint creak. He cracked the door just enough to peek outside. The coast was clear.

"Come on." He slid the door wider.

Mia followed as they hopped out.

He scanned the deserted gravel lot bordered by trees, with no sign of their captors. The voices had faded to the left, so he motioned her to the right.

A faint crunching caught his attention. Mia kicked off her heels and carried them as she ran in her stockinged feet. Smart, he thought, not breaking stride.

The trees loomed ahead, dark and thick, and his mind raced. They'd escaped the van, but now what? All that mattered was staying ahead of whoever had taken them. And figuring out why they'd been taken in the first place.

CHAPTER 16

OUTDOOR MALL

OLIVIA

The outdoor mall bustled with shoppers. The scent of roasted coffee and fresh pastries mingled in the crisp January air. Strings of white lights woven through the trees shimmered in the warm afternoon light. Olivia stepped out of her car, and the mild breeze brushed against her face as she scanned the café patio.

There.

Falcon sat at a corner table, exuding the effortless confidence of a man who belonged wherever he chose to be. His dark trench coat hung over the back of his chair, and a cup of tea steamed by his elbow. Tea, not coffee. Olivia almost snorted. Typical.

She lifted her phone. "Gotta go." A swipe ended the call, and she slid the device into her coat pocket before striding toward the café.

Of course, Raven was already there, seated across from Falcon, her expression unreadable as she cradled a steaming cup. Olivia joined them, easing into the metal chair, which scraped against the stone patio. A server appeared and set down a fresh coffee without Olivia needing to ask.

Falcon barely acknowledged them, his gaze fixed on the distant storefronts as if something beyond the rows of boutiques and holiday shoppers held his attention.

"It's been a while. You two look good." Olivia sipped her coffee. "So, what are you here for, other than tracking Marlowe?"

The two operatives exchanged a glance—quick, but telling. Raven was the first to speak. "Marlowe's been keeping a low profile, staying one step ahead of anyone watching. We're just trying to suss out his next move."

"Would you be willing to work with an elite FBI task force to track Marlowe? If we pool our resources, we stand a better chance of getting ahead of him."

Falcon arched an eyebrow. He glanced at Raven, who gave the barest of nods.

"A joint effort makes sense." He swirled the dregs in his cup. "But we need to tread carefully. Marlowe's been cleaning house. His inner circle's shrinking, and the ones left aren't the sort to ask questions." He studied Olivia. "A guard with access to something valuable was meant to sell it to Marlowe. But someone got to him first."

Olivia's grip tightened around her cup. "Who?"

"That's the question, isn't it?" Raven finished her cup of tea, the feathery edges of her short-cut black hair suiting her code name. "The deal fell apart before Marlowe could get his hands on what he wanted. Whoever stepped in did it fast and left no trace."

Falcon leaned back. "Marlowe's next move depends on who took it. If it was competition, he'll be looking to reclaim it. If it was law enforcement… well, he'll be looking to vanish."

Working through the implications, Olivia kept her expression neutral. They were fishing, testing to see what she knew. And they hadn't mentioned the book directly, a deliberate omission.

"Interesting," she said. "But Marlowe's still out there. Any idea where?"

Falcon huffed. "Not yet. He's cautious—burner phones, disposable motors. We've turned a low-level bloke in his network, but he doesn't know much." He set his cup aside. "I was hoping you might have resources that could help."

"I'll see what I can do." She let the steam warm her face. "We need to move fast. Clock's ticking."

Raven wiped the lipstick from her cup rim. "Falcon and I will keep digging into Marlowe. That's our brief."

They were being careful—too careful. If they'd been tracking Marlowe this long, why were they so focused on this one failed deal? If they knew about the guard, they had to know what he was selling. And yet, they hadn't said a word about it.

"Good. I'll handle my end."

Falcon continued assessing her. "Alone?"

Olivia smirked. "I'll have backup."

He gave a slight nod and reached for his tea. Only to find his cup empty.

"I'll keep you posted if anything new comes up on Marlowe."

"Of course," Raven said.

The three of them rose in near unison, their movements seamless, practiced. No wasted motion. They knew their roles and the urgency of what was at stake.

As Olivia started toward the exit, her phone chimed. Jay—4:36.

She waved the others ahead and answered, clearing the encrypted line. "I'm about to meet O'Shea."

Jay's voice was sharp. "Not exactly."

CHAPTER 17

MORRISON & ASSOCIATES

OLIVIA

Olivia's breath hitched as she approached the CPA office building. Jay's words echoed in her mind: *"Secure the intel, and you know what else to do."*

She adjusted her gloves, fingers curling into fists before she released a breath and hurried up the steps. The stoplights cast wavering shadows against the glass façade, stretching the moment thin.

Inside, the building was eerily quiet for an office complex. An elevator hummed into the silence. When the metal doors slid open, her pulse ticked higher.

The fifth floor beyond was dim, lit only by sterile, bluish emergency lights. Nothing seemed disturbed at first glance. Where was the body? Her nose picked up a familiar scent, something metallic—*blood.*

Her instincts sharpened.

One step. Then another.

Her hand drifted to the holster at her waist as she moved deeper into the office.

Inside one office, the crime scene took shape—an overturned desk, a lamp flickering on the ground, the eerie quiet pressing in around her.

No movement. No sounds beyond her own controlled breaths.

Whoever had been here hadn't left quietly.

She edged through the wreckage. Her fingers brushed across the desk, disturbing a layer of dust except where a smudge stood out—a partial fingerprint? Maybe. But that wasn't hers to analyze. A filing cabinet hung open, its folders bent and spilling out.

This wasn't a random break-in. The place had been searched with precision.

They were looking for something specific.

On the desk blotter, an indentation marked the leather. She tore a sheet from a notepad, grabbed a pen, and scratched on the indentation to reveal a name. A name she wasn't expecting to see. Fr. Phil?

No time to speculate.

After smoothing out the indentation, she crouched by the filing cabinet and rifled through the mess. Nothing useful. Whoever had come before her hadn't been searching. They'd known what they were after. The intel was gone.

Olivia exhaled and stood as her mind worked through the next move.

Moving to the bookshelf, she scanned the titles for anything out of place. Was that a slim journal wedged between two larger books? She slid it free and flipped through its pages. Hmm, nothing but personal notes.

At the desk, a half-empty coffee cup near the corner didn't look like it'd been left by the desk's owner. A risk. Too easy to lift prints from. She left that for the cops. She wasn't here for the murder.

The distant sirens sent a jolt through her chest.

Time's up.

She scanned the room one last time. Whoever killed him took O'Shea's laptop. And possibly the intel. But O'Shea wouldn't have left classified information on his laptop. And Jay already wiped O'Shea's phone remotely.

The red-and-blue glow of police lights flickered against the glass walls.

She slipped through the office and out the door.

At the stairwell, she hesitated, glancing back at the disheveled scene. She had noticed the tan sedan parked in the lot, but she hadn't paid any attention until the Evergreen State license plate frame and the M&M parking decal caught her attention. It wasn't Dylan. Despite the slim chance another employee came from Washington State, she'd bet it was Tommy. So, why was his car here? And where did he go?

CHAPTER 18

INDUSTRIAL PARK

TOMMY

Tommy's breath puffed out in short bursts. The late afternoon air slapped at his face as he and Mia darted down a cracked asphalt road. The sun hung low in the sky, and shadows stretched across the industrial park like reaching fingers. Golden light painted the warehouses' corrugated metal walls. Overhead, a jet streaked across the sky, its contrail glowing in the orange haze.

The streets twisted like a maze, the repetitive layout of warehouses and empty lots offering no clear landmarks.

"Any idea where we are?"

Mia's head swiveled as she ran beside him. "Not really. Looks like some kind of industrial area."

"Thanks for narrowing that down." His muttering only netted him a sharp glare before she refocused on their path.

He checked his pockets for what felt like the tenth time. Still empty. No wallet, no phone. The goons who ambushed them must have taken everything. Mia's phone and purse were gone too, considering how light her hands looked.

Ahead of them, the road curved into another row of abandoned warehouses, their steel doors dressed in graffiti. A chain-link fence loomed by the street, stretching in either direction like a metal barrier to freedom. And to make things worse, razor-sharp barbed wire topped it.

"Great." He threw up his hands. "It's like they want to keep us here."

"There!" Mia pointed to a spot farther to the west. "Does that look like a hole?"

He squinted against the sun's glare. Sure enough, a small section of fencing swayed with the breeze. It was a crude attempt at an opening, the chain links bent back and fastened with a rusty wire to form—a pet door?

"Only one way to find out." He sprinted toward it.

When they reached it, she knelt to inspect the hole. "Someone's been sneaking through here."

"Good for them. Hope they left instructions." He hunkered beside her and tugged at the makeshift door. It moved, but not enough for him. "You first."

She hesitated, glancing toward the faint voices and running footsteps somewhere in the distance. Then she lay flat on the ground and wiggled into the gap. The loose gravel scraped against her navy dress, but she squeezed through.

He crouched down before the opening. It seemed much smaller now.

"I'm not fitting through that." He kicked the hole. The chain links rattled but held firm.

"Kick harder!" She grabbed the edges and pulled as he aimed another kick. This time, a few links gave way, widening the gap.

"Come on, you oversized gorilla!" Mia urged, her tone part frantic, part teasing.

"Oversized? I'm average height." He rammed it with another hard kick. The hole widened enough to fit his shoulders.

"There they are!" a voice shouted.

Tommy's stomach dropped.

Footsteps pounded louder against the pavement. Mia reached through. "Come on!"

He slammed himself to the ground and shoved his arms through, wiggling like a worm on a hook. The jagged metal snagged his shirt, but Mia gripped his hands and yanked with all her strength. His shoulders scraped against the opening, and for a horrifying moment, he thought he might get stuck.

"Pull harder!" He kicked his legs wildly as if that would help.

"I'm not letting you get caught." She grunted. Digging her heels into the gravel, she gave one final tug.

With a lurch, he popped through, tumbled onto the ground, and landed in an undignified heap at her feet.

"Graceful." She deadpanned, already hauling him to his feet.

"I'll take graceful over dead." He rubbed his sore shoulders.

"Run!" Still holding his arm, she tugged him forward.

They bolted down a narrow alley between two warehouses, their footsteps thundering. Their pursuers were closing the distance, their shouts growing more distinct.

"Any other bright ideas?" Tommy pumped his legs faster.

Her gaze darted around. "There!" She pointed toward wooden pallets stacked against one building.

"Hide behind those?"

"No, climb them, genius!"

She leaped onto the first pallet and scrambled up like a pro. He followed, his hands slipping on the worn wood. At the top, she pulled him onto a narrow ledge running alongside the building. The voices below grew louder as their pursuers reached the alley.

"Where'd they go?"

"I don't see them!"

They pressed against the cold metal wall, barely daring to breathe. He whispered, "Well, at least they're as lost as we are."

She rolled her eyes, but a small smile curved her lips. "Let's hope it stays that way."

For now, they were safe. But their luck wouldn't last forever.

CHAPTER 19

MORRISON & ASSOCIATES

RON

R on adjusted his tie as he stepped out of the unmarked car, the cooling afternoon air brushing against his face. The soft hum of squad car radios and murmured conversations filled the parking lot. Lights from police cruisers flashed against the building's façade.

"What a circus!" Charlie muttered. His gaze swept over the parking lot, the Medical Examiner's van pulling in behind them, and the growing cluster of officers. "How many people does it take to look at one body?"

Ron ignored the comment, leading the way with Tanner and Charlie close behind. Ana went to follow up with the British folks. As special agent in charge, Ron rarely ventured out into the field. This wasn't just any case—it was *sensitive*. His job wasn't just solving a murder—it was navigating the treacherous waters between the local police, the federal agents, and the spooks.

They entered the building and badged their way past a wary uniformed officer. The elevator ride to the fifth floor was tense, silent except for the machinery's whir. Order came straight from the deputy director who hadn't shared much, only that the victim was somehow tied to classified operations. Ron had questions, but the answers would have to wait.

He glanced at his phone. Hmm, 4:51. It would be a long night.

The elevator doors slid open. Officers milled around the hallway, murmuring in low tones, while plainclothes detectives examined the scene and the techs photographed evidence and collected samples. A detective stormed toward them, his round face flushed.

Detective Spaulding. Of course.

"Hey, you guys are fast." The detective held up a hand. "We just got word to play nice."

Ron pulled on protective gloves and put on booties, along with his agents. "So, what do we know?" he asked Spaulding.

"Nothing much yet. Got an anonymous call about the body. Vic is Adam O'Shea, in-house counsel for the firm. Single gunshot wound but looks like there was a struggle first. The death investigator just arrived." He gestured toward where Tanner stood. "That's my new partner, Detective Kylie Cassidy, over there with your agent."

"What happened to Detective Monnin?" For the last couple of years, Monnin always accompanied Spaulding.

"Moved up the coast to a beach town. According to her, nothing much happens. Shoplifting and auto thefts, like that." He tapped Ron's elbow. "The irony is KC, uh, Cassidy, she goes by KC, came here from a small town. Pine Grove."

Now the name clicked. So, that was KC, Tanner's girlfriend. No time to dwell on that.

Ron surveyed the disastrous room, the overturned desk and scattered papers. The faint smell of blood and cordite lingered, mixing with the acrid odor of spilled coffee. Technicians snapped photos, bagged evidence, and otherwise documented the scene.

The ME's investigator, a woman with a dark ponytail, knelt by the body. She stood and jotted on her tablet as Ron approached.

"Excuse me." He flashed his credentials. "Time of death?"

Her gaze flicked to the badge. "Judging by body temp and early rigor, I'd say about one to three hours, give or take. The ME will confirm after the autopsy but cause of death appears to be a single gunshot wound."

Ron crouched beside the body as the investigator stepped aside. Adam O'Shea lay face down, his suit rumpled and blood-stained.

"Okay to turn his head?"

She nodded and flipped the body. "Based on the entry wound, he was likely standing and perhaps walking when he was shot. Then he fell forward face down."

His face was battered, suggesting a struggle before the fatal shot. The entry wound was clean, close to the shoulder. There were no obvious signs of anything unusual, no hidden clues tucked into his pockets or under his body.

"Anything else stand out?" Ron asked.

"Not at the moment. You'll get the full report after the postmortem."

Ron straightened as the technicians moved in to lift the body onto a gurney. As they did so, something caught his eye. He bent over a ballpoint pen. Not just any pen, but one with the M&M logo on it. His first thought was Dylan. This would be the kind of trouble the young tycoon found himself in. *What did you get yourself into now?*

Although tempted to call Dylan then, he'd wait. The desk was searched. Techs were getting prints. "No laptop?"

"Nope, killer must have taken it. No phone either," Spaulding offered. "The pen could be a marketing thing. I get pens sometimes from charity organizations."

"Yeah, maybe." Ron surveyed the room one more time, then

stepped out. He pulled out his phone, scrolled to Dylan's number, and hit Call. It rang a few times. He was about to hang up when someone answered. "Agent Peters."

Background commotion intruded, but it sounded like Dylan. "Where are you?"

"At the hotel. It's our annual party."

"Okay, have fun."

"Hey, why'd you call?"

"Making sure you're staying out of trouble." He almost pressed End when he thought of something. "Do you guys send out promotional pens with the M&M logo?"

"I don't think so. Not since I started. There are some floating around here. Tommy likes them though. He has a stash in his desk and always carries one."

"Is Tommy there with you?"

"No, he left about an hour ago with Mia. They were stopping by Morrison to pick up something before going to dinner or something."

No!

CHAPTER 20

RESORT HOTEL FOOD COURT

ANA

Ana Ruiz bit into her double chocolate chip cookie, letting the rich sweetness dissolve on her tongue as she scanned the bustling food court. The scent of fried food and freshly brewed coffee mixed with the hum of conversation. Her fingers drummed against the table as she reread Olivia's text. The British operatives were en route.

During Ana's monthslong suspension, the agency had called on her for a few selective ops as some sort of contractor. She didn't know how the technicalities worked, but it was good to stay in the game.

A couple moved toward her. The man carried a tray with sandwiches and drinks, walking with a casual ease that belied his sharp, observant eyes. Falcon. She recognized him from the art gallery. She'd known him as Collins. He looked much the same —slim, average height, more gray hairs peppering his temples. The woman at his side was on the thin side, her skin pale, short-cut black hair feathering her forehead. Her gaze swept the area as if memorizing every detail before she took her seat.

"Hello, Ana." Falcon set the tray down. "This is Raven."

Of course. They only used code names. The names suited the duo.

Wisps of short black hair curved along her neck as Raven inclined her head, her expression neutral but watchful. "Pleasure."

Ana nodded in return. "Appreciate you meeting me." She leaned forward, voice lowering enough to keep their conversation private. "I need intel on Victor Marlowe."

Falcon exchanged a glance with Raven before answering. "As we told Olivia, we have a low-level bloke inside Marlowe's organization. I've been handling him."

"Can he get me anything useful?" Ana asked.

"Marlowe's careful." Raven spoke this time, her British accent subdued. "Right hand wouldn't know what the left hand is doing. Only the top echelon has the full picture."

"Okay."

Falcon set one drink in front of Raven and sipped his own. "Marlowe's inner circle is tight. Luca is his bodyguard and right-hand man. Marlowe doesn't go anywhere without him."

"Nobody else?" Ana finished her last bite of cookie, hardly tasting the gooey chocolate now.

"Ringo is one of his top lieutenants," Falcon confirmed. "Also a bodyguard. If Marlowe breathes, one of them is nearby."

"And the auction?" Ana wiped greasy crumbs from her fingertips. "Do you have anything?"

Raven's lips pressed into a thin line. She peeled the paper from her straw. "All we know is that Marlowe doesn't have what he listed."

Ana's brow lifted. "Then why is he still hosting it?"

Falcon unwrapped his sandwich, one of those healthy things with sprouts. "Here's my understanding. Whoever stole the book, I assume is a guard, was selling it to him, but your agency guy got to him first."

Olivia didn't say anything about that, but then again, that was how the spooks worked. "Did Olivia know this operative?"

"Yes." Raven poked her straw into her drink cup. "But I think she only found out today."

Falcon pushed wayward sprouts back between the bread. "Anyway, Marlowe is scrambling to get his hands on it before the auction date. If he doesn't, he'll lose credibility."

Ana frowned. "That makes him dangerous."

Falcon bit into his sandwich, then added, "More unpredictable than usual."

CHAPTER 21

TASK FORCE OFFICE

OLIVIA

The moment Olivia stepped into the task force office, the stale coffee scent assaulted her. The hum of electronics and the murmur of agents working the weekend filled the air, but her focus zeroed in on Ana's empty desk. Ana must not be back yet from meeting with Raven and Falcon. While Olivia waited, she found Deanna in the lab.

The forensic scientist sat at her desk in the back, fingers flying on the keyboard.

"Hey, Deanna." Olivia approached.

Deanna looked up. "Oh, hi."

"Would you mind pinging a phone number?"

"For a case?"

"Yes, the Marlowe case." A bit of a stretch, but Tommy's car was there.

"We don't even have a case number yet. Let me open a file."

Olivia waited.

"Okay, let's see." Deanna entered the number and did her magic. "It's off now. But the last known location was Morrison."

"Do you think you can pull footage of the building's security cameras? Maybe street cam?"

Fingers danced some more on the keyboard. "Hmm… security camera feed has a gap of about twenty minutes. Let me see. Here we go. Here's from a camera across the street." She hit Play.

Tommy's car parked in the lot. He and a woman then went inside. Eight minutes thirty-four seconds later, two goons came out with them. Both looked drugged or unconscious. They were tossed in the back of a van.

"Can you—?"

"Bad angle. Can't get the plate."

Olivia asked to watch the footage again. "Pan out a bit and start ten minutes before they get there." There, a sedan idled by the curb. "Can you punch in here?" She pointed at the car. Two figures were inside. One in back and one in the driver's seat. She made the one in the driver's seat a bodyguard—head on a swivel, his build. A man, another bodyguard type, came out to talk to the man in the rear, returned inside. A minute or so after Tommy got there, they took off.

"Go back and get a shot of that vehicle's plate. Then let's see where they went."

Deanna got up. "That was Tommy, wasn't it?"

"Yeah."

"Let's take it to the wall screen." Deanna led her to the lab and went to the keyboard on the counter.

Moments later, a slew of camera feeds was projected on the screen. But before Olivia could look further, Ana texted her.

"I got to go upstairs. Let me know if you find the van?"

"Will do."

Olivia thanked her and headed back up to the bullpen. She joined Ana at her desk. "So, how did your meeting go?"

"The only news is that he said Marlowe didn't have the book. But Raven gave me this." She held up a nondescript flash drive before plugging it into her system. The screen flickered, and a list of encrypted files populated the monitor. She clicked through them with practiced efficiency.

The first file loaded. Text came on the screen, a dossier filled with Marlowe's personal details, spanning years.

One hand braced on the desk, Olivia leaned toward the screen.

"Marlowe keeps a clean public image," Ana muttered. "On paper, he's a wealthy businessman with investments in high-end art galleries, import-export firms, and luxury goods. His tax records are spotless, and his businesses look legitimate."

Ana scrolled further, opening an image file, a surveillance shot of Marlowe shaking hands with a man.

"Davor Iliev," Olivia whispered. A known trafficker with ties to arms deals and underground auctions.

"This was taken in Vienna two months ago."

"I wonder what else Marlowe had in his pipeline." Olivia pushed off the desk and straightened her spine. "Anything on the book?"

Ana clicked through all the files. "Nothing."

Olivia's phone rang. Lily. "Excuse me. I need to get this." Kids never called unless it was urgent.

"Hey, Mom. What's going on? Did something happen?" Lily's questions poured out once Olivia answered.

"Slow down. What are you talking about?"

"Agent Peters called Dylan just now. Really strange. He asked about promotional pens and if Tommy was with us. He never asks about Tommy. What's going on?"

Oh, Ron, now you poked the bear. Those two are gonna play detective again.

"I'm sure it's nothing."

"Mom!"

She sighed. "I haven't talked to Ron yet. But I think he just wanted to make sure Tommy was okay."

"Why wouldn't he? What…"

Dylan's voice intruded in the background.

Then Lily gasped. "We saw the headlines. There's some kind of crime at Morrison? Now Dylan said Tommy isn't answering his call or responding to his text. I just tried Mia and hers went to voicemail too."

"Listen to me, Lily and Dylan. You two, stand down. We will find Tommy. If you hear from either of them, let us know." About to disconnect, she paused to say it again. "Stay put."

After she hung up, she called Ron and left a message to call her. Then she briefed Ana on the crime scene.

"How is Tommy involved?" Ana frowned.

"No doubt, he's not involved. Probably wrong place, wrong time. The footage shows two goons took him and Mia, I guess his date. Deanna is monitoring the camera feeds. Would you please follow up with her and check in with Ron? I need to follow another lead."

"Of course." Ana bobbed her head. "We all know him. We'll find him."

Olivia nodded her thanks, her mind already on the next task. Fr. Phil.

CHAPTER 22

INDUSTRIAL PARK

TOMMY

A ir, thick with dust and the acrid scent of motor oil, clogged Tommy's lungs. He pressed himself against the cold wall, heart hammering. He could feel Mia's shallow breaths beside him, both of them wedged in a narrow space between the stacked pallets and concrete.

Footsteps had passed close, too close, followed by a tense silence. Then the distant rumble of engines fired up.

A sharp crack, perhaps a door slamming, snapped the silence in two.

Tommy exhaled, straining to catch any lingering voices. None.

Mia's wide eyes met his, questioning. Was it safe?

They couldn't wait any longer.

With careful movements, he shifted and braced his hands against the wooden slats. His muscles burned from holding still for so long, but he pushed through, clawing his way up and over the stack. He swung his legs free and landed in a crouch.

The moment his boots hit the ground, tension snapped into urgency.

Dirt clung to his palms as he reached back and grasped Mia's arm. The engines outside roared, a signal they were running out of time.

"Come on!" he urged.

They ran into the industrial wasteland, their footfalls echoing against the looming structures. Rows of dilapidated warehouses and rusted shipping containers rose like silent sentinels, their shadows stretching long in the afternoon light. The air smelled of oil and decay, and the occasional clang of unseen machinery echoed eerily in the distance.

Tommy didn't know where they were going, just that they had to keep moving. The engines revved louder, and the sound sent ice down his spine. Vehicles. Coming closer.

"Why are they chasing us?" he muttered, half to himself. "We didn't see who killed the lawyer. We didn't—"

"Tommy," Mia interrupted.

He glanced at her. They couldn't outrun vehicles, not in this labyrinth of metal and concrete. His lungs burned, his legs ached, and his hopelessness pressed down like a weight.

"We need to stop." He grabbed her hand to slow her down. "Find a place to hide and figure out our next step."

She shook her head, her ponytail whipping across her face. She didn't slow but pointed ahead with her free hand.

"See that crane?" She panted, her words coming in short bursts. "There's a tarp over it. I think… I think we can hide there."

Tommy squinted through the golden light of the afternoon. The crane loomed like a skeletal giant at the edge of a deserted lot, its rusted frame stretching into the sky. Below it, he spotted what Mia meant—a massive tarp draped over what looked like a pile of cement blocks.

It might work. If their pursuers didn't see where they went...
If they could buy themselves time...

"Good idea." He nodded. "But we need to lose them first.
Let's cut through here. Cars can't follow us."

He veered toward an opening between two hulking warehouses, hauling Mia with him. She slipped on her heels just in
time. The passage was tight, littered with broken pallets, and
glass shards crunched underfoot. The sound made him wince,
but he kept going, weaving through the debris maze.

Behind them, the engines grew louder, joined now by faint
shouts, angry, purposeful.

"They're close!" Mia gasped, glancing over her shoulder.

"Just keep going." He pulled her along.

They emerged beyond the buildings, the crane now closer, its
shadow a stark silhouette against the low-hanging sun. The tarp
fluttered in the breeze, flapping like a beckoning hand.

"This way." He led her around the back.

The tarp wasn't draped over the crane itself, but over the
cement blocks near its base. Up close, it was filthy and riddled
with small holes, the smell of damp concrete wafting from
beneath it. He crouched, lifted one edge, and gestured for her to
crawl inside.

"Hurry," he whispered.

Mia scrambled under, her breath ragged as she squeezed into
a space between the blocks. He followed and tucked the tarp
down to avoid leaving it askew. In the stifling space beneath, the
edges of the cement dug into his back as he shifted to settle
beside her.

All he could hear was their breathing, loud and uneven in the
claustrophobic darkness.

Then the engines drew nearer.

Tommy held his breath, his heart pounding so hard it might
betray their hiding spot. Through one of the tarp's holes, he saw

headlights sweep across the lot, the beams slicing through the afternoon shadows like searchlights.

A vehicle rolled to a stop just beyond the crane, its engine idling. Voices barked orders, though he couldn't make out the words. Who were these people? What did they want? And why were they so determined to catch them?

Mia shifted, her hand brushing his arm. The dim light filtering through the tarp highlighted the terror on her face.

"What now?" she mouthed.

He swallowed hard, forcing himself to stay calm. "Wait," he whispered, barely audible.

Footsteps crunched on the gravel. He froze, every muscle taut as a bowstring. A shadow passed inches from their hiding spot, blocking out the faint light for a heartbeat.

"Nothing here!" a gruff voice shouted.

Another voice responded, sharper. "Check the crane! They couldn't have gone far!"

Tommy's pulse thundered in his ears. If they looked closely enough, they'd see the tarp wasn't flush with the ground. They'd find them.

Mia's hand gripped his arm, her nails digging into his skin. He wanted to reassure her, to say something, anything, but he didn't dare make a sound.

The footsteps drew closer, and his breath caught as a boot kicked the tarp, sending a cascade of dust and gravel into their hiding spot.

Time stretched unbearably.

Then, miraculously, the boot retreated.

"They're not here," the first voice grumbled.

"Spread out!" the sharper voice demanded. "They're on foot. They couldn't have gone far."

Tommy exhaled, his body sagging against the cement blocks.

"Are they gone?" Mia's voice trembled.

"Not far." His gut twisted. "But we can't stay here."

He shifted, peering through the hole in hope the coast would soon be clear. "If they go far enough away, we'll need to find somewhere safer before they come back."

One thing was clear: Whoever was after them wouldn't stop until they were found.

And he wasn't sure how much longer they could keep running.

CHAPTER 23

CHAPEL, MIRROR ESTATE

PHIL

The shadows stretched long across the road as Phil drove toward Mirror Estate. He gripped the steering wheel tightly. The golden sunset was at odds with the questions churning his mind. The anonymous 911 call had been necessary. But why? Why had O'Shea contacted him?

He replayed the events in his mind. He tapped the dash control to pull up the call logs and listened to the vague voicemail again. O'Shea had been deliberate, reaching out to him. But why? Did O'Shea know about his past with Vatican Intelligence? Or had he been a desperate man clutching at straws?

The flash drive in the cupholder, its black plastic exterior unassuming, might hold the answers he sought. Or at least the breadcrumbs leading to them.

He parked at his spot beside the chapel, killed the engine, and sat in silence. Scanning his surroundings, he confirmed no one was in sight. Satisfied, he pocketed the drive and stepped out. Gravel crunched underfoot, breaking the stillness.

At the chapel doors, a faint shuffle caught his attention. Diane Giordano, one of his elderly parishioners, emerged from the main church. Clutching her oversized handbag, she moved at her usual glacial pace.

"Fr. Phil!" she called.

Phil forced a smile. "Diane, good evening. Here for evening prayers?"

She nodded, her silver hair catching the last rays of sunlight. "I was, but now I need to, ah, use the facilities. These old bones don't move like they used to."

"Of course." He stepped aside to let her through. "It's just down there."

"Oh yes. I know." She shuffled off.

He waited until she disappeared around the corner. Time wasn't on his side, and he couldn't afford interruptions. He entered the rectory and headed straight to his office.

Once inside, he locked the door. The quiet click brought small relief. The office was simple, just a wooden desk, a leather chair, and a modest crucifix hanging above shelves filled with theology texts.

At the desk, he opened his laptop. His fingers moving deftly, he logged into the secured Vatican Intelligence network. The familiar interface loaded quickly, a stark contrast to the slow tension in his chest.

He retrieved the flash drive, pausing to study it. Although nothing was remarkable about its appearance, the weight of its contents was undeniable. With a steady hand, he plugged it into the laptop.

The screen lit up, displaying a security scan in progress. Lines of code scrolled by, the system verifying the drive's integrity and searching for potential threats. He leaned back in his chair, his gaze fixed on the screen as the seconds stretched into what felt like hours.

Finally, the scan completed, and a notification appeared: Drive Secure. Access Granted.

He clicked on the newly opened folder. Inside were several files, all labeled with terse, cryptic names: Project Aegis, Coded Log 47, and Archive II.

He hesitated before opening the first file.

Project Aegis.

The document loaded slowly, revealing a series of seemingly unremarkable photographs—snapshots of a normal life. But the precision was too deliberate, the progression too methodical. Someone had been watching.

The first image showed her as a child, maybe four or five, in the arms of a smiling woman. A birthday party. Bright balloons, a homemade cake, an ordinary suburban backyard. The woman, presumably her mother, had kind eyes.

He scrolled to the next. Age eight. A school picture. Hair neatly brushed, a navy uniform, the kind worn in private academies. The background was crisp, professionally done. She had the easy, confident smile of a child who felt safe, who believed she belonged.

Another image. Twelve. Seated on a porch swing, a book in her lap. The house behind her was large, secluded, the kind that offered privacy rather than opulence. A dog lay at her feet. Everything spoke of stability. A carefully curated life.

Then fourteen. A family photo—posed, warm. Her hair was lighter now, subtly dyed.

He clicked the most recent image. Seventeen. Close to eighteen. The change was subtle but noticeable. Her features had refined, her gaze held more awareness.

Only a few people knew the girl's identity. He was one of them. But why were her photos here?

Before he could dwell on the question, a knock at the office door made him freeze.

"Fr. Phil?" Diane called from the other side. "I left my prayer book in the pew. It's locked now."

He suppressed a sigh, closed the laptop, stood, and headed to open his office door when he heard, "I'll unlock it, ma'am."

"Thank you, Leo," Phil called out.

Back at his desk, he reopened the laptop. The files were still waiting, their secrets pressing in on him, ghosts from a past he thought buried.

He clicked on the next one.

Coded Log 47.

The document opened to a stark white page, a simple list of names. Four in total.

He scanned them. Phil Shagley. His own name near the bottom.

Above it, Michael Donovan, his mentor. The man who had guided him both spiritually and through the shadowed corridors of Vatican Intelligence. Fr. Donovan had passed away some years ago.

The next name: Jean-Claude Marchand.

Jean-Claude was dead to the world—officially, at least. He disappeared years ago.

The last name was marked only with initials: GLR.

Grim realization settled over him. Jean-Claude, Fr. Donovan, and Phil himself all knew the existence of the girl and the secret. By extension, GLR must be another operative who also knew the secret. But who was this person? Why wasn't he made aware of him?

Archive II.

The file required another password.

The document opened, revealing a set of audio files. Each was marked with a timestamp and a cryptic label.

He hesitated, then clicked on the first one.

A faint crackle of static, followed by muffled voices. Three men. The recording quality was poor, but their words were unmistakable.

"We don't have much time." He recognized Fr. Donovan's voice. "If we do this, it has to be clean. No loose ends."

"Agreed." That was Jean-Claude's voice. "But relocating the wife complicates things. She'll need a new identity, full sweep. Guardian, can you manage it?"

A pause. A third voice, the guardian's. Scratchy, somewhat mechanical. Was it altered? "It'll be done. The wife and the girl disappear together. We control the narrative."

The audio cut off.

His pulse quickened, and he clicked the next file.

More static. This time, the conversation was sharper, more urgent.

Jean-Claude: "She'll be looking. She has resources."

Donovan: "We knew she'd come for the child. That was the point."

A pause.

Guardian: "And when the time comes, she'll have no choice but to listen."

Silence. Then an exhale, almost imperceptible.

Jean-Claude: "And if she refuses?"

Donovan: "She won't."

The recording ended.

Phil ejected the drive and held it, pondering. Why would there be recordings of clandestine meetings? At least, he believed they were clandestine. Yet, someone recorded them. And how had that ended up in the archives? And now, someone had stolen it, and O'Shea had gotten hold of it? Nobody could know this, especially—

A soft closing of a door.

He froze. He locked the drive in his desk drawer, got up, and moved to the door.

"Who's there?" he called.

Silence.

Maybe it was the wind he heard. He went back to his desk. He needed to find out how O'Shea got the drive. Was he killed because of that? Or something else? But most importantly, Phil was no closer to finding the book.

CHAPTER 24

MORRISON & ASSOCIATES

RON

The crime scene pulsed with controlled chaos. CSU techs moved with precision, snapping photographs, dusting surfaces for prints, and bagging evidence. The quiet murmur of forensic teams, the occasional click of a camera shutter, and the low hum of conversation added to the sense of efficiency.

Ron beckoned Tanner who'd finished a conversation with KC. "Tanner."

Tanner turned. "Yeah, boss?"

"I think Tommy was here earlier. With his date. Mia, I think. Dylan said she was picking up something."

Tanner cocked his head slightly. "Tommy? So, Mia works here?"

"That would be my guess. Find out. If they were here earlier, where did they go? Locate him."

"Yeah, boss. What makes you think he was here?"

"A pen with the M&M logo on the floor. Dylan said Tommy had a stash of them. Hopefully, I'm being overly cautious."

"Let's hope it's not wrong-place, wrong-time kind of thing."
Tanner pulled out his phone. "I'll get right on it."

Before Ron could step away, Spaulding called, "Agent
Peters!"

Ron walked toward him as a man entered, his casual attire—
jeans and a polo shirt—at odds with the scene. His thinning hair
looked mussed, and he carried himself with a mix of discomfort
and authority.

"Mr. Rupin?" Spaulding stepped forward.

"Yeah." The man nodded. "Nelson Rupin, managing partner.
Security company called me."

Ron extended a hand. "Special Agent in Charge Ron Peters,
FBI. Thanks for coming in."

Rupin shook his hand, his grip firm but distracted. "Yeah,
well, this is a nightmare. I was out with my kids when I got the
call. Never expected something like this to happen here."

"Did you know Adam O'Shea?" Ron cut to the point.

Rupin's expression shifted, unease crossing his face. "Of
course. Adam's our in-house counsel. Been with us for years.
You're saying... he's the victim?"

"That's correct," Ron said. "When was the last time you saw
him?"

Rupin rubbed the back of his neck. "It's been a while. Adam
was on vacation. He wasn't supposed to be back in town for a
few more days."

"You know where he went?"

"No. Adam wasn't the type to share personal details. I know
he has a wife—she's a magazine writer, I think—but that's
about it."

Before Ron could press further, Rupin cleared his throat. "I
should also let you know—our senior in-house counsel from
another office is on her way. She said I need to remind you about
the firm's obligations. Law enforcement can examine the scene,
catalog evidence, and take anything in plain sight. But files,

computers, phones, or anything that could contain privileged information—those are off-limits without a warrant."

"Understood."

Rupin hesitated. "She also mentioned coordinating with you to ensure privileged material isn't mishandled. She'll oversee the process to protect lawyer-client confidentiality."

Spaulding raised an eyebrow. "What happens if we come across something that looks… relevant, but might be privileged?"

Rupin pressed his lips into a thin line. "She said she'd work with you to flag anything that could fall under privilege. But anything improperly seized could have serious legal consequences for the firm and our clients."

Ron gave a curt nod. "We'll handle it carefully. I'll speak with her when she arrives."

Spaulding crossed his arms. "What kind of work does this office handle, Mr. Rupin?"

"Corporate accounts, mostly. Tax law, compliance, audits." Rupin glanced sideways at the scene. "Nothing that would"—he gestured toward the mess—"lead to something like this."

Ron studied him. "Did Adam seem worried about anything before his vacation? Was he acting out of the ordinary?"

"No." Rupin shoved his hands in his jeans pockets. "Adam was steady, reliable. If something was bothering him, he didn't let it show."

"Did he have any enemies?"

"Not in the office, no. But outside of work? I wouldn't know."

"We'll need to speak with his wife."

"Of course, whatever you need. Let me, uh, check with HR to get the personnel information." His shoulders slumped. "If we're done, I need to notify the partners about this… situation."

"Go ahead. If anything else comes to mind, contact us."

After Rupin stepped out, Spaulding turned to Ron. "You think the counsel's gonna be a pain?"

"Maybe. Luck of the draw. Some are nice and some not so much."

KC sidled up, flipping her notebook open as she spoke.

Spaulding interrupted her. "Meet my new partner, Detective Kylie Cassidy. She goes by KC. And this is FBI Special Agent in Charge Ron Peters."

"I know who you are, sir." She lowered her notebook. "Tanner told me. Nice to meet you."

"Likewise." He offered his hand. "Keep him in line for me, will you?"

She smiled, then seemed to remember why she was there. She cleared her throat and gestured toward the evidence bag one CSU tech held up. Inside, a delicate silver loop earring gleamed under the overhead lights.

"Found it in the corner of the office. Could've been yanked off in a struggle or just came loose during a fall. CSU's bagging it now. We'll run it for prints and DNA."

Spaulding nodded. "Good."

She continued. "Already got officers canvassing the neighborhood. They're checking trash bins, dumpsters—anywhere someone might've ditched evidence in a hurry."

"Let's hope they find something useful," Spaulding muttered.

She didn't slow down. "I'll have the techs check for security footage—inside the building, street cams, anything that might've picked up movement before or after the murder. We're looking at a tight window, so whoever did this had to come in and out fast."

Ron, standing just within earshot, listened to her run through her list of action items. She was thorough. Efficient. No wasted steps.

He nodded his approval. Good investigator material.

"All right." Spaulding exhaled, rubbing his chin. "Keep me

updated on the footage. If CSU finds anything on that earring, I want to know ASAP."

"Got it." KC jotted a note before snapping her notebook shut. She pivoted and strode off, already flagging down a CSU tech.

Ron let out a low whistle. "She always this on top of things?"

"Beats me. First major case with her." Spalding's fingers rasped over his jawline again. "Makes me feel old. Don't you get that feeling? You're working with all these young bucks?"

"They come in handy, like reading small print."

That drew a laugh out of Spalding who mumbled something. But Ron's mind was on the pen and the earring. It sounded more and more like Tommy and Mia were here earlier. And if the earring belonged to Mia, there must've been a struggle. But since there was no other body here, did the killer take them? Why?

CHAPTER 25

TASK FORCE OFFICE

OLIVIA

The task force office monitors cast elongated shadows across the desk Olivia borrowed as she tapped through the agency's secured server. The search bar flickered, awaiting input. She typed deliberately: Shagley, Philip.

The system processed before a file loaded on her screen.

Thin.

Too thin for someone with his background.

She scrolled through the limited information. Former military —Navy SEAL, honorably discharged. A handful of commendations, vague references to operations in classified regions. No official documentation on his post-military work, but Olivia had seen enough sanitized files to know when something had been scrubbed.

For a time, he had been attached to the Vatican. The record didn't say in what capacity, but she had her suspicions.

Vatican Intelligence.

His status was listed as inactive, but *inactive* in intelligence work rarely meant *uninvolved*.

Her fingers tapped idly on the desk. Adam O'Shea was dead. The only clue to retrieving the intel was the priest.

A peek at the clock told her she could still make it before the sun set or close. If she moved now, she'd get to the chapel before twilight.

She shut the file, grabbed her coat, and walked out.

CHAPEL, MIRROR ESTATE

The January air had a crisp coolness, rare for Orlando but pleasant, with temperatures dipping just enough to make a jacket necessary. Olivia pulled into the church parking lot alongside the first wave of parishioners arriving for evening Mass.

The setting sun cast long shadows over the pavement, stretching past the trimmed hedges bordering the chapel grounds. Olivia scanned the area out of habit, her trained eye noting details. An older couple, their steps slow but steady. A teenager scrolling on his phone near the side of the building. A woman guiding a restless child toward the doors.

Normal.

She stepped out of the car, the pavement still holding the sun's warmth beneath her boots. As she entered the chapel, the familiar scent of polished wood surrounded her, a stark contrast to the sterility of the task force office.

A glance toward the altar confirmed what she needed—Fr. Jeremy was preparing for the evening liturgy. That meant Fr. Phil was likely free.

Pivoting, she moved toward the rectory, her steps quiet against the hallway's aged wooden floors. The air felt different here, more insulated. She reached a closed door, warm light spilling into the dim corridor.

She knocked. Twice.

"Come in," came the response.

She pushed the door open.

Fr. Phil sat behind a mahogany desk, his laptop closed in front of him. His gaze lifted as she entered, coolly observant, the lamplight catching the silver at his temples. His posture was relaxed but alert.

Then a slight smile.

"Olivia," he greeted, his voice smooth, deliberate. "Not going to Mass?"

She closed the door behind her. "No. I'm on assignment."

He gestured toward the chair across from him. "Sit."

She did. He watched, calm, waiting.

"I have a name for you," she said. "Adam O'Shea."

A flicker. Barely noticeable, but it was there.

And, just as quickly, he shook his head. "I don't know him. Why do you ask?"

Answering with a question.

"His body was found this afternoon."

Phil exhaled and lowered his gaze.

"Lord, have mercy," he muttered under his breath. A reflex. A prayer.

"Why would O'Shea have your name if you didn't know him?"

His eyes lifted again, steady. Unreadable. "I have no idea."

"Priests aren't supposed to lie," she reminded him.

"I'm not lying."

Silence. Thick, charged.

Until he spoke again. "What's your mission, er, assignment?"

She blinked. "I'm afraid it's classified."

A slow nod, as if that was the only answer he expected. "Then let me save you some trouble." He leaned forward, hands clasped, forearms on the desk. "If this has anything to do with the rumor about a book or a list of names of covert operatives, you can forget it."

Her pulse ticked up. "And why's that?"

"Because it's just that, a rumor. The list doesn't exist."

Her jaw tightened. "How would you know?"

His smile was faint, measured. "Just trying to save you some time."

She let the words settle. He wasn't dismissing her. If anything, he seemed to be warning her.

"You'd do better finding out who killed O'Shea," he added. "The answer might lie with that."

CHAPTER 26

INDUSTRIAL PARK

TOMMY

The air under the tarp felt thick and suffocating, a mix of damp concrete and the faint, sour tang of sweat. Every breath Tommy took was shallow and deliberate, his ears straining to pick up the movements outside. Gravel crunched intermittently, boots scraping the ground. The occasional bark of orders punctuated the silence, each sharp word sending a jolt of urgency through his chest.

"Spread out. Check everything. No one leaves this lot!"

Tommy glanced at Mia. Her wide, fearful eyes locked onto his, her face pale in the faint light filtering through the tarp's tiny holes. She looked like she might shatter any moment, but her trembling fingers, gripping his arm like a vise, told him she was holding on. Barely.

"We can't stay here," he whispered, the words barely more than a breath.

Mia gave a jerky nod, her lips pressed together so tightly they were bloodless. "Where do we go?"

Tommy peered through a hole in the tarp. The industrial park stretched out in a mess of shadows and skeletal structures. Beyond a stack of barrels, something dark caught his attention. He squinted, the shape resolving into a low, boxy form partially obscured by debris.

A van.

It looked ancient, its paint scuffed and dull under the faint glow of distant floodlights. The back doors were secured with a heavy chain, but the driver's door was slightly ajar.

"There." He tilted his head toward it.

She followed his gaze. "That thing?"

"It's our best shot."

Ignoring her skepticism, he lifted the tarp an inch to check the surroundings. The footsteps and flashlights were moving away, deeper into the lot. He motioned for Mia to follow, slipping out and crouching low. The crunch of gravel under their steps seemed loud as they crept toward the van.

"Over here! Check the crane again!" a voice shouted behind them.

Tommy froze, grabbing her arm. They ducked behind a stack of crates, hearts pounding in unison. The flashlight beams arced close, too close, illuminating the shadowy gravel where they'd just been.

Her breath came in short gasps, her panic palpable. "Tommy…"

He covered her mouth.

They waited, crouched in the shadows, until the beams moved on. He nudged her, and they darted to the van, keeping low and close to the stacked debris. Up close, the vehicle looked even more beat-up, its side panels scratched and dented.

He reached for the driver's door and pulled. It creaked open with a metallic groan.

He slid inside, the old vinyl seats cracking under his weight. He scanned the dashboard. No keys, of course. His fingers brushed over the steering column, his mind racing.

"Hot-wiring. Okay. I've seen this in movies." He yanked at the plastic panel below the wheel.

"Do you know how to hot-wire it?" She stood outside watching.

"Uh… no." He winced as he struggled to pry the panel off.

She shoved his hands aside and pushed him along. "Move."

"What?"

"Move over!" She climbed up to the driver's seat.

He had no choice but to slide over to the passenger side, gaping as she reached under the column. Her fingers pried away the panel with a deftness that made his jaw drop.

"How do you—"

"Don't ask," she cut him off. She twisted two wires free and yanked them apart, exposing their copper ends.

He leaned closer. "Is this something I should be worried about?"

She didn't look at him, her focus laser-sharp. "Just something I picked up. I'm not proud of it, okay?"

The wires sparked as she twisted them together. The engine sputtered but didn't turn over.

"Come on," she muttered, low and urgent. She tried again, this time tapping the wires together with precision. The engine roared to life, its guttural sound cutting through the night like a gunshot.

His relief was short-lived.

"There!" a shout rang out from behind them. "They're in the van!"

"Go, go, go!" he yelled.

She didn't hesitate. She slammed the van into gear, the tires screeching against the gravel as they lurched forward. Their pursuers' headlights swung wildly, illuminating the van's rear window as it sped away.

A sharp crack split the air, a gunshot, and the rearview mirror exploded, shards of glass scattering onto the dashboard.

"Duck!" He grabbed Mia's shoulder and pulled her down as another shot hit the side panel.

She peered over the dash to steer. Her hands clenched the wheel. "I've got this!"

The van barreled through the lot, bouncing over potholes and dodging debris. She swerved around a stack of barrels, the tires skimming close to a ditch.

"They're gaining!" He glanced back.

"Not for long."

A narrow service road opened ahead, barely wide enough for the van. He pointed it out, but she already veered onto it, the van scraping against branches and bushes as they sped through.

Behind them, the pursuing SUV hesitated, its headlights stopping at the narrow path.

"They're stuck." His whole body went shaky with relief.

"For now." Her knuckles whitened on the wheel. "But we need to keep moving."

As they burst onto a deserted back road, the industrial park fading behind them, he slumped in his seat, his chest heaving. "You hot-wired that like you've done it a hundred times."

A humorless smile tugged at her lips. "Not everyone grew up in a nice house with a picket fence. I used to hang out with the wrong crowd. Hot-wiring a car is one of those things I picked up."

Was she serious? "Well, anyway, it saved our lives."

They drove until the van started to protest. The engine coughed. The vehicle lurched forward, then stuttered. She tapped the gas gauge, and his stomach dropped.

CHAPTER 27

MORRISON & ASSOCIATES

RON

R on couldn't believe how long he had been on scene. The day already bled into twilight. Soon, the city skyline would be a mosaic of glowing office windows and distant traffic lights. Time had stretched in that way it always did on homicides —one moment racing, the next dragging, like it was trying to disorient them.

Inside the CPA firm's sleek offices, the crime scene remained active, complete with the hum of forensic techs, the snap of cameras, the murmurs of investigators. Somewhere down the hall, the faint scent of printer toner clung to the air, mixing with the acrid tang of coffee that had gone stale hours ago.

Ron had just finished dealing with the press—or as he preferred to think of them, vultures with microphones. They had pounced the second word got out that someone had been murdered in a prestigious accounting firm. But he'd shut them down, for now. No comment. No details. Just a firm "We're investigating."

Now, as he made his way back upstairs, he found Veronica Hess waiting in the conference room.

She was every inch the corporate legal powerhouse—late forties, maybe early fifties, light-brown hair pulled back into an unforgiving bun, her sharp navy suit tailored to precision. A woman who negotiated in absolutes, who saw the law as both a shield and a weapon.

He and Spaulding stepped in, shaking her hand.

Hess didn't waste time. "The firm will do anything within its power to assist with the investigation."

Then she laid out the rules.

"Anything not within plain sight requires a warrant."

Ron and Spaulding exchanged a glance but let her continue.

"Any files law enforcement wants to review will come through me first. I need to ensure our clients' confidentiality is safeguarded."

The implication was clear. She wasn't just here to cooperate —she was here to control.

Ron let the silence stretch for a beat. He would indulge her for now. Then he gave her a nod. "Understood."

Spaulding jotted something down. "Let's start with the basics. How well did you know Adam O'Shea?"

Hess exhaled through her nose, like she had expected the question but still found it tedious. "He was one of our in-house counsels. Handled compliance, contract disputes, and some more complex financial cases. Not a litigator—his work was behind the scenes."

"Was he working on anything sensitive?" Spaulding asked.

"Everything he worked on was sensitive." A dry, practiced response.

Ron wasn't biting. "Anything that might have made him a target?"

Hess pursed her lips. "Agent, detective, I don't look over my staff's shoulder. So, I can't say for sure. All I can tell you is that he was methodical, didn't take shortcuts. If something was wrong, he wouldn't have ignored it."

"When was the last time you saw him?"

"About two weeks ago, maybe longer. Before he went on vacation."

Ron tapped his fingers on the table. He'd sent Charlie to track down O'Shea's wife. Maybe she could tell them something Hess wouldn't.

Ron barely had time to register the heavy silence settling over the conference room before KC walked in, a file in her gloved hands.

She placed it in front of Hess. "Found this on the floor, in plain sight. Not far from where we found the earring."

Ron's jaw tightened. The earring—the only personal item near the body.

Hess flicked open the folder and scanned the pages inside. Her brow furrowed.

Ron and Spaulding leaned in. The words on the paper jumped out.

Two different financial statements.

Same company—Obsidian Rare Works. That was Marlowe's legitimate business or the front of his underground work.

Same reporting period.

Different numbers.

At the bottom of one version—a signature.

Mia Granger—one of the firm's CPAs. And wasn't she Tommy's date? His girlfriend?

His gaze flicked to the detective. Deanna had reported that Olivia asked her to pull street cam footage. Tommy and Mia were seen being taken. Abducted. Until now, they'd been victims.

But this?

This was something else.

His gut churned. Was she not as innocent as he thought? Was she involved in this somehow?

Spaulding broke the silence first. "What exactly are we looking at?"

Hess flipped through the pages, her frown deepening. "I'm an attorney, not an accountant. They look like financial statements, but I have no idea why there are two versions."

No hesitation. No shift in her tone. She really didn't know.

Still, his instincts refused to settle. He tapped the file with his index finger. "We'll have our finance guys check them out."

Then his jaw hardened as he met Hess's eyes. "Tell us about Mia Granger."

CHAPTER 28

MIRAGE FINE ARTS

ANA

A na stepped into Mirage Fine Arts just before its closing time. The gallery was quiet at this hour, with only a few patrons admiring the curated collection. Warm light glowed on the oil paintings and their ornate frames. The entire space exuded exclusivity, the kind of place where whispers carried more weight than voices.

Hugo Perez emerged from behind the main counter, his salt-and-pepper hair suave, his welcoming smile settling his sharp features. "Ana! It's been too long."

She returned the smile. "Hugo. I appreciate you making time for me."

"For you? Always." He gestured toward a door marked Private. "Come on back."

She followed him past sculptures under glass cases to an office stacked with catalogs, leather-bound volumes, and framed photographs of Hugo with various collectors and artists. Amber lamplight reflected off his mahogany desk.

"Can I get you something? Tea? Coffee?" He gestured toward the worn leather chair opposite his.

"I'm good, thanks." She sat. "How have you been?"

Hugo took a seat. "Busy. You know how it is. The art world never stops. You?"

"Same. I wanted to ask you about someone. Victor Marlowe."

His expression didn't shift, but he paused before he spoke. "Marlowe? Everybody in the art world knows of him."

"But do you know him personally?"

He shook his head. "Never met the man."

Despite the straightforward answer, something in his tone—a tightness, a precision—told her there was more to it. She let the silence stretch, waiting. The trick with people like Hugo wasn't to push, but to let them fill the quiet.

He rubbed the back of his neck. "There was something. A situation a few months back. I wasn't sure what to make of it."

She leaned forward. "Tell me."

He glanced at the office door, then lowered his voice. "A man came in, a collector, claiming to have an old master painting that had been in his family for generations. Wanted to sell it."

"Did you authenticate it?"

"I started the process. Did a preliminary examination. It looked promising, but when I asked for provenance—bills of sale, shipping records—he gave me a familiar excuse. Said the documents were lost in the war."

She arched a brow. "Which war?"

"Didn't specify. Just 'the war.'" He gave a dry chuckle. "Happens more often than you'd think."

"So, what did you do?"

"Told him I couldn't proceed without proof. Suggested alternative evidence—family photos with the painting, old letters mentioning it, anything." Hugo tapped a finger on his desk. "He agreed, said he'd see what he could find. But he never came back."

"And then?"

"A few weeks later, I saw the same painting being listed for sale by Obsidian Rare Art. This time, it had a certificate of ownership. Looked official enough, but I had my doubts."

She frowned. "You think the certificate was forged?"

"I can't prove it. But something didn't sit right."

While art fraud wasn't her primary focus, her team was pursuing Victor Marlowe and the elusive auction item. This connection could be a valuable lead.

"Have you ever conducted business with Obsidian Rare Works?"

He nodded. "We've had a few transactions. Mostly smaller pieces, nothing of this magnitude."

"Do you have any records of these dealings?"

"Of course." He woke his laptop, typed something, and tilted it toward her.

The screen displayed the PDF of an invoice. When she touched the arrow, it showed a shipping document. Several of them.

"I also have hard copies."

"This is good. Can you send this folder to me?"

"Of course."

She continued to scan the documents. One shipping invoice stood out. It listed a warehouse address different from Obsidian's known gallery location.

"This address." She angled the laptop his way. "It's not their main gallery."

He peered at the screen. "Ah, that's their storage facility. We had a piece shipped from there once."

She straightened up. "And about the possible forged provenance, would you be willing to speak with our Art Crime Unit about this?"

He tilted his head. "You think it's worth investigating?"

"It might be. Even if it doesn't tie to my case, they'd want to know."

"All right. I'll cooperate."

"Thank you."

As she walked out of the gallery, her phone dinged with a text from the task force.

CHAPTER 29

ON THE ROAD

TOMMY

N*ow what?*
Tommy's pulse thundered in his ears. His breath came fast and shallow as his mind clawed for options, but all he could think was, *Oh God, help, please!*

Wait. Where did that come from?

He gave his head a hard shake to shove the intrusive plea away. This wasn't the time for prayers. This was the time for action.

He faced Mia whose lips moved soundlessly. Her hands still gripped the steering wheel so tightly that her knuckles remained blanched white.

"Are you okay?"

She nodded, eyes still fixed ahead. "Just praying."

Praying. He wanted to say something about that, but now wasn't the time. They had bigger problems.

His gaze darted across the road ahead, searching. The dashboard fuel gauge was low, the needle quivering near empty. They had minutes, if that. His heart kept pounding as he scanned their surroundings for an escape route.

Then he saw a mall, Colonial Market Square, ahead. He pointed to its parking lot. "Do you think we have enough gas to get there?"

She didn't take her focus off the road. "I don't know."

The van jerked. The power steering fought her grip, the wheel resisting as she twisted it. The entire vehicle shuddered—once, twice—before lurching to a dead stop.

Her shoulders sloped. "Guess not."

He didn't wait, shoved the door open. The street was empty, but that meant nothing. Sound carried.

"Let's hope they don't notice the van," he muttered. "We need to move."

Mia swung the door open and hit the pavement, slipping on her shoes.

Then—the sound.

A deep, steady rumble.

Tires crunching on asphalt.

A vehicle slowing. Searching.

His stomach twisted into knots. His instincts screamed at him before his brain caught up. He spun around, his pulse jumping to full throttle.

A black SUV.

Not just any SUV—the same one from earlier.

They'd found the van.

She must have seen it too because her fingers clamped onto his wrist. Her grip was damp—sweat or fear or both.

They ran.

Through the grass. Up the embankment. The damp earth sucked at his shoes like quicksand, dragging them down, fighting them.

Behind them, the SUV screeched to a stop.

Doors slammed.

Footsteps. Fast. Urgent. Too close.

Tommy didn't dare look back. Looking back meant slowing down. Slowing down meant death.

They reached the parking structure, Mia half a step behind him. As they cut into the shadowed concrete, she stumbled —hard.

He turned back to pull her up. "What—?"

She dropped to one knee, yanking at the heel of her right shoe.

His brain barely kept up. What was she doing?

A sharp crack.

The heel snapped clean off, the sound echoing in the empty parking structure. Her fingers moved fast, prying something loose from the hollowed-out space inside.

A tiny black flash drive.

"I thought I was paranoid backing up my work in an external drive, in addition to the company's backup." He pointed to the flash drive. "Now, that's next-level paranoia."

She looped the drive onto a plastic spiral bracelet, the kind that looked like an old telephone cord, and slipped it onto her wrist. The translucent coil blended in, cheap and forgettable, nothing to draw attention. Nothing to suggest the data it carried could get them both killed.

She exhaled. "It's safer this way. Easier to hand off."

"Hand off? What are you—"

A sharp whistle split the air.

Not the wind. A signal.

The bad guys had seen them.

A voice barked—low, commanding. "Hey!"

Footsteps—fast. Close. Getting closer.

"Go!"

He pulled her forward, zigzagging between the rows of parked cars.

Too loud. The gravel crunch of their steps. The ragged rasp of their breathing. The pounding of their hearts.

Another shout behind them. Closer.

They cleared the lot and hit the stairwell, their only escape to the skybridge between the parking structure and the shopping mall.

She threw a desperate glance over her shoulder. "They're gaining."

He didn't look. He knew. He could feel it.

He yanked open the fire door and shoved her inside. It clanged shut behind them, the echo bouncing through the stairwell like a gunshot.

They bolted up the stairs, two at a time. Harsh fluorescent lights flickered overhead, and jagged shadows made his skin crawl. At every flicker, every movement in the corner of his vision, his gut screamed, "Ambush!"

Third floor. Almost there.

Then—the heavy door below them burst open.

Footsteps—pounding up the stairs.

"Faster!"

Mia pushed harder, breath coming in sharp gasps.

They hit the top landing and shouldered through the door.

Bright lights. Crowds. The shopping mall swallowed them whole.

Tommy forced himself to slow down, to breathe, to blend in.

Normal. They had to look normal.

The artificial hum of mall life surrounded them. The overwhelming scent of coffee, cinnamon, and overpriced perfume hit him like a brick wall. Families strolled. Teenagers loitered by the fountain. A sale sign flashed in garish red behind a designer boutique's glass window.

A world away from the one they were running from.

He forced his hands to unclench. He wiped the sweat off his brow. Breathe. Stay casual.

Mia, her face too pale, her shoulders too tense, did the same.

Then—her fingers dug into his arm.

Tommy stiffened.

He pivoted. Followed her frozen stare.

His throat clenched.

At the top of the escalator.

They were here.

CHAPTER 30

MARLOWE'S HOME BASE

MARLOWE

The monitor's screen cast harsh shadows over Marlowe's angular face, the light flickering as the numbers on the screen climbed higher. His lips curled in satisfaction. Interest in his listed item exceeded expectations. More bidders, more desperation, more power in his hands.

Now he just needed the book.

A sharp rap on the doorframe cut through his focus.

"Boss."

Luca's interruption grated. Marlowe didn't turn, letting his underling feel his silence before glancing up. Luca stood at the threshold, hands shoved into his leather jacket's pockets, trying to look casual. He wasn't.

"The couple escaped." Luca shifted his weight. "But the team is getting close to capturing them."

Marlowe's fingers froze on the keyboard. He cursed. "How is that possible?"

Luca shrugged. "They seem to be resourceful. We'll get them back."

"They *seem* to be resourceful?" Marlowe repeated. He pushed back his chair and stood, his movements deliberate, controlled. Dangerous. "I don't pay you to *guess*, Luca. I pay you to *ensure* accidents don't happen."

"They might've just been in the wrong place at the wrong time."

His eyes narrowed. "You believe that?"

Luca didn't answer right away. Smart. The silence stretched between them, heavy and suffocating.

Marlowe moved closer, slow, predatory. "The fact that the team doesn't have them yet tells me they're more than office worker bees. Maybe they were poking their noses where they shouldn't have. Maybe they know something."

"We're on it." Luca nodded. "They won't get far."

Marlowe stared at him a second longer, then ran a hand over his jaw. "And the priest?"

Luca sucked in a breath. "Yeah, about that... It's a bit tricky."

Marlowe's jaw tightened. "Tricky how?"

"The chapel is close to the Mirror Estate. And, you know... the Marino family—"

He pivoted. "I thought they'd gone legit."

"They have. But the Ghost." Luca let the name hang in the air.

Air whooshed out through Marlowe's nose. The Ghost. That woman had been a problem for years. Locked up, but still pulling strings. Worse for others, but great for her. More and more of her competitors got arrested or put in the ground. The Feds were busy closing up shop for many others.

His fingers curled into fists. He'd been careful, meticulous. He didn't like forces he couldn't control.

"Should we ask her?" Luca asked.

Marlowe didn't answer. His gaze drifted back to the screen, to the ever-growing list of interested parties in his dark-web auction. The book was the key. It would cement his position, secure the leverage he needed.

But first, he had to get it.

He exhaled. "No." He glared at Luca. "We don't ask. We *take*."

Luca gave a slow nod.

Marlowe drummed his fingers against the desk. Then he smiled. It wasn't friendly.

"Let's invite the priest here."

CHAPTER 31

CHAPEL, MIRROR ESTATE

PHIL

The key burned like a brand against his palm. Phil rubbed it between his fingers. The cool metal grounded him amid the uncertainties. What did it unlock? That answer remained elusive. And he had to deal with his guest.

"Be that as it may, we can't ignore such a so-called rumor," Olivia insisted. "What if the list does exist? We have to find it. Or find evidence to the contrary. And rest assured, we will find justice for O'Shea."

A tightness gripped the edges of her mouth, and determination glinted in her eyes. She had been in the intelligence game long enough to know even whispers could carry deadly weight.

His right fingers clenched around the key. "I understand." He drummed his left fingers on his closed laptop. "What do you know about the attorney's last days? Have you traced his movements?"

"Not yet."

"If he'd had anything, that would be a good way to know when and where he lost it."

Her lips pressed even closer together. She had already calculated that much, of course. But she wasn't getting what she wanted from him. Not yet. She stood and adjusted her jacket, conceding the conversation.

"I'll keep you updated." She eyed him as if measuring his secrets. "Take care, Father."

"You too."

The door clicked behind her. Alone in the stillness, he turned his attention to his laptop, its glow cutting into the dark room. O'Shea had been careful, his online presence minimal. No social media, no careless posts. But others weren't as cautious. A few tagged photos, grainy but useful, led him to the lawyer's wife, Stephanie Carr.

A travel magazine writer currently in town. Maybe she knew something.

O'SHEA/CARR RESIDENCE

Phil drove to the O'Shea/Carr residence, per the address his contacts yielded. In the upper-middle-class enclave, the houses were what realtors would call executive homes—pristine lawns, brick façades, and long driveways for luxury sedans. He scanned for house number 4953.

A car was already in the driveway. He pulled up next to it, shut off the engine, and stepped out, smoothing his clerical collar. The key in his pocket felt heavier now, but he pushed the thought aside as he rang the doorbell.

The door opened to reveal a middle-aged woman with light-brown hair. Her eyes red-rimmed and glistening, she clutched a tissue. Her gaze flicked to his collar before meeting his eyes.

"Yes, Father?"

"Ms. Carr? I'm Fr. Phil with the Holy Angels Chapel." As a priest, he was no stranger to grief-stricken families, and he played the part well. "I wanted to offer my deepest sympathies for your loss."

Confusion flickered in her eyes before her posture relaxed, and she stepped aside, gesturing for him to enter. "Thank you, Father. I didn't realize Adam attended services there."

"Well, he had called just the other day. And when I heard about his passing, I thought I'd come to offer any spiritual assistance you might need."

"Oh, thank you. Please, come in."

Inside, the tastefully decorated house bore signs of recent distress—an untouched cup of tea on the coffee table, tissues scattered near the couch. In the living room, a man stood as Phil entered. He had the look of law enforcement—broad shoulders, alert gaze, and faint air of suspicion.

"Father, this is Special Agent Charlie O'Rourke," Carr introduced.

The agent gave a nod, possibly assuming this was a routine chaplain's visit. "I was just leaving. Thank you for your time, Ms. Carr. And, Father, good to meet you."

Phil returned the nod. He couldn't be sure, but he thought O'Rourke was supposed to be in Italy. Why didn't anyone alert him of his relocation? No time to dwell on that.

The key didn't look like a safe-deposit-box key, so he'd already ruled that out. Now, as Carr led him to sit, he took note of anything that might hint at what it unlocked. But nothing unordinary stood out, just the normal family photos on the mantel, books on a shelf, framed certificates on the wall.

"This must be an incredibly difficult time. Tell me about Adam."

Tears welled in her eyes. "He was a good man. Dedicated. Honest. He worked so hard. He didn't deserve…"

Her voice faltered, and Phil offered some comforting words while steering the conversation toward O'Shea's last days.

"Did he mention any concerns before he passed? Something troubling him?"

She hesitated. "He had been distracted, but he didn't tell me why. I thought it was work stress. He had to go to Europe for work. Now I wish I'd gone with him. It was so strange that Agent O'Rourke thought he had been on vacation."

"Is that right?" He could think of few reasons O'Shea would lie to his wife. Infidelity wouldn't be the case, this time.

As their conversation drew to a close, a small pile of mail on the side table, particularly the piece on top, caught his eye, a bill for one of those private vault places.

Carr turned away for a moment, giving him just enough time to snap a photo with his phone.

He rose, offering a final prayer for comfort before excusing himself. As he stepped out into the brisk air, he checked the image on his phone. The address could be the key—literally.

CHAPTER 32

TASK FORCE OFFICE

RON

F inally, Ron was back in the office. He'd get an update and send his team home. They'd come back with fresh eyes. That was the plan, anyway. His team stood gathered around the large screen, as expected. No one was lounging. No one was relaxed.

"Update!" He strode toward them.

Tanner's hands worked the stress ball, fingers clenching and releasing in rapid succession. "Canvass turned up something." He freed up one hand, clicked a few keys, and two grainy images filled the monitor. "These are Mia Granger's and Tommy Rivers's phones. Found them shattered on the sidewalk two blocks from the CPA office. I think even our Deanna can't resurrect them."

Ron's jaw tensed. That wasn't good. "What else?"

"Mia's purse and Tommy's wallet were in a trash can a block away. Completely cleaned out—no cash, no cards, nothing but some crumpled receipts. Cops aren't looking at them as victims anymore. They're considering them persons of interest."

A beat of silence passed before Deanna scoffed. "Do they seriously think Tommy had anything to do with this?"

Ron exhaled through his nose. "We know Tommy, but we don't know Mia."

Deanna opened her mouth but shut it again. Mia was still a question mark. If there was even a small chance she was involved, they couldn't ignore it.

"Did anyone get ahold of financial crimes?" he asked. "The two statements?"

"Ah, yes, boss." Tanner put the stress ball on his desk and checked his phone. "I sent them copies. Kyle said it looked like someone was cooking the books."

Ana reported the findings from her meeting with Hugo earlier. Then she typed something on her phone. "I think I just tripped a wire when I looked up Mia Granger in the database."

"The plot thickens." Tanner tossed his stress ball up.

After a beat, Charlie started. "O'Shea's widow, Stephanie Carr, is devastated. Had no clue what was going on. She thought he was in Europe for work."

"Work?" Ana repeated, frowning. "Not vacation?"

"Nope," Charlie confirmed. "Straight-up told her it was business."

That got the team murmuring.

"If the CIA's involved, then O'Shea had to be an asset or a spy," Hernandez reasoned.

"So what was he doing in Europe?" Deanna asked.

"Could've been meeting an informant," Tanner suggested. "Or doing a side job the agency didn't sanction."

"Maybe he was burning a contact," Charlie threw in.

"Enough." Ron's patience snapped. "That's above our pay grade."

But he was wondering the same thing. O'Shea lying to his wife about his reason for being in Europe? That was significant.

If he was on Agency business, why not just tell her he was traveling? Unless…

Unless Carr was also an asset.

Ron made a mental note to dig deeper.

"The Brits shared their intel on Marlowe." Ana cut in, shifting the conversation.

That got everyone's attention.

She clicked on the screen and flipped through a set of surveillance images, grainy, high-contrast photos of a man with a sharp jawline, cropped silver hair, and deep-set eyes. "This is our guy."

"Looks like someone's grandfather," Deanna muttered.

"MI6 has a low-level guy on the inside, but nothing close to Marlowe himself."

Ron studied the images, filing away the details.

"Anything else?"

Hernandez raised a hand. "Auction's still on schedule. The listing's been viewed hundreds of times in the last few hours."

A muscle ticked in Ron's jaw. That wasn't good either.

Hernandez continued. "Bidding starts Monday at noon."

That gave them less than two days.

Then Deanna spoke up, her voice tight. "I found a better image of the van." She clicked again, bringing up a pixelated but sharper photo.

It still had no plate, but—

"There." She pointed. "A decal."

She clicked to enlarge it.

Obsidian Rare Works.

Ron's breath slowed.

"Isn't that—" Charlie started.

"That's Marlowe's legit or front company, isn't it?" Tanner was scrolling his phone.

It was all coming together now. O'Shea's murder. Tommy's and Mia's disappearance. The auction. Marlowe.

Somehow, they were all tied together.

Now they just needed to figure out how.

CHAPTER 33

COLONIAL MARKET SQUARE

TOMMY

Tommy's heart pounded out a drumbeat in his chest. He checked over his shoulder. A man in a dark jacket and baseball cap, with eyes like a hawk, met his gaze. Their pursuer. He knew it. The man didn't break stride, but his intent was clear.

"Not good," he muttered.

Mia's hand shot out, grabbing his arm like a lifeline. "This way!" She tugged him forward, jolting him into motion.

His legs felt like lead for the first few steps, but adrenaline kicked in, pushing him to keep up. They weaved through the bustling mall, dodging shoppers, strollers, and holiday displays. The air smelled of cinnamon pretzels and desperation.

Tommy risked another glance back, his head swiveling. Two men now.

"Don't look back!" she snapped.

"I—" He opened his mouth to respond but nearly collided with a mother juggling shopping bags and a toddler.

"Excuse us! Coming through!" Mia called out. She darted ahead, zigzagging like a runner cutting corners on a track.

He struggled to match her pace. His shoulder clipped a rack of overpriced handbags.

Who was this woman in Mia's shimmery navy dress? He never would've envisioned her to hot-wire a car, hide a flash drive in her heel, and who knows what else she had in mind. It was like a switch flipped when they were in the van. A different Mia took over.

"Keep moving!" she ordered, her grip a vise on his wrist.

Ahead, she zeroed in on an unassuming door marked Mall Employees Only. Without breaking stride, she shoved it open and dragged him inside.

"What are you doing?" His voice rose. "This is for employees!"

Already halfway down the dim hallway, she called over her shoulder. "You want to argue about rules or lose these guys?"

He hesitated, his breathing uneven, but the distant, purposeful footsteps snapping on tile decided for him. He followed her, the door clicking shut behind them.

The gray cinderblock walls stretched on, oppressive beneath the flickering fluorescent lights, and the faint smell of cleaning chemicals stung his nose.

"Come on. There it is." She nodded toward the door ahead marked Locker Rooms. Nearby, janitorial supplies cluttered a rack, and a mop bucket sat idle in the corner.

"Okay, what now?" he asked. They might be able to hide here for a while.

She turned to him, jerking her head toward the safety vests on the rack. "Put one of those on. Lose your tie. Go into the men's locker room. Change into something casual."

He blinked. "What? Are you serious? We're not in high school playing pranks, Mia."

"Do I look like I'm joking?" She tried the women's locker room, but it was locked. That didn't deter her. She headed to the janitorial supplies, rummaged around, and pulled out a putty knife.

"What are you doing?"

She slid the knife under the latch. And just like that, the door opened.

She then marched toward the men's locker room and did the same trick. "Now, get moving! They're probably seconds away."

Before he could argue further, she disappeared into the women's locker room, leaving him standing there like a deer in headlights.

He swallowed hard and pushed into the men's locker room. The door creaked shut behind him, muffling the distant mall noise. His gaze darted around the empty room where metal lockers surrounded a bench. The smell of sweat and disinfectant hung heavy in the air.

"Okay, okay." He forced his legs to move. Uniforms hung on a rack: blue janitor shirts and pants.

He grabbed a set, praying it wouldn't be too small or too big. The fabric was rough against his skin as he changed out of his clothes as fast as his shaking hands allowed. Dressed in the uniform, he glimpsed himself in the mirror above the sinks. He looked… ridiculous, but unrecognizable.

"Better than being shot." He ran a hand through his hair before stepping back into the hallway and remembered to put on a vest.

She emerged at the same time, wearing a similar janitor outfit. She'd also found shoes. She, too, grabbed a vest. "Ready?"

"Define 'ready.'"

She rolled her eyes. "Just act natural. Blend in. No sudden moves."

Mia strode ahead, her posture relaxed. Tommy followed, his hands shoved into his pockets.

"Why do I feel like this isn't going to work?" he whispered.

"It will," she whispered back. "Now smile and keep walking."

They exited the back hallway and moved through the crowd, their pace slow and steady. His heart threatened to hammer its way out of his chest as he scanned the faces around them. Were their pursuers already here? Watching them?

Beside him, she tightened her grip on her visor, her voice barely audible over the din. "Don't look around too much. You'll draw attention."

"Right. Sure. Blend in."

Movement in his peripheral attracted his attention—dark jackets, purposeful strides. The men were there, just feet away, their focus sweeping the crowd.

His knees wobbled.

Mia's hand brushed his arm, a silent warning. "Stay cool," she murmured.

He nodded. His pulse roared in his ears as they headed toward the nearest exit, their steps as casual as they could manage.

The exit was ahead—freedom, steps away.

Then something caught his eye.

Beyond the wide glass storefront of an electronics store, a row of TVs blared muted news footage. Bright-red text crawled across the bottom: "Persons of Interest in Ongoing Investigation." Beneath it, two faces flickered onto the screen—his and Mia's.

His stomach bottomed out. His breath hitched, and his steps faltered.

His face on a news broadcast twisted his insides into knots. Their driver's license photos were on display for all to see. He looked normal in his, clean-shaven and clueless. But the words *persons of interest* made him look like a suspect. A criminal.

He'd never been in trouble with the law. Not once. Not even a parking ticket. And now, his face was on TV? His heartbeat slammed against his ribs, air coming in shallow gulps.

He pivoted to Mia, his pulse roaring in his ears. "Mia—Mia, we're on the news." His voice came out hoarse, too loud. "That's us. That's our faces."

She barely glanced at the screen. "I know."

"You know? What do you mean, you know? This is bad. This is really, really bad." He gestured at the TV, scanning the surrounding area. So far, no one had connected the people on the screen to the two janitors standing near the exit. But how long before someone did?

She grabbed his wrist and tugged him toward the doors. "We need to go to Arlin's."

His brain stuttered. Arlin's?

He yanked his hand back. Had she lost her mind? "Now?" He lowered his voice but couldn't keep the disbelief out. "You want to go to a bar now?"

"Yes, come on." She didn't hesitate, didn't explain. She just pulled him forward, her grip firm, her posture determined.

He resisted for a second. The newscasters had moved on to another story, but that didn't mean people hadn't seen. That didn't mean someone wasn't already making a phone call. His hands felt clammy inside the janitor's gloves.

Her voice cut through his panic. "Tommy."

He met her eyes, and there was something in her expression —certainty, urgency, control. She had a plan.

He exhaled. "Fine. Let's go."

Together, they pushed through the exit door into the cold evening air. The smell of asphalt and city smog hit him, mingling with the scent of fried food from the vendors parked outside the mall. The neon glow of storefront signs flickered against the pavement.

Then he remembered their stolen van had run out of gas, and they had no money or phone. "And how do you suppose we do that? Walk?"

"I believe that's the last of your worries," a voice behind him said, followed by the unmistakable sound of metal clicking.

CHAPTER 34

CHAPEL, MIRROR ESTATE

PHIL

Phil eased his car into the detached garage behind the rectory, the engine's soft purr fading as he pressed the button. The night was still, the darkness thick and undisturbed. He sat there, his fingers drumming the steering wheel as he went over his plan for tomorrow.

The address on the envelope. Maybe it would give him some answers. Maybe it would tell him what the key was for.

He sighed, pulled the handle, and stepped out into the cool evening air. The scent of damp earth and faint gasoline from the garage clung to the breeze. His footsteps echoed against the concrete, but something else lingered, a prickling sensation that tightened the muscles in his shoulders. A warning.

His instincts, long buried beneath clerical robes and years of peaceful routine, stirred. He scanned the area, his eyes adjusting to the dusky shadows draped over the backyard. The rectory stood just ahead, its windows dark, lifeless. The street beyond was quiet. Nothing moved. Nothing seemed out of place.

Maybe he was being paranoid.

Still, he couldn't shake the feeling. His gut told him to be careful. He continued toward the house, his ears tuned to the slightest sound.

Then a flicker of motion.

A figure emerged from the shadows and stepped into his path like a phantom. "Mr. Marlowe would like a word with you, Padre."

Phil's eyes narrowed. "Who?"

"Victor Marlowe."

The name meant nothing to him, but the man's stance and squared shoulders, the slight bulge beneath his jacket—this was someone accustomed to getting his way.

He forced a calm smile. "I keep a full schedule. Perhaps Mr. Marlowe can make an appointment through my office."

The man didn't move. "I'm afraid he needs to see you now."

So this wasn't—and wouldn't be—a negotiation. Phil studied the man's stance, the balanced posture, the calluses on his knuckles, the way he scanned his surroundings. Special ops, or something close. He was about to respond when he caught the subtle shift in the man's posture—the tightening of his stance, the flex of his fingers. Years of training screamed at him. *Move!*

He twisted as a fist came barreling toward his face. It skimmed his jaw instead of landing full force, but a sharp sting flared along his cheekbone. In the blur of motion, the needle meant for him somehow twisted in the man's grip, jabbing into the attacker's forearm. He yanked it out with a curse, but the damage was done.

The man was strong, built like a soldier, and still moved with precision, though now a slight hesitation crept in. Phil countered with a jab to the ribs, but even with the drug starting to work, the blow barely made his attacker flinch.

A forearm slammed against his chest, forcing him backward. He gritted his teeth, using the momentum to shift his weight and pivot, barely avoiding another strike aimed at his gut.

He wasn't as quick as he once was. The years had softened him, made him slower. His attacker, despite the growing sluggishness in his movements, knew it too.

A fist caught his side, knocking the wind from his lungs. He stumbled, and his back slammed against the garage door. He barely had time to recover before another blow struck his ribs. Pain seared his torso, but he pushed through it, grabbed the man's wrist, and twisted. His opponent grunted, his reactions now delayed as he jerked free before slamming a knee into Phil's stomach.

The ground tilted beneath him. His vision blurred.

He hit the pavement hard.

Dazed, he rolled onto his side and struggled to push himself up. His attacker loomed over him, ready to finish the job, though his movements were becoming more unsteady.

Then—a blur of movement.

A shadow launched out of nowhere and collided with the man like a battering ram. Between the drug now coursing through his system and the impact, his balance failed. The force sent him stumbling back, his previous grace gone.

A sharp crack echoed through the night.

The attacker was on the ground now, groaning, the drug and the impact leaving him inert.

Phil blinked, his vision clearing as his rescuer stepped forward.

"Are you okay, Phil?" The familiar voice cut through the haze.

Jeremy.

Phil took the offered hand and let Jeremy haul him up. His ribs ached, and his face throbbed from the hit. But he managed a nod. "Yeah. Thank you."

Jeremy nudged the groaning figure on the ground. "He's out cold. What is going on? We need to call 911."

Phil's jaw tightened. "I don't know what's going on. But I'm okay."

Jeremy's eyes darkened. "You should get inside before he wakes up. I'll find something to tie him up."

Phil nodded. Victor Marlowe, whoever he was, had sent a clear message.

CHAPTER 35

COLONIAL MARKET SQUARE

TOMMY

The chill of the gun aimed at Tommy's back sent his pulse into overdrive. His brain screamed at him to move, to do something, but one wrong step could get them killed.

Mia, standing beside him, was as still as a statue.

"Turn around. Slowly."

The voice, so calm and controlled, was worse than if the guy had been yelling.

Tommy swallowed hard and turned enough to see the man behind him—plain clothes, a hard expression, and a steady hand on a compact pistol. Not a cop. Not security. Someone worse.

"We're just leaving," he said.

The man smirked. "I don't think you are."

Mia made her move.

Fast.

She pivoted on her heel, grabbed a nearby trash can, and threw it at the guy's chest. It wasn't heavy, but it was enough to make him flinch. Enough to break his focus.

That was all they needed. They bolted.

A gunshot cracked behind them, too close, too loud. The bullet whizzed past his shoulder, nicking his sleeve before punching into the brick wall.

Adrenaline surged through his veins.

Keep moving.

They tore across the parking lot, dodging between parked cars, Mia keeping a step ahead. Behind them, the gunman cursed, recovering fast, but Tommy didn't look back.

Then—sirens.

Loud. Close. Too close.

Flashing red-and-blue lights painted the lot in frantic bursts of color as two cop cars screeched to a stop right in front of them, blocking their path. Uniformed officers jumped out, weapons drawn.

Tommy's stomach clenched as doors flew open.

"Freeze! Hands where we can see them!"

Mia didn't stop. She caught his wrist and yanked him left between two SUVs.

He barely managed to keep his footing. Why were they running from potential rescuers? As if they were criminals, not just persons of interest. Did she not trust the police? His heart pounded as they zigzagged through the parked cars, trying to break the officers' line of sight.

Then—a silver car barreled toward them.

His eyes widened.

Dylan. And Lily.

They weren't stopping, but slowing down.

Mia ripped open the back door the second the car skidded close enough. "Get in!"

Tommy threw himself inside, barely dodging another shouted order from the cops. Lily, in the passenger seat, looked shocked. Dylan slammed the gas pedal before the doors even closed.

The tires screeched. The world blurred as they sped off.

"What in the world is going on?" Dylan demanded, his gaze flicking between them in the rearview mirror and the way ahead.

Tommy twisted to the back window. The cops were in pursuit, sirens wailing.

Lily turned around in her seat. "You guys are persons of interest. What happened? Agent Peters called Dylan. I called Mom. They all asked about you."

"Long story. Come to think of it, how'd you find us?" Tommy gulped hurried breaths.

"Your watch. It was glitchy or something. Didn't get a good location until the Colonial Square."

"The industrial park." He touched his watch. He'd only just realized it was still on his wrist. "Probably because the signal was lousy there."

"Oh no. You're bleeding." Mia pried at his sleeve.

He lifted his arm. The bullet hadn't hit him, but the graze had ripped through his sleeve and left a shallow, stinging wound. Blood smeared his skin, but he barely felt it. "I'm fine."

"I need to go to Arlin's." Mia told Dylan.

"What?" Dylan eyed her in the rearview mirror.

"Why?" Lily gaped.

Mia crossed her arms. "Let me make a phone call. Can I borrow a phone, please?"

Lily narrowed her eyes, hesitated, then offered hers.

Mia made a call.

Tommy grabbed some tissue to wipe his wound. His ears still rang from the gunshot.

He couldn't hear the other end of the conversation, only Mia's voice—low, urgent.

"Yeah. Okay." A pause. "Okay." She disconnected and handed the phone back to Lily. "Please take me to the police station."

CHAPTER 36

ORLANDO PD – CENTRAL DISTRICT

RON

R on adjusted his coat and stepped into the station. The dim hum of overhead fluorescents buzzed in the background, casting harsh white light over the precinct's polished floors. It was going to be a long night.

He'd barely sent his team home when the alert came in. Tommy and Mia had turned up at the station. Now, walking past the bullpen, he spotted them, the risk-taking duo. Dylan and Lily.

Olivia waved him over. "Simon just walked into the room."

Ron barely nodded. Of course, Dylan wouldn't let Tommy say a word without an attorney present. Smart move. The kid had good instincts. He listened as Olivia filled him in. Dylan and Lily had tracked Tommy via his watch and found them first. They'd managed to bring them in without incident. Since Tommy and Mia were only persons of interest, there hadn't been any trouble. For now.

He glanced across the room and found Spaulding and KC leaning against a desk, deep in discussion. They hadn't gathered much new information since Morrison. The puzzle remained incomplete.

Simon then emerged from the interrogation room, straightening his tie. His expression gave nothing away. "We're ready. They'd like to be questioned separately."

Interesting.

Ron stepped back as KC led Mia into another room. Through the one-way mirror, he studied Tommy's body language. His shoulders were rigid, his hands clasped so tightly his knuckles had gone white. His chest rose and fell in uneven breaths, but beneath the lingering panic was something else—a relief in his steady gaze, as if he was still grappling with the fact that he was here, alive, and not lying dead somewhere.

Then KC joined Spaulding, and detectives launched in. Ron listened. Olivia, whom the cops knew as an FBI agent, stood beside him.

"You were in the building," Spaulding stated. "Right place, wrong time?"

As coached, Tommy looked at Simon before answering. When he saw the nod, he said, "I was supposed to have a drink with Mia after our company party. She needed to pick something up at the office, so we left early and stopped by Morrison. That's when we saw the body."

"Who was the meeting with?" KC pressed.

Another check with Simon before answering. "There was no meeting. We weren't expecting anyone to be there."

Spaulding leaned forward. "And when you found the body?"

At Simon's nod, Tommy exhaled. "I checked for a pulse. He was barely alive. I asked Mia to call 911, but then I heard this thump, turned, and saw her go down. Next thing I know, I was out."

KC pushed a piece of paper in front of Spaulding, and he dipped his head. "Yes, we got the video footage." He went on to ask where they were taken to and how they escaped.

Ron listened, but Tommy wasn't involved. Still, Ron would have his agents talk to Tommy again tomorrow after he'd had a chance to rest. Maybe then he'd remember something else.

Before Ron could dwell on the thought, hurried footsteps approached.

Lily whispered, "Fr. Phil got attacked."

"What? When?" Olivia spun toward her daughter.

Ron demanded, "Is he okay?"

Dylan caught up with Lily. "According to Dante, Fr. Phil is okay. Paramedics treated him. Some cuts and bruises. And Dante figured the attacker came in from the north. Our patrol only covers the estate grounds. The chapel campus is just outside of the perimeter."

"Did they catch the guy?" Olivia asked.

Dylan rocked off his toes, adrenaline obviously leaving the boy jittery. "Yeah, the cops showed up. Fr. Jeremy subdued him somehow. I didn't get the details."

After a beat, Olivia announced, "I'm going to check on him. You two, stay with Tommy. He'll need a ride back."

"Keep me posted." Ron called after her.

Minutes later, the detectives gathered in the adjacent room. Ron lingered in the doorway, observing.

"You're not going in, counselor?"

Simon shook his head. "She declined representation. At least, not yet."

KC leaned in. "Mia, we need to know what happened tonight."

Nothing. She didn't even blink.

"This isn't helping you," Spaulding added.

Still nothing.

Ron rubbed his jaw. From her posture and calmness, this wasn't her first dance. She must've been arrested before and knew the drill.

Then from the front desk—

"I need to speak with someone in charge!" The authoritative bellow cut through the tension.

Ron stepped out to assess the situation. A woman in a crisp navy suit stood with another man. Both flashed DOJ credentials at the front desk.

"Ashley Fleming." The speaker then tilted her head toward the man beside her. "Brad Lane, DOJ legal counsel."

Ron scanned their credentials. By now, Spaulding had stepped out, likely responding to the desk sergeant's summons. Before Ron could respond, another man strolled in, also extending his credential pack, this one bearing Homeland Security Investigations.

Wesley Holt.

Now Ron was intrigued. What had gotten their attention?

"Ron Peters, SAC, FBI." He fished out his own cred pack.

"Detective Rick Spaulding," the detective added. "How can we be of service?"

On cue, Lane handed a folder to Fleming. She offered it to Ron while giving Spaulding an apologetic smile.

"For SAC Peters's eyes only. Classified." Her gaze swept between Ron and Spaulding. "Ms. Granger is not under arrest. She hasn't been charged, and as far as federal jurisdiction goes, she's under government protection."

Ron skimmed the memo. Mia Granger was an asset in a Homeland Security operation. That explained Holt's presence. He must be her handler. Ron met Holt's gaze. "You're here for Ms. Granger."

"Yes, sir." Holt nodded. "If I may ask, are you in charge of Task Force 629?"

Ron frowned.

Fleming interjected. "SAC Peters, I suggest you chat with Agent Holt. You're chasing the same criminal."

CHAPTER 37

CHAPEL, MIRROR ESTATE

OLIVIA

Olivia weaved through the dusky streets, the city stretching out in eerie silence. Her car's engine hummed low, the only sound breaking the still evening. She'd pushed the speed limit getting here, her grip tight on the wheel, her mind spinning faster than the tires.

As she neared the chapel, something felt off.

She had expected to see squad cars, but nothing.

She killed the engine, sitting motionless, scanning the street. Nothing but shadows. The air hung heavy, thick with damp earth and lingering incense. A deep breath. Then another.

She slipped out of the car, closing the door softly. Her boots crunched against the gravel, each step amplifying the silence. A shiver coiled down her spine. She knocked on the rectory door. Waited. Nothing.

Her stomach twisted.

She knocked again, harder. Still nothing.

Her pulse climbed as she pivoted toward the adjacent house.

A faint glow flickered behind the curtains. Someone was home. This time, her knock was firm. Urgent.

Seconds dragged.

Then—metal scraped. The door eased open a crack, revealing Fr. Jeremy. Surprise flickered in his eyes before settling into something guarded. *"Olivia?"*

At his hesitant tone, she forced a smile. "Sorry for showing up this late." A beat. "I heard about Fr. Phil. I wanted to check on him."

Fr. Jeremy hesitated, his grip tightening on the door.

Then movement came from the dim hallway. A shadow shifted. Fr. Phil stepped into view.

Heat flared through Olivia's chest—part anger, part concern.

A dark bruise marred his left cheekbone, the swelling bleeding into the creases around his eye. A cut at his temple had started to scab over, raw against his pale skin. His collar sat askew. His stance stiff. Like he was hiding more injuries than he'd admit.

"Olivia," he greeted, his gaze steady despite the night's violence. "Come in."

The warmth of the house wrapped around her as she stepped inside. The common room was small, lived-in—book-lined walls, worn furniture, soft lamplight pooling in cozy corners. The faint scent of old paper and coffee lingering in the air.

Fr. Jeremy gestured toward the couch.

She stayed standing. "What happened?"

Fr. Jeremy gave a curt nod and disappeared into his side of the house.

Sinking into a chair, Phil exhaled. "It was… unexpected."

He recounted the attack. She pieced it together. The precision. The strength. A professional.

"Any idea why he came after you? Sounds personal."

"I don't know." Phil ran a hand over his face. "It doesn't make sense. He said Malone wanted a word with me."

Her spine stiffened. Malone? "Are you sure that's the name?"

A headshake. "Something like that. Victor Malone, I think. Never heard of him."

Crossing her arms, she perched against the couch arm. "I think you mean Victor Marlowe."

His head cocked, his eyes brightening. "Yeah. That's it. Who is he?"

Fr. Phil had been trained. He wasn't easy to rattle. But she believed him.

"A criminal. And if you didn't know him, then he's not your mission?"

He didn't answer.

She narrowed her eyes. "You told me the book didn't exist. If Marlowe wasn't your mission, then what is?"

His jaw muscle convulsed. "I never said the book didn't exist. I said the list didn't exist."

She scoffed. "Semantics."

"Hardly." His tone was even. "The list you're thinking of, a list of covert operatives, doesn't exist."

She let his words sink in. "So, there is a book. And that's your mission."

Silence.

Time to change tactics. "Let's go back to the attack. I think your attacker was one of Marlowe's enforcers. Can you describe him?"

Phil leaned back, eyes distant. "Tall. Well-built. Military bearing. Moved like he knew what he was doing." He nodded toward Jeremy's side of the house. "If Jeremy hadn't been there…"

Olivia clenched her teeth. If Fr. Jeremy hadn't been there, Fr. Phil might not have been sitting here at all.

Her fingers twitched with the urge to move. Time was slipping away.

"I'm glad you're okay." She pushed off the couch.

When she stepped out into the night, the door clicked behind her. The local police station was next. Before she looped Ron in, she needed confirmation.

MARIAN POLICE STATION

The Marian Police Station claimed a quiet street corner, a squat, gray-bricked building that had probably been around longer than most of the town. A single floodlight above the entrance buzzed, scarcely illuminating the worn concrete steps before the heavy glass doors. A squad car was parked out front, its engine still warm, a sign someone had just come in.

Olivia eased her car into an empty space, killed the engine, and took her usual moment before stepping out. The air was crisp, the scent of rain lingering. Then she walked up to the entrance, her boots making sharp taps against the pavement. The glass doors swung open under her grip, and she stepped inside the outdated station.

The burnt-coffee scent hit her first. Metal chairs lined the wall opposite the front desk where a tired-looking desk sergeant behind thick plexiglass flipped through paperwork.

A man in a rumpled windbreaker sat slumped in one of the chairs. A uniformed officer stood near the hallway, chatting with a second officer pouring coffee. The whole place hummed with the quiet exhaustion that settled into police stations after-hours.

Olivia approached the desk, slid her FBI credentials from her coat pocket, and held them up for the sergeant to see. "Olivia Tso, FBI. I need to speak to the detective handling Fr. Phil Shagley's assault case."

The sergeant looked at her badge, then at her, before he grunted and leaned back in his chair. "Give me a minute."

He reached for the phone, pressed a button, and mumbled into the receiver. She tapped her fingers against the desk. Seconds later, the hallway door creaked open, and a man in a wrinkled button-down and slacks walked out, running a hand through his graying hair. He looked like he'd been working this beat for years, the lines on his face deep, his expression carrying that specific brand of skepticism that came with the job.

He approached her with a measured stride, sizing her up before extending a hand. "Detective Lloyd Sweeney. You're FBI?"

She shook his hand. "That's right."

"What's the Bureau's interest in a simple assault case?" He hooked his thumbs in his belt loops.

"It's part of an ongoing investigation involving a high-value target," she said. "I need to question the suspect you have in custody."

Sweeney scoffed. "Yeah, good luck with that. Guy was out cold at the scene. Paramedics gave him something, probably woke him up enough to get him stable. He only came around a little while ago. Clammed up the second I started questioning him. Didn't say a word except to ask for a lawyer and his phone call."

"I figured as much." She crossed her arms. "Can I at least see him?"

Sweeney eyed her, then shrugged. "No skin off my back. Come on."

He led her down the hall, past empty desks and a full bulletin board crammed with wanted flyers and department notices. The holding cells were at the back of the station, past an old metal door with a keypad entry. Sweeney punched in a code, the door buzzed, and he pushed it open.

The hallway was dimmer here, the overhead lights flickering. Only one of the three cells was occupied.

A man sat on the bench, his hands resting on his knees, his head bowed. He was built like a soldier—broad shoulders, strong posture even in stillness. His face was shadowed, but Olivia's pulse ticked up. She'd seen that stance before. She wasn't sure, but could he be one of the men in the security footage outside Morrison's?

Sweeney watched her. "Ring a bell?"

She kept her expression neutral. "Do you have a booking photo?"

"Sure. Might not be uploaded yet, though."

"I'd like a copy."

"I'll get you one."

"Did the prints get any hits?"

"Oh, yeah." Sweeney grabbed a folder and opened it. "Ramon Vega, aka Fat Boy. Former US Special Ops, specific unit is redacted."

Special Ops guy. Fr. Jeremy was lucky to have restrained him. She gave the suspect another lingering look, noting the set of his jaw, the fingers tapping his knee, the faint scar cutting through his left eyebrow. Then she turned back to the detective.

"Appreciate it."

"Don't say I never did the Feds a favor," he muttered.

It didn't take long for him to get her a printout. The image was grainy, but it was clear enough. Olivia studied it, then folded it, and slipped it into her coat pocket. "Thanks, Detective."

Sweeney waved her on. "Good luck getting anything out of him. You ask me, guys like that don't talk unless they want to."

She gave him a curt nod, then walked out of the station, her mind already working three steps ahead. Once inside her car, she pulled out her phone and texted the image to Deanna and Ron.

Olivia: *Deanna, match this against the Morrison footage. I need confirmation.*

Then she followed up with a call to Ron.

He picked up on the second ring. "Tell me you've got something."

"You're not gonna believe it. Marlowe is behind the assault."

"What's the connection?"

"Working on it. Will let you know. Tommy still there?"

"We let him go. Turns out Mia is a Fed asset. Long story. I'll have to check if you have clearance to be read in. Anyway, Dylan put her up in the hotel. I posted agents there."

Asset. Interesting. If the Fed was already running an op targeting Marlowe, why did the Ghost give her the name? Coincidence? No, the Ghost had an agenda. What was it?

CHAPTER 38

TASK FORCE OFFICE

RON

R on stepped up to the retinal scanner, leaning in as the light flickered across his eye. A soft beep, then a mechanical click. He pulled the door open and moved aside, letting Holt in first. The SCIF door shut behind them with a finality that sealed them from the outside world.

Spacious for a SCIF, the room hosted workstations along the walls and large screens mounted around the perimeter. Ron nodded at the few personnel inside, signaling for them to clear the room. They filed out. He then gestured to the table in the center.

Holt dropped his bag onto the surface, unzipped it, and removed his laptop. "Give me a few minutes to go through what Mia handed over."

"Help yourself." Ron stood back.

Holt inserted the flash drive and clicked through folders. His expression unreadable, he scrolled through file after file, but Ron caught the subtle shift—Holt's fingers hesitating over certain documents, his jaw tightening.

Ron paced behind him, catching glimpses of the file names under the Obsidian Rare Works folder: Transactions, Bank Deposits, Cross-Reference, Provenance Records, Red Flags. The documents were dense—financial statements, wire transfers, asset logs. A forensic accountant's treasure trove.

Holt skimmed the numbers, speaking as he worked. "She came highly recommended by Judge Elaine Hargrove."

"How long have you guys been after Marlowe?" Ron pulled out a chair.

"Over a year," Holt said without looking up. "Your Art Crime Unit opened the file first, suspected him of dealing in stolen rare books, old masters with murky provenance, black-market antiquities. But they never got anywhere. Marlowe was too careful. No paper trail, no loose ends."

Finally, Ron sat beside him. "Then HSI got involved."

"We stepped in after overseas transactions flagged customs. Looked like Marlowe was moving high-value items across borders, but nothing ever traced back to him. HSI and the Art Crime Unit originally worked the case together—until the sting."

Folding his arms on the table, Ron narrowed his eyes. "What sting?"

Breath hissed past Holt's teeth. "We set up a buy. Someone inside Marlowe's network was supposed to hand over records proving he was dealing in stolen goods. But Marlowe got wind of it and disappeared before we could move in."

Ron muttered a curse. "So someone leaked."

"After that, both agencies started pointing fingers. HSI blamed the Bureau for getting bogged down in red tape. The FBI thought we were sloppy with sources. End of the day, the case fell apart, and Marlowe vanished for months."

Ron rubbed his jaw. "So you cut the FBI out."

"Pretty much." Holt tapped the screen. "We kept digging, but we had no way in. Not until Mia."

The table edge cut into Ron's forearms. He scooted back in his seat. "What did she find?"

"She was assigned to M&M Enterprises, Marino Hotels, but she also handled smaller accounts, including Obsidian Rare Works." Holt tapped the screen again. "She flagged anomalies in their financials. Nothing outright illegal, but things that didn't track. The problem? The books were too clean."

Ron studied the on-screen numbers. "Explain."

"The numbers lined up too perfectly," Holt said. "Most businesses have minor inconsistencies—rounding errors, unexpected costs, minor write-offs. But not this one. Every dollar had a place. Like someone went out of their way to audit-proof it."

Ron huffed. "Marlowe wanted it to pass scrutiny."

"Exactly. But Mia's a forensic accountant. She doesn't just look at what's there. She looks for what isn't." Holt scrolled down. "Then she found something else. These deposits? Large amounts labeled as Sales. On paper, Obsidian sold artwork, each piece supposedly worth five figures. But Mia had third-party appraisals done. Turns out, the art was worthless, barely fifty bucks apiece. When she flagged it, I told her to stall the audit. HSI wants all the ducks in a row before making a move."

Ron racked a finger down the document. "Found any evidence on forged provenance records?"

"Yes, that too." Holt clicked another file. "And then there's this—insurance records. Mia noticed some pieces were 'insured' before they were even reported as purchased. That's not normal. You don't insure something you don't own yet—unless you already have it under a different name."

Ron swore under his breath.

Holt sat back. "I was supposed to meet with her tonight for our weekly check-in, but she called first. And then I see her face blasted all over town as a person of interest."

Ron clenched his jaw. "So you directed her to the police station."

"Figured she'd be safer there than running around town." Holt met his gaze. "As for why someone's after her and her boyfriend, assuming he is her boyfriend, I have no idea."

Mia's audit hadn't made her a target. Not at first. But she and Tommy walked into Morrison's just after Marlowe's people killed the lawyer. That changed everything.

"They think she and Tommy saw something," Ron muttered.

CHAPTER 39

MARINO HOTEL

DYLAN

On the quiet drive back to the hotel, exhaustion pressed like a weighted blanket. The city lights blurred past, golden reflections on the sleek black car windows. Dylan kept his hands firm on the wheel, eyes sharp, mind running through security measures even as the hum of the road invaded the silence.

At the Marino Hotel, he pulled into the private underground entrance, bypassing the main lobby. Security cameras watched their every move, and the guards would already be on alert. He wasn't taking any chances.

"Agent Peters knows you're staying with me." Dylan led them into the elevator. "The hotel's fully booked. I could bump someone, but that's bad business. Just crash at my penthouse."

No one argued. They were too tired for debate, and, truthfully, there weren't many safer places than the hotel.

Tommy ran a hand through his hair, gripping it before he exhaled and released his clutch. Mia stood close to him, arms crossed, gaze darting toward every exit like she couldn't let her guard down. Lily leaned against the elevator wall, her expression unreadable.

When the doors opened to the grand atrium, Lily tugged on Mia's sleeve. "Come on. You need a change of clothes."

Mia blinked. "Huh?"

"There's a boutique on this level. We'll grab you something before heading up."

Dylan met Tommy's questioning glance and shrugged. "They won't take long. We'll meet them upstairs. Besides, I'm sure Agent Peters has plainclothes agents around. Now you know what it feels like."

"What?" As soon as the doors slid open, they stepped out and crossed to the private elevator, which required a key card. Dylan swiped his, and the doors opened to take them to the penthouse.

"To be chased. Now that you're safe, I'll say I'm glad it was you and not me."

Again, the elevator doors opened. This time, to a sleek, modern living space.

"I don't know how you and Lily do it." Tommy followed him inside. "It was terrifying."

Dylan switched on the lights. "We should give Mia the room, so I hope you don't mind the couch. Or you can crash in the loft with me. On the floor, though."

Tommy plopped onto the leather couch. "This is fine."

Lily and Mia returned, a shopping bag swinging at Lily's side. Tommy stretched, then pushed himself up from the couch. "I'm taking a shower in your bathroom," he called over his shoulder on his way to the loft.

"Just make sure you don't flood the floor," Dylan yelled.

Lily showed Mia the guest room and the adjacent bathroom. "You can shower in here."

Mia grabbed the shopping bag and headed to the bathroom.

The distant hum of running water echoed through the penthouse. Dylan braced against the kitchen island and motioned for Lily to sit. "Wanna know about my meeting with my aunt?"

She arched a brow, but sank onto the plush sofa, and tucked her legs beneath her. "Of course."

"She let something slip about the hidden treasures she's been searching for. If she's right, they could be stolen artifacts from World War II."

Her mouth parted. "You mean like… pilfered art? Nazi loot?"

"Maybe. I don't know for sure." He drummed his palms on the countertop. "But it's all just talk. We still haven't made any progress on the map or the code."

She patted the seat next to her. Once he sat, she snuggled up to him. "I'm sure we'll find something. She may know more than she's willing to tell you."

"That's what I need her to tell me." He draped his arm over her, her familiar lavender scent comforting.

"Did she say anything else? Do you think she's behind what happened to Tommy and Mia?"

He braced his cheek against the top of her head, breathing in that scent. "That's what I want to know, if she had any part in it."

Lily scooted away and furrowed her delicate brows beneath those new curtain bangs of hers. "I don't get it. How is she even communicating with the outside world? Everyone who works in that facility is vetted. No unauthorized calls, no mail without heavy monitoring."

He smirked. "You think that's stopped her before?"

"I thought the Feds cracked down after the last time she tried using her attorneys as messengers."

"Yeah, well, with the Ghost involved, you never know." He snugged her back into his arms. "She could have found another way."

CHAPTER 40

CHAPEL, MIRROR ESTATE

PHIL

Dawn had barely touched the sky when Phil swung his legs over the edge of his bed, the wooden floor cold beneath his bare feet. The routine was ingrained. Years of discipline made waking early second nature. But as he stretched, a persistent throb along his ribs reminded him of last night's attack.

His fingers brushed the swelling along his cheekbone. He winced at the tenderness. The cut at his temple had scabbed over, but the sting told him it hadn't healed enough. It didn't matter. He had Mass to say, and whatever aches and pains followed him to the altar were secondary.

Jeremy was about to pull on his vestments when Phil entered the sacristy. "What are you doing up? You should rest. I'll take the Mass."

Phil shook his head, having already donned his garb. "I need to fulfill my obligation anyway. You take care of the next one."

As he stepped onto the altar, curious eyes tracked him. Parishioners weren't subtle when something was amiss, and the bruises on his face weren't minor. If he didn't address it up front, he'd be fielding questions the entire morning.

He took a deep breath and offered a reassuring smile.

"Before we begin"—his steady voice carried through the church—"I want to put your minds at ease. I had a bit of a mishap last night, but I assure you, I'm fine. Nothing serious. I'll be more careful in the future. Now, let's turn our hearts toward the Lord."

It wasn't a lie. Just not the whole truth.

The explanation seemed to settle them. As the Mass continued, he focused on the rhythm of the liturgy, and the familiarity of Scripture and ritual steadied him.

But afterward, he couldn't avoid the inevitable.

Jan approached first. "Father, are you sure you're all right?"

"I promise, Jan, I'm fine."

She pursed her lips. "You don't look fine."

Behind her, a cluster of parishioners nodded.

"It's nothing a few days of rest won't fix," he reassured them.

Felix, a retired firefighter, clapped a firm hand on Phil's shoulder. "You need anything, Father, you let us know. My wife's chicken soup can heal just about anything."

Others chimed in, suggesting remedies and home-cooked meals.

"We'll pray for your swift recovery," Jan offered to murmured agreements.

"That means a lot." Phil inclined his head. "Thank you."

After several more reassurances, he made it back to the rectory. He rubbed a tired hand over his face. The concern was touching, but he had other worries. And he needed a distraction.

He changed from his vestments and went to his office. At his desk, he pulled out his phone and searched for Sentinel Vault & Locker's hours. They wouldn't likely be open on a Sunday, but it was worth checking.

Then his phone rang.

"Father." The voice on the other end was strained. "It's about Sam."

His heart clenched.

"What happened?"

"He… became aggressive. One of the visitors must have upset him. We had to calm him down, but when we administered the sedative… he went into cardiac arrest. The paramedics took him to the hospital, but—"

The breath hitched in Phil's throat. He already knew what was coming next. "Which hospital?"

"Marian Hospital."

"I'll be there."

MARIAN HOSPITAL

When he arrived, the sterile scent of disinfectant and stale air pressed in around him. The fluorescent lights buzzed overhead, cold and clinical. He was no stranger to hospitals, especially this one.

He approached the front desk. "I'm here for Sam Rhodes."

"He's in 2B, Father."

He hurried over. A team hovered around the bed, but it didn't look promising. Nurses were pulling the tubes out, and technicians were unplugging the equipment. His heart sank. He was too late.

"Doctor!" He caught the doctor as he was walking out of the room. "Phil Shagley, Sam's next of kin."

"Father, I'm so sorry. We did all we could." He shook his head.

"I'd like a moment with him, please."

A hesitation. Then a nod. "Of course." The doctor then whispered something to a nurse who herded everyone out.

Phil walked in. He stood there, his throat tight, his breath uneven.

He'd promised. Fr. Donovan had entrusted Jean-Claude to him. And now...

"I failed him."

The words burned, but he swallowed them down. Then he stepped forward and began to pray.

"'Eternal rest grant unto him, O Lord, and let perpetual light shine upon him'..." His fingers traced the sign of the cross over Jean-Claude's forehead. "'May his soul, and the souls of all the faithful departed, through the mercy of God, rest in peace.'"

He lingered, searching the still features of the man who had been, in many ways, more than a responsibility. Jean-Claude had secrets, that much was certain. Now those secrets died with him.

The memory came unbidden, sharp and clear despite the decades in between. A rainy afternoon in Rome, three months after Phil joined Vatican Intelligence. Jean-Claude, younger but already gray at the temples, pacing before him in that cramped apartment serving as their unofficial training ground.

"You're thinking like a soldier," Jean-Claude had said, his accent thickening. "Always the direct approach. Always the obvious route." He'd tapped his own temple. "In this world, Phil, the quiet path is often the only path that keeps you alive."

Phil had been stubborn then, still carrying the confidence— arrogance, really—of his SEAL training. "With respect, sir, I was taught to eliminate threats efficiently."

Jean-Claude had smiled, not unkindly. "And how many of your operations were compromised because someone else was watching? Someone you never saw?"

Phil remembered shifting uncomfortably, unable to answer.

"This isn't the battlefield you know." Jean-Claude had then

*retrieved a case from the shelf. He'd removed a simple rosary.
"Our enemies don't wear uniforms. They sit beside you at
Mass. They smile as they pass you communion. They hear
confessions while planning assassinations."*

"Seriously? Priests?"

*Jean-Claude merely glanced at him. "Lots of things will
surprise you. Wolves in sheep's clothing. I'm not saying all are
bad, but enough."*

*His mentor pressed the rosary into Phil's palm, closing
Phil's fingers around the beads with surprising gentleness.
"Never trust blindly, Phil. Even inside the Church—maybe
especially inside the Church. The stakes are too high, the
consequences too grave."*

That night, Jean-Claude had taught him how to build a dead
drop inside a rosary, a technique Phil would use countless times
in the years to come. But the lesson that stayed with him wasn't
about tradecraft. It was about discernment. About seeing beneath
surfaces. About understanding that even the holiest façades
could conceal the darkest intentions.

Now, with Jean-Claude's still form before him, those words
resounded. His mentor hadn't been lost in that nursing home.
He'd been where he needed to be. Hiding. Watching. Protecting
secrets someone had decided were worth killing for.

Phil needed the Lord. There was only one place to go.

The hospital interfaith chapel was small but inviting, its dim
lighting a stark contrast to the hallways' harsh brightness. He
sank onto a wooden pew, his head bowed.

He failed. Did he make the wrong decision to follow Fr.
Donovan way back when? What if he'd been a regular parish
priest all these years? He wouldn't have known anything about
the book, the deal, and all the secrets. He thought he'd be able to
protect Mickey, but... He'd failed him and now Jean-Claude.

You are not a failure. And you still have Dylan.

But I can't do this alone.

You're never alone. Remember "My grace is sufficient for you." Arise, my child!

Yes, he couldn't sit here. There would be time for mourning. Now he had work to do. He straightened. He needed to request an autopsy.

"Excuse me, Father." A nurse approached.

"Yes?"

"I thought you should know... your uncle's last words."

His pulse jumped.

"He said something?"

The nurse nodded, shifting. "He kept mumbling something. He was insistent."

Phil stood. "What did he say?"

She hesitated. "Find phone. Book. I hope that makes sense to you."

Find phone. Book. What did it mean? He understood finding the book, but phone? He would have gotten his phone when he collected Jean-Claude's belongings later. So, why so specific? He needed to go to the nursing home where it happened.

"Thank you." He went in search of the doctor to request an autopsy.

CHAPTER 41

TASK FORCE OFFICE

RON

R on pulled at his tie, loosening it as he walked into the task force office. The place was still mostly empty, the quiet punctuated only by the distant hum of the building's heating system.

Church with Sheila. Not his usual Sunday routine, but she'd asked—one of the "requests" she'd made when they started hanging out again. A loaded phrase if he'd ever heard one.

Hanging out.

Like they were friends.

Like he was some teenager afraid to commit.

He rubbed a hand over his face as he made his way to his office. Not the time to dwell on that. He had about an hour before the team rolled in. Might as well make good use of it.

At his desk, he eyed the performance evaluations. If he ever needed proof paperwork was a necessary evil, this was it. Did anyone read this stuff? He doubted it.

Still, a job was a job. He grabbed a pen, flipped open the first file, and forced himself to focus.

The phone rang. Phil.

His brows furrowed. Why was he calling this early?

He swiped to answer. "Hey, Phil."

"Ron." The priest's voice was steady, but something was off about it.

He leaned back in his chair. "Heard about the attack. Olivia updated me. How are you holding up?"

A pause. Then, "I'm fine."

"Look, I'm glad you're okay, but I doubt you called to reassure me."

A breath on the other end of the line.

"My friend passed away."

They had known each other since their military days. He knew a bit about a particular friend, Sam, pretending to be his uncle. "Sam?"

"Yeah." Another pause. Phil then explained the circumstances. "By the time I got to the hospital, he was already gone."

A familiar knot formed in Ron's gut. "I'm sorry to hear that."

"Something doesn't sit right with me."

"What are you thinking?"

"I asked for an autopsy."

"And?"

"I don't know if the hospital will comply. I don't know if they'll even consider it." A beat. "I need you to light a fire."

An autopsy request meant Phil suspected something. And if he suspected something, that meant Ron had a new problem on his hands.

"Tell me straight. Do you think someone helped him along?"

A hesitation. Then a quiet response. "I don't know. It's not like him to act belligerent. And then a cardiac arrest right after getting a sedative?"

"It does sound fishy. Which hospital?"

"Marian."

"All right. I'll make some calls."

He could hear Phil's exhale.

"Thank you, Ron." He disconnected.

Ron set the phone down, but the unease didn't leave. It coiled deeper. Something about this didn't feel right.

And if Phil was coming to him, asking him to push for an autopsy...

The priest wasn't just feeling grief. He was feeling suspicion.

And Ron couldn't ignore that. He grabbed his phone and made a call.

CHAPTER 42

THE BREAKFAST GROVE

OLIVIA

The incense lingered in Olivia's senses as she stepped into The Breakfast Grove. Mass with Simon had been a grounding moment, an hour where she could breathe, listen, and let the past week settle in the presence of something constant, unshakable.

Faith was her anchor. Even in the darkest corners of her work, it never left her. But the moment she walked into the restaurant, the shift was immediate.

The low hum of conversation, the scrape of cutlery against plates, the rich aroma of coffee and buttered toast. Normal, easy things.

Two exits. Five windows.

Mapping the space—an ingrained habit, drilled into her bones. She counted egresses, noted obstacles, calculated the fastest exit if things went sideways.

And she wasn't the only one.

At the corner table, Raven and Falcon—her British counterparts—had positioned themselves with their backs to the wall, eyes on the doors. Even now, they were watching, assessing.

Olivia nudged the seat across from them sideways enough to keep the room in view.

By the time Olivia's coffee arrived, Ana showed up. She gave a subtle flick of her gaze to the exits before she joined them.

They were all wired the same way.

Olivia set her coffee cup down. "Any updates?"

Falcon leaned in, his voice pitched just low enough. "Our man inside picked up something interesting. Marlowe's inner circle is spooked."

Raven feathered her fingers through her short black hair, the bangs looked longer than she was comfortable with. Probably hadn't taken time for a cut lately. "One of his top lieutenants got picked up. No confirmation yet on who grabbed him, but it's rattled them. The auction is moving forward, but there's uncertainty in the ranks."

Her mind spinning, Olivia kept her expression even. She had woken up to a text from Deanna, confirmation that Fr. Phil's attacker had been one of the men from Morrison. The same crew that had taken Tommy and Mia.

And now, a lieutenant in custody?

She didn't believe in coincidences.

But she wasn't about to tell Raven and Falcon. Not yet anyway.

They were after Marlowe—or so they wanted her to believe. But they weren't telling her everything. No matter how well they worked together, and despite the close ties between their countries, they were still from different intelligence agencies. Some things would always be kept under wraps. That was how the game was played.

"The auction is still on, then?"

"As far as we know," she confirmed. "But Marlowe's moving

differently. He's shutting people out, and some of his usual operatives have gone dark."

That meant something.

Ana sat forward. "We've been checking industrial parks,
warehouses, loading docks—anywhere that could be used as a
staging ground. He's not using his usual spots."

Which meant one thing.

"He's being careful," Olivia murmured. "Or he's planning
something we haven't seen yet."

Ana's nod bounced her ponytail. "We'll keep digging."

Silence settled, heavy and thoughtful.

Then Falcon spoke, tilting his head. "We need to figure out
who has the lieutenant. If it's someone we can work with, we
might be able to get access."

Olivia barely reacted, though her gut coiled.

The Brits didn't want Marlowe. They wanted the book, like
they did.

Raven added, "If it's someone who won't play nice, we'll
need another plan."

Olivia curved her fingers around her coffee cup. Warmth
seeped into her palms, but couldn't ward off the inner chill. She
already had her theory.

If the man in custody was Fr. Phil's attacker, that changed
everything. He wasn't just another enforcer. He was close to
Marlowe—trusted, maybe even a handler for something bigger.
Could they flip him?

CHAPTER 43

SUNSET NURSING HOME

PHIL

P hil stepped into Sunset Nursing Home's lobby, the scent of antiseptic and faint lavender mixing in the air. The atmosphere, usually subdued with the hum of distant conversations and the occasional beeping of medical equipment, now felt thick, tense.

As he crossed the threshold, an anxious-eyed nurse hurried toward him. "Father, I'm so sorry." Sally wrung her hands together.

He placed a reassuring hand on her shoulder. "Thank you, Sally. Did you see what happened?"

"No." She tucked her hands in the pockets of her scrubs. "I'd just wheeled Sam out to the garden. He likes it out there in the mornings, you know? But then another resident called for me, so I went back inside. The next thing I knew, Sam was making a ruckus. By the time I got out there, one of the visitors was holding him, trying to stop him from hurting himself—or anyone else."

"A visitor?" Phil frowned.

"Yeah, I'd never seen him before." She squinched her brow, then shrugged. "Sam was so agitated. Kept pointing at the guy, yelling. We had to sedate him... and then—" She swallowed hard. "That's when he went into cardiac arrest."

Phil frowned, his lips pressing together. Jean-Claude—or Sam, as the staff called him—was not prone to outbursts. Something had set him off, and Phil needed to know what.

"Do you have security footage of the incident?"

Sally's face fell. "I don't know, Father. You'd have to talk to Ms. Yang. She came in because of the incident."

Phil thanked her and made his way to the administrator's office.

Ms. Yang, a composed woman in her early fifties, offered him a polite nod upon his arrival. "Fr. Phil, I'm so sorry for your loss. Sam was a special man."

"Thank you." He took the seat across from her desk. "I was wondering if I could review the security footage from this morning. I need to understand what happened."

Ms. Yang's expression gave way to regret. "I wish I could help, but we don't have cameras in the garden. There's a motion light out there, but the only surveillance we have is for the front and back entrances."

Phil exhaled through his nose, keeping his frustration at bay. "I appreciate your time, Ms. Yang."

Back outside, he approached the garden. The morning light had softened into an afternoon glow, and elongated shadows stretched along the pathways. He walked slowly, scanning the area.

Then movement caught his eye. A woman stood inside one room, watching him through a sliding glass door. Her lanai had a perfect view of the garden.

He approached, offering a friendly smile. The woman hesitated but finally slid the door open.

"Hello," he said. "I'm Fr. Phil."

She studied him before responding. "Kim. I was just visiting my mother."

An older woman exited the bathroom, her face wrinkled but kind. "Joanne," she introduced herself.

Phil took in the resemblance—the same sharp gaze, the same wary stance. "Joanne, Kim, I was wondering if either of you saw what happened in the garden this morning?"

Both women shook their heads, but then Joanne pointed toward a tree just outside the lanai. "My son installed a camera there," she said. "I wanted to record the hatching of the eggs."

"She's a birdwatcher." Kim hugged her mother's waist. "Mom doesn't know how to work her phone to check the footage, though. We were waiting for my brother to come by. But… I can do it."

"Would you mind taking a look?"

Kim retrieved her phone and tapped at the screen while Phil waited. Moments later, she turned the device around, and the grainy footage began to play.

Jean-Claude sat in his wheelchair, his hands resting in his lap. A man approached from behind. The resolution wasn't great, but something about the way the stranger moved sent unease crawling up Phil's spine.

Then Jean-Claude reacted.

The old man swung his arm, knocking against the visitor. He pushed himself up, unsteady but determined, arms flailing. The visitor grabbed him, at first appearing to steady him. But something wasn't right.

Phil replayed the footage and paused at the crucial point. The man's hand emerged from his pocket.

Something gleamed in the filtered light.

A syringe? A small object of some kind?

His pulse quickened.

"Kim, can you email me this video?"

"Of course." She started tapping away.

After he thanked them, he planned to find the phone. Instead, he veered back to see Ms. Yang. This time, he asked for the footage of the front and back entrance. It might have a better picture or angle of the man who showed up behind Jean-Claude. Ms. Yang obliged and called the tech person to email the footage to him.

Now, ready to look for the phone, he found Sally and asked if he could see Sam's room. She said of course, in fact, he would have to claim Sam's belongings once the staff completed a list. He thanked her, waited for her to walk away before searching the room. After a thorough search, he came up empty. And then it hit him—Jean-Claude might have had his phone with him this morning.

Phil pulled his phone out to watch the footage again. Yes, Jean-Claude's phone was with him. So, he went back to the garden to look. From the video, he found where Jean-Claude's wheelchair had been. He followed the path to go back inside. Then he spotted it.

The phone was in a planter. It was open. To keep up his appearance, Jean-Claude had a flip phone with large buttons. It was open with the numbers 66825 on the screen. He frowned. It wasn't a phone number. He pocketed it anyhow.

CHAPTER 44

MARLOWE'S HOME BASE

MARLOWE

M arlowe stalked the length of his hidden office, each measured step pressing deep into the worn Persian rug. The dim monitors cast shaky shadows across the mahogany desk, their screens depicting feeds of city streets, alleys, and doorways—all of them useless. Somewhere out there, his men had lost the couple, and now Fat Boy was sitting in a cell.

He ran a hand down his face, the tension tightening his jaw like a vise.

How had this happened?

Fat Boy—a misnomer if there ever was one, the man was built like a truck, not an ounce of fat on him—getting pinched was bad enough. But the timing had Marlowe's blood running hot. First, the couple had slipped through their fingers. Now one of his most trusted men was locked up. He didn't believe in coincidences.

The soft creak of the door barely registered, but the scent of coffee told him Luca had entered.

"Boss." Luca set a steaming mug on the desk. "Fat Boy's still inside, but he's keeping his mouth shut."

Marlowe didn't acknowledge the coffee. His focus stayed on the monitors, sharp and unrelenting. "And?"

Luca shifted, his broad frame tense. "Ringo's on the line with our guy now. Said the station's crawling with Feds, but no one knows why."

Marlowe's fingers curled into a fist. His gut twisted with something dark and dangerous.

"Marian? That's where Fat Boy is, right?"

"Yes, I mean, the station here where the couple went is crawling with Feds."

He remembered seeing the pictures on TV. Mia Granger. The auditor. "They're there for her."

Luca didn't argue.

A phone buzzed.

Luca pulled his out and checked the screen. "Ringo." He put it on speaker.

"The couple got picked up, questioned." Ringo's voice crackled through the line. "Not arrested, but they were at the station. Our guy says the Feds came in late last night. There was some kind of standoff before they all worked together. Then the couple was gone."

Marlowe straightened, his fist slammed the desk. "Gone?"

"Vanished," Ringo confirmed. "Our guy didn't get close, but the whole station's been on edge ever since."

Marlowe inhaled, controlling the fury. The couple had been right there, and then they'd disappeared.

"They gotta be under federal protection now." Luca rubbed a hand over his jaw. "Feds don't swoop in like that for nobodies."

Marlowe turned away from the desk, pacing toward the monitors. If the Feds were there, the auditor was working for the Feds. Had she found something?

He waved to the TV, his voice low, lethal. "Find them."

Luca nodded once. "Already on it."

Marlowe picked up the coffee mug and tested a slow sip as silent, grainy images flowed over the monitors. Somewhere in those streets, the couple was hiding, thinking they'd escaped.

They hadn't.

They were just running on borrowed time.

CHAPTER 45

MARIAN POLICE STATION

OLIVIA

Olivia stepped out of The Breakfast Grove, planning to head to Marian Police Station. But a thought hit her. She pulled out her phone and dialed Ron as she got in her car.

"Yes?" Ron greeted.

"Here's what I think. We need to flip him, the suspect in Fr. Phil's case. He's one of Marlowe's top lieutenants. He made it clear when he told Fr. Phil that Victor Marlowe wanted to have a chat with him. If we play this right, we can get him to roll over."

"It's not my case."

"No, but it ties back to Marlowe. You could bigfoot in, take jurisdiction." She scanned the lot out of habit. "We both know local PD isn't going to squeeze him like we can. Besides, they think it's a simple assault case."

"True. But as you say, a simple assault case. Is he likely to budge?"

She shrugged, even though he couldn't see her. "Probably not, but you know me. Ana and I will bluff a bit."

There was a pause, then the sound of shuffling papers. "All

right. Let me get in touch with my DOJ contact. Let's hope he answers on a Sunday." A few minutes later, he came back on the line. "The US Attorney's Office signed off on a proffer session. We have legal grounds to interview him before arraignment."

"That'll help. Ana can come with me?"

"Yeah. I'll have the paperwork ready."

Ana came out of the restaurant and headed to her car.

"Appreciate it." Olivia ended the call and honked to get Ana's attention.

Ana turned toward the sound, spotted her, and walked over. "Yes?"

"Just got off the phone with Ron." Olivia briefed her on Fr. Phil's attack and what the suspect said. "The US Attorney approved a proffer session. We get first crack at the suspect before arraignment. Can you pick up the paperwork and meet me at the Marian Police Station?"

Ana nodded. "Sure."

About forty minutes later, Olivia strode into the station. The scent of industrial-strength cleaner and sweat hit her as she passed the metal detector. The front desk sergeant barely looked up before directing her down the hall. "Sweeney's out." He didn't bother to remove his reading glasses. "You'll talk to Detective Kenny Summer."

Soon, Detective Summer, a Black man in his thirties, emerged from his office, his tall frame blocking the doorway. His sharp gaze flicked between Olivia and Ana as he approached.

"Detective Summer." Olivia flashed her badge. "Agent Olivia Tso, FBI. This is Agent Ana Ruiz, Defense Intelligence Agency liaison."

Summer raised an eyebrow but didn't comment as he shook their hands. "I heard you were coming." He gestured for them to follow. His office, cluttered but organized, bore the signs of long hours—stacks of case files, a half-empty coffee cup perched precariously atop them, take-out containers in the trash.

Olivia slipped the official paperwork onto his desk. "We need to arrange a proffer session with your suspect. The US Attorney's Office approved it. The suspect has ties to Victor Marlowe, and we believe he has actionable intelligence. We need to coordinate with his attorney before proceeding with an interview."

Summer slid into his chair, then took the papers. His lips pressed together. He tapped his pen against the desk. "Not often we get Feds swooping in on something like this."

"It's connected to a federal case." Ana, still standing by the door, clasped her hands in front of her. "One that falls under our task force's jurisdiction."

Shaking his head, he tapped the papers against his desk. "Fine. But if you break him, I want to know what he says."

Olivia gave him a knowing smile. "We'll see what he has to offer."

He pushed back his chair, then grabbed a key ring from his desk. "All right. Let's confirm his status and make sure his attorney is contacted."

He led them down a drab hallway, explaining as they walked. "We haven't heard from his attorney yet, but he knows he's got federal attention now."

Only one cell was occupied. A man sat straight on its bench, his gaze flicking up as they passed. The air carried a faint mix of disinfectant and stale sweat, the floor scuffed from years of wear, but clean. The quiet hum of the station settled over them, broken only by the occasional rustle of paperwork from a nearby desk.

Summer stopped near the holding cell, gesturing toward the occupied bench. "Figured you might want to see him, get a read on his state of mind before the lawyer gets here." He hesitated. "You sure about this?"

Olivia met his gaze. "Absolutely."

She observed the suspect's posture, not slouched, and his gaze darted toward them. She exchanged a look with Ana. "We'll see how cooperative he is once his lawyer is in the room."

When they were ready to leave, a middle-aged man in a pressed suit strode in, briefcase in one hand and phone in the other. Summer nodded toward him. "That's his lawyer."

Summer stepped forward, holding out the paperwork. "Your client has been made an offer—a federal proffer agreement. Thought you should be aware before you talk to him."

The lawyer's spine straightened, his expression guarded but not unreadable. He then skimmed the paperwork before he barely acknowledged his client and made a beeline for the nearest corner, phone pressed to his ear. His voice was low, urgent, but Olivia couldn't make out the words.

She and Ana shared a look. "Wonder who he's calling before even speaking to his client."

CHAPTER 46

MARINO HOTEL

TOMMY

Tommy's head throbbed as consciousness crept in. A dull ache pulsed at his temples while he drifted toward wakefulness. Sunlight sliced through the floor-to-ceiling windows, forcing a wince. He blinked bleary eyes at his surroundings—the sleek leather couch, high-end hardwood flooring, and classy decor. Dylan's penthouse. Then yesterday's events sharpened in his mind: the escape, the questioning, the endless reexplaining. It all felt like a fever dream.

What day was it? He reached for his phone before he realized his phone was gone, likely destroyed. His sluggish brain churned through the fog until Sunday. Right. Dylan never missed church.

He shifted on the couch, the plush cushions doing little to help the dull ache in his body.

A sigh escaped him as he scrubbed a hand down his face. He'd barely remembered crashing here last night. He hadn't had a real moment to breathe since it all went sideways.

Coffee. The lifeline beckoned. He pushed himself upright,

rolling his shoulders before trudging toward the kitchen. The penthouse was quiet, the only sounds coming from the city below. No Dylan. No Mia.

Where was Mia? Had she gone to church? She'd crossed herself yesterday, hadn't she? Okay, maybe she did go.

He went through the motions—mug, dark roast pod, button press. The machine whirred to life, emitting the scent of something warm and familiar. He leaned against the counter, staring at the city skyline through the massive windows.

The black TV screen on the wall stared at him as if telling him "watch me." He picked up the remote and flipped through channels until he landed on a sports recap. Nothing stuck. His mind kept running through the past day, no closer to making sense of it all.

By the time he finished his coffee, the elevator chimed.

Footsteps. Voices.

Lily's laughter drifted in first, followed by Dylan's easygoing voice. "—not my fault he shook the collection basket like that. You saw it."

"Poor guy looked terrified." Amusement rumbled through Mia's tone.

Tommy swiveled toward the entryway as they walked in. Lily, casually elegant as always. Dylan, already rolling up his sleeves, loosening his Sunday-best look. And Mia, hair tousled from the breeze outside, looking far more refreshed than anyone had a right to after what happened.

"You guys are back." Tommy made another cup of coffee.

She grinned and set her purse on the counter. "Yep. Mass was good. You should've come."

"Maybe next time."

Dylan stared at him, then Mia before Lily smacked him and nudged a bag toward Tommy, wafting the enticement of fresh pastries. "We brought breakfast."

"You're a saint." He reached for the bag. "I thought you went home last night."

"I did. Dylan picked me up, and we met Mia at church. She came back with us."

"Wait." Midbite, Mia lowered the pastry. "I didn't know you had a mole there."

Before Mia could touch the mark, Lily's hand shot out and caught her wrist. "Hold on." Her brows furrowed as she studied the underside of his forearm. "Tell me again, did the dead guy grab you?"

Tommy's pulse kicked up. Unease upended his gut, but he couldn't place why.

"Seriously," Lily pressed. "Did he touch your arm?"

"Yeah, he…" The memory crystallized. "He grasped my arm. Muttered something I couldn't understand."

Lily's expression grew grave. She hesitated before speaking. "I've seen something like this before." Her words were measured, but Tommy knew what she wasn't saying. "It's designed to mimic skin, with a microstorage unit embedded beneath a biopolymer layer." She turned her gaze to Mia. "I'm calling Mom."

His breath shuddered out. "You think the guy gave me some storage device?"

Lily was already tapping her phone, her shrug not quite hiding her tension. "Only one way to find out."

She ran a hand through her hair, gaze darting to the window before focusing on her phone screen.

"Mom? Yeah, it's about Tommy." Lily paced the living room, her free hand gesturing. "Remember how you removed my… special delivery? We might have another one."

Tommy's skin crawled. The spot on his arm seemed to burn now that he was aware of it. He remembered the dead man's grip —cold, desperate, purposeful. Not the random grasp of a dying man after all?

"Yes, exactly." Lily's voice pulled him back to the present. She wedged the phone between her ear and shoulder, heading to the bathroom. "Hold on. Let me check… yes! Found it."

She returned with a lotion bottle, the label worn away. "Mom says she's coming to the hotel right now, but we should try to remove it ourselves." She set the phone on speaker and placed it on the coffee table.

"Tommy?" Olivia's query crackled through the speaker, accompanied by the soft whoosh of traffic.

"Yes?" His voice came out hoarser than he'd expected.

"Don't move your arm too much. If this is what we think it is, we don't want to damage it."

Dylan appeared from the kitchen with rubber gloves and a bowl. "Here. Should we clear the coffee table?"

As Dylan set down a bowl and gloves, Mia leaned forward, eyes wide. "This feels like surgery prep."

"Something like that." Lily snapped on the gloves. When Tommy flinched at the sharp sound, she gave him a reassuring smile and softened her voice. "Sorry. Okay, Tommy, put your arm on the table."

He complied, trying to steady his breathing as Lily uncapped the bottle. His nose tingled at the lotion's odd smell.

"You okay?" Dylan squeezed his shoulder.

"Yeah, just… weird to think I've been walking around with potential classified intel stuck to my skin."

"Welcome to my world." Lily's lips quirked. She applied the lotion around the mark. "Mom, it's reacting just like mine did."

Sure enough, the edges of the "mole" started to lift. Tommy felt a slight tugging sensation, but no pain. He watched, fascinated despite his unease, as Lily worked the substance loose.

"Got it!" She extracted a small, flesh-colored disk no bigger than a pencil eraser. "Mom, it's the same design."

"I'm about fifteen minutes out." Olivia turned stern. "And, Tommy?"

"Yes?"

"Next time someone's dying in front of you, maybe check for sleight of hand?"

He exhaled a shaky breath, forcing a smirk. "Yes, ma'am."

He fixated on the disk in Lily's gloved hand. What secrets did it hold? And more importantly, who else knew he had it?

CHAPTER 47

BUNKER, MIRROR ESTATE

PHIL

Phil navigated the winding roads back to the chapel, preoccupied with the footage he just sent Ron. He trusted Ron's team to clean it up, but he couldn't shake this... urgency. He needed clearer visuals now. As he passed the estate's perimeter, he sighted Alex's SUV near the bunker's entrance.

The young IT consultant. Phil had heard about Alex's upgrades to the estate's network. If anyone could enhance the video, it was him.

Phil turned the wheel and guided his car toward the bunker parking area—calling it a "lot" would be too generous. Dylan had only cleared enough space for a handful of vehicles.

Phil parked beside Alex's SUV, climbed out, and approached the bunker's reinforced steel door. A keypad was affixed to the side. He pressed the call button, waiting as static crackled.

"Oh, Fr. Phil, come in." Alex's voice came through the speaker, followed by the mechanical click of the lock releasing.

Phil pulled open the heavy door, stepped inside, and descended a few steps. The air cooled as he moved deeper into the underground facility, the faint hum of electronics growing louder. He found Alex in the computer room, surrounded by an array of monitors and keyboards, their screens flickering with feeds of estate security footage.

Alex spun his chair around, offering a casual nod. "Didn't expect you to drop by, Father. Everything okay?"

Phil sat next to him. One screen displayed Latin and Greek alphabet characters and Roman numerals.

Alex must have noticed his curiosity. "Grace found some interesting symbols last year. I've been trying to decode them when I have time. Are you familiar with Latin?"

"Yes, we had to study Latin in the seminary and Koine Greek, New Testament language."

"Maybe you can help—"

"I'd love to, but I'm afraid it'll have to wait a bit. What I need is urgent." In fact, looking at all of them on the same screen reminded him of what Dylan had asked him to look at long ago. He'd have to get back to that when he could. But now, he needed to focus on the current issue.

"Oh, right, of course."

"I've got some video footage that needs enhancing."

Alex's brows lifted. "Enhancing? You mean, like, sharpening images? Removing noise?"

"Exactly. The footage is from a nursing home and a nearby birdwatcher's camera. A visitor caught my attention, but the quality's too poor to make out details."

The young man swiveled back toward his screens. "I can help with that. Just email me the files."

Phil slid out his phone and forwarded the footage. "Sent."

Alex cracked his knuckles and got to work, his fingers flying across the keyboard. Screens flickered as the raw footage loaded. Then he tapped a key. "Let's see what we've got here."

The videos played on the main monitor. After a few flickers,

Jean-Claude shuffled across the screen. He looked weary, but then his body language shifted, his posture stiffened.

Alex leaned forward, adjusting the resolution. "See that? He tensed up before the guy even got close. That's instinct. He knew something was off."

"Play that again, please."

Alex rewound the footage and slowed it down. Jean-Claude's hands twitched at his sides. Then a blurred figure closed the gap between them. A struggle. "Was that—? Wait." Alex toggled something, enhancing the brightness and contrast. "It almost looks like the guy stabbed him with something."

Phil's gut clenched. He had suspected foul play, but seeing it unfold made his stomach churn. "Can you zoom in on the suspect?"

Alex adjusted the frame, isolating the attacker. But the angle remained unhelpful. Shadows and poor lighting obscured the finer details.

Alex muttered a curse. "He's positioned just right to keep his face out of view."

Phil rubbed his temple, frustrated. "Can you check the front and back entrance footage?"

Alex switched screens, summoning the cameras positioned at the nursing home's entry points. Visitors entered and exited, but nothing seemed out of the ordinary. No suspicious loitering, no sudden departures. Whoever the attacker was, he hadn't walked through the front or back like a normal visitor.

"This doesn't make sense." Phil let out a heavy breath. "If he didn't come through the front or the back, then how—"

"Hang on," Alex interrupted, his fingers flying over the keyboard. "Let's try something different."

He played the garden footage where Jean-Claude had been attacked. A new set of measurements appeared on the screen.

"What's this?" Phil asked.

"I'm running a height estimation based on the shadows and

surrounding objects. If we can get an approximate height, we can compare it to the people who entered through the main doors."

Lines and grids formed over the attacker's figure, calibrating against the environment. A number flashed on the screen.

"Got it." Alex swiveled his chair side to side. "Roughly five foot eleven. Now, let's check the entrance footage."

The system cross-referenced every person who entered and exited, filtering out anyone who didn't match the estimated height. The algorithm found a match.

CHAPTER 48

TASK FORCE OFFICE

RON

R on leaned back in his chair, his gaze sweeping over the squad room as his team trickled in, one by one. Low conversations filled the space, the occasional shuffle of papers and clatter of keyboards adding to the rhythm of a morning settling in. He gave them fifteen minutes, enough time to grab coffee, set up laptops, and brace for the day. Then he pushed back from his desk, collected his notepad, and strode out.

The squad room quieted as he approached. They knew the drill. When Ron called a meeting, there was work to be done, and no one would be leaving anytime soon. He didn't bother with pleasantries.

"All right, listen up." His voice cut through the last murmurs. "Before I forget, Tanner, make sure to brief Agent Berrigan on everything. I met with an HSI agent last evening. Now, tell me about Mia and Tommy."

Tanner stirred his coffee. "They're secure at Dylan's penthouse. We've got a plainclothes agent tailing Mia. This morning, he followed her to church. Another agent is stationed inside the hotel with Tommy. Nothing unusual so far."

Ron processed that, then shifted his focus. "Local PD?"

Tanner clattered the spoon onto his desk. "Nothing new."

"Ana went to the Marian police station with Olivia, following up on Fr. Phil's attacker," Ron told them.

Charlie cleared his throat. "I dug into Obsidian Rare Works." He clicked a few keys. A satellite image appeared on the large screen. "They've got a small storefront, but this"—he pointed to a much larger building on the screen—"this is their warehouse listed on one invoice Ana got from that gallery. Way too big for the kind of inventory they claim to be moving."

Ron studied the image, a slow unease creeping into his gut. "You planning to check it out?"

"Yeah." Charlie braced against the desk behind him. "Thought I'd take a drive out there, see what's what."

"You're not going alone." Ron looked at Tanner. "Go with him."

Tanner frowned at the map. "Could be something. That industrial area could be where Mia and Tommy were taken to."

Ron released a long breath. "Then let's not waste time. You two head out as soon as we're done here."

Hernandez and Deanna exchanged a glance before Hernandez spoke up. "We're still monitoring the auction. It's active."

Ron nodded to Deanna. "Did you get the video footage?"

"Just got it." She pushed her glasses up the bridge of her nose. "I'll clean it up, run facial recognition. Should have something soon."

"You know the drill. If it turns out to be anything of use, we need to request those through the official channel."

"Aye-aye, sir."

His phone buzzed in his pocket. He fished it out. A text from the medical examiner.

MORGUE

The scent of antiseptic and something more unpleasant, a metallic tang mixed with the chill of the morgue, hit Ron as he stepped inside. His stomach tightened. He'd been here more times than he cared to count, and each time, the walls pressed in a little closer. He tightened his coat around himself as he approached the examination table where Dr. O'Bannon was already bent over the body.

The assistant, a wiry young man with tired eyes, waved Ron in without looking up. O'Bannon straightened and pointed at the corpse's neck.

"Come here," he beckoned.

Ron hesitated. He preferred to keep his distance when he could. The dead didn't bother him, but the stories their bodies told—that was another matter.

"Ron," O'Bannon pressed, gesturing toward the screen. "You'll want to see this."

Ron shivered and stepped forward, his gaze shifting from the deceased's pale skin to the monitor. A magnified image displayed an almost imperceptible mark on the victim's neck. A tiny puncture nearly lost among the natural folds of the skin.

"Injection site."

"Looks fresh."

"Indeed." O'Bannon grabbed a stylus and circled the area on the screen. "Not in a place where any lifesaving measures would be administered. No IV line, no emergency intubation, no medical reason for it."

"Meaning—"

"Meaning someone put it there on purpose," the ME confirmed. He set the stylus down and straightened. "The body got here about a half hour ago. I'm just getting started—gross examination, preliminaries—but this jumped out at me. I'll run a full tox screen. Not just routine, but broad-spectrum. Some of the more sophisticated compounds out there can mimic cardiac arrest, slip past a standard panel. If something's there, we'll find it."

Ron nodded. Someone had wanted this death to look natural. Someone had taken great care.

O'Bannon moved to the body's torso and folded down the sheet to expose the upper chest and arms. His gloved fingers traced a faint discoloration along the wrist. "These bruises. See here?" He pointed to a cluster of contusions near the forearm, then another along the shoulder. "Signs of a struggle. Defensive wounds."

Ron's gut clenched. Jean-Claude had fought. Had known something was coming.

O'Bannon snapped off his gloves. "Pending a full autopsy, I'm inclined to rule the manner of death as homicide."

Ron didn't speak right away. His instincts had already been screaming the same thing, but hearing it confirmed... Phil had been right.

"That's the part where you say, 'Thanks, Doc.'" O'Bannon smirked.

"Thanks, Doc." Ron turned serious. "I mean it, thank you, Tim. I didn't think you'd do the post yourself, and so quickly." He had called the hospital. But it was a Sunday. Most office staff were off, as well as the pathologists. And then Phil sent video footage that hinted at something kicky. So Ron had asked Deanna to enhance the footage. And alerted Tim.

O'Bannon waved to dismiss it. "One assistant ME is on vacation, and another out sick. I gotta come in anyway."

"Thank you all the same."

Over the past year, Ron and the medical examiner had built a decent rapport, mostly thanks to O'Bannon's wife and Sheila. Sheila had pulled off some kind of miracle when O'Bannon's daughter's wedding nearly fell apart.

Ron headed toward the exit. He needed to update Phil.

CHAPTER 49

ON THE ROAD

OLIVIA

Olivia stepped out of the Marian Police Station with Ana, the late morning air thick with the promise of rain. They walked in silence toward their cars, but Ana must be thinking the same thing Olivia was.

"That lawyer," Ana said. "Something's off."

"Alonso Carter." Olivia unlocked her phone.

Ana leaned in as Olivia typed. The search results loaded, and both of them scanned the screen.

Ana let out a low whistle. "Cartel ties. Multiple investigations. And now he's Vega's lawyer?" She glanced at Olivia. "Marlowe sent him."

"Has to be," Olivia agreed. "And that phone call he made? He wasn't checking in—he was reporting."

"Carter's the kind of guy who doesn't step in unless it's high stakes. Marlowe must really want Vega protected."

Olivia locked her phone. "We were leaving separately anyway. You're heading back to the task force office?"

"Yeah. I'll see what I can dig up on Carter and any connections to this case." Ana started toward her car.

"See you." Olivia unlocked her car and got in. She pulled onto the road. Could Carter get a judge to have a bail hearing on a Sunday? Would Vega walk before they could talk to him?

Her phone buzzed. Lily.

Olivia tapped the dash to answer. "Hey."

"Mom? It's about Tommy. Remember how you removed my... special delivery? We might have another one."

She frowned. Now, why wouldn't her daughter—ah, Mia! Lily wasn't sure if Mia should hear about it. "The microchip I had you bring over to this country? Disguised as a mole?"

"Yes, exactly."

"Okay, do you have any lotion handy?"

Moments later, Lily's voice came through. "Yes, found it."

"Remember how we removed it? Remove it, but be careful."

Lily must have put her on speaker then. Olivia could hear the commotion in the background. She needed to caution these kids. "Tommy."

"Yes?"

"Don't move your arm too much. If this is what we think it is, we don't want to damage it." She veered into the exit lane.

After a brief pause, Lily said, "Got it! Mom, it's the same design."

Finally, something was going right. This had to be the intel. "I'm about fifteen minutes out. And, Tommy?"

"Yes?"

"Next time someone's dying in front of you, maybe check for sleight of hand?"

"Yes, ma'am."

She disconnected and pressed harder on the gas. Fr. Phil's words popped into her mind. *The list doesn't exist.*

We'll see, Father. We'll see.

MARLOWE'S HOME BASE

Marlowe set his phone down and smiled. Carter had worked his magic, and now Fat Boy was out. The pieces were falling into place, as intended. But before he could savor his small victory, Ringo stepped into the sunlit room, his expression tight.

"Boss, we got a problem."

Marlowe arched a brow and gestured for him to continue.

"Our guy at the police station just sent word. That girl, Mia Granger? Turns out she's not just any office bee. She's the auditor for Obsidian Rare Works."

"I noticed that when I saw her name on TV." Marlowe leaned back in his chair, fingers laced in his lap. "What happened to the other guy? Our old CPA?"

Ringo shrugged.

Luca blew out some smoke. "He got transferred. We don't have anyone else in that firm."

"She's working for the Feds." Marlowe muttered a curse. "Has to be. So, where is she?"

"That's what we're trying to figure out," Ringo said.

Luca perched by the window, a cigarette dangling from his fingers. "They're in the Marino Hotel."

"They checked in?"

"Not exactly." Luca flicked ash onto the tray he'd balanced on his knee. "Our guy says they're in the building, but no sign of them at the front desk. No reservations under their names either."

Processing this, Marlowe frowned. "So someone else is covering for them. Could be nothing, or it could mean they're hiding. Either way, I want to know why."

He jerked his thumb toward Ringo. "You and Fat Boy—go

take care of them. I want eyes on every exit. If they're holed up in there, they won't stay forever. Find their room, but don't go in blind. If they have protection, I want to know before you make a move. Understood?"

Ringo nodded, his expression grim. "Got it."

Marlowe held up a hand. "If Mia Granger is sniffing around, we shut it down. Make sure it's handled clean. No mess. No trails."

Ringo gave a sharp nod before leaving. Luca stubbed out his cigarette and started making calls, setting things in motion.

Marlowe swiveled the chair toward the rising morning light filtering through the blinds. The day had taken a turn, and he didn't like surprises. "We still need to find the book. So, let's talk to the priest."

CHAPTER 50

ON THE ROAD

PHIL

The computer screen flickered as the results came in, a ping confirming the match. Phil leaned in, his eyes narrowing as the grainy image sharpened, bringing the man's face into focus. His stomach coiled.

He knew that face.

His fingers tightened on the edge of the desk. Recognition came with an uneasy weight pressing against his ribs.

"Good work, Alex."

Alex rotated his chair. "You sure about him?"

"Yeah." Phil stood, his chair scraping against the floor. "I've seen him before. Thank you." No time to linger. He needed solid confirmation.

The chapel was quiet when he reached it, the soft glow of votive candles casting flickering shadows against the walls. The scent of melting wax mingled with old wood and incense, a familiar mix that usually brought peace. Not tonight.

Jeremy stood near the office door, keys in hand, turning the lock. Steps away, Leo adjusted a candleholder, adjusting one that had tilted.

"I can finish up here," Leo offered.

Jeremy handed over the keys. "Thanks, Leo."

Phil waited until Leo stepped away before moving in, lowering his voice. "Jeremy, I need you to look at something."

Jeremy blinked, straightening. "What is it?"

Without answering, Phil took out his phone, tapped the screen, and turned it toward him. The cleaned-out sharper footage began playing, the man's face clear.

"That's him." Jeremy's reaction was instant. He inhaled, pointing at the screen before Phil even finished asking. "That's the guy from the golf club."

Grim satisfaction settled in Phil's chest. *So, I wasn't wrong.*

"You're sure?" he pressed, needing to hear it again.

"Positive. He was watching us."

Pocketing his phone, Phil exhaled. Confirmation.

"Thanks." He spun toward the door.

Jeremy frowned. "Hey, are you okay?"

Phil paused, aware of how tense his shoulders were.

"You should rest." Jeremy frowned at him. "You were just attacked. Now you've been running around all morning."

"I'm fine." Rest wasn't an option. Not yet.

Jeremy didn't look convinced but let it go.

Outside, the air had cooled, though the humidity still clung to Phil's skin. He climbed into his car and gripped his phone, ready to call Ron. He needed to update him, show him the footage.

Then his fingers brushed against something in his pocket.

The key.

His pulse picked up. The vault place.

With fresh urgency, he drove onto the road, the streets stretching ahead in silent anticipation. Who was that man? Jean-Claude's enemy? He looked too young. A hired gun? Nobody should have known about him, so how did he do that?

A thought hit him like a tsunami. He pulled to the side, checked all over his car, and found it hidden in one of the wheel wells. It had to be the man in the golf club. He'd been tracking Phil. That was how he found the nursing home and Jean-Claude. Phil bet anything the man did his own research into the nursing home residents. Anyone who looked into Phil's life would know he had no uncle.

Phil rubbed his eyes. He was really losing it after years out of the game. This would never have happened way back when.

Lamenting would do no good. He stood up and dropped the tracker in a dumpster nearby. He got back in the car in time to hear his phone buzz.

Ron.

He hit the answer button. "Hello."

"Hey, Phil. Deanna found a suspect in the footage."

He straightened, gripping the wheel tighter. "That was fast." He had no idea Ron's team worked so quickly. He swallowed what he was about to tell Ron.

"She's running facial recognition now. So, your gut feeling was right. It's looking like a homicide. The ME is leaning that way. Pending tox screen and full autopsy."

He groaned. He'd led the killer to Jean-Claude.

Forgive me, Lord.

It is not your fault. Focus.

When Phil didn't say anything, Ron said, "At least we've got momentum. Pieces are coming together."

"Yeah." Phil nodded, even though Ron couldn't see him. "I'm going to check something."

"All right."

The call ended, leaving Phil alone with his thoughts.

Sentinel Vault & Lockers came into view, the brass signage blending into the sleek façade. No neon Open sign, just a frosted glass door with a keypad entry for after-hours access. A security camera blinked above the entrance, its red light a silent sentry.

He parked.

Inside, the lobby was quiet, the air cool and sterile, carrying the faint scent of polished steel. No rows of mailboxes, no clutter. Minimalist reception desk and a reinforced glass door leading to the private locker vault. The attendant, a bored-looking man in a navy blazer, barely glanced up from his phone.

Phil stepped toward the counter, palming the key in his pocket, his thumb running over the ridges.

No box number.

His gaze flicked toward the secured locker vault, visible through the reinforced glass. Inside, floor-to-ceiling walls of metal safe deposit boxes lined the space, each identical in size, the doors unmarked except for their numbers.

A needle in a haystack.

The numbers 66825 left on Jean-Claude's phone…? But no, that was too long. A code, not a box number. Besides, Jean-Claude wouldn't have known about this place.

A sigh threatened to escape, but then—an image.

Phil scrolled through the pictures on his phone until he found it. The flash drive. He had wondered why a number was engraved on it—197.

His pulse quickened.

He approached the secured access panel beside the vault entrance and swiped his rental key card. A soft beep, followed by the click of the lock releasing. He stepped through, the heavy door sealing behind him.

Row after row of identical metal doors stretched before him. He moved down the aisle, scanning—

There.

Box 197.

The key slid into the lock with ease. A faint tick.

The door creaked open.

CHAPTER 51

MARINO HOTEL

DYLAN

As Lily peeled away the fake mole, Dylan felt a strange sense of déjà vu. Not from anything as simple as watching someone remove an adhesive. No. This ran deeper. Watching the careful, deliberate way Lily worked, the sharp focus in her eyes, brought him straight back to when they met.

Everything in their lives changed around then.

He had only just uncovered the truth about his family—his grandmother, the empire, the criminal past—when he'd been sent to Hong Kong to bring Lily here. And she? She had just found out that her entire life had been built on lies—lies for her protection. Her parents were alive and well, her mother a spy for the US, and her father a sitting senator.

Two lives flipped upside down.

And now, here they were, gathered around an unassuming object, a fake mole. And once again, nothing was as simple as it seemed.

Lily held it between her fingers, turning it under the light. "It's more than just a disguise."

Frowning, Dylan leaned in. "Could it be tracking?"

Tommy, seated nearby, expelled a shaky breath. "Let's hope not. If it is, we're all sitting ducks."

"I doubt it. The dead guy put it there." Mia put her hand on Tommy's shoulder. "He wouldn't be tracking from the grave."

Dylan didn't like that thought anyway. He had made sure his suite was secure—top floor, private elevator access, high-end security. But he still wasn't about to take any chances. He had called ahead to authorize Olivia a key card.

His phone dinged. A security alert flashed on his screen.

Someone was coming up.

"I think your mom is here."

A second later, the metal doors slid open with a smooth mechanical hiss. Olivia stepped out, moving with purpose, her expression taut with focus. She wasn't one to waste time. Her sight landed on Mia. "You must be Mia. Pretty gutsy to go after Victor Marlowe."

A bashful smile appeared on Mia's face. "I just did the audit."

"Show me." Olivia held her hand out. When Lily handed her the small object, Olivia turned it over in her palm, then brought it closer to her face, studying it under the chandelier. Her brow furrowed slightly. Then she exhaled. "It's a storage device."

Silence settled over the room for half a beat.

A storage device. Not just a fake mole. If the dead guy did it on purpose, it had to mean something.

"What's on it?" Tommy stared at the mole in Olivia's hand.

She shook her head. "I won't know until I access it. But I need to take it to a secure location. Did he say anything at all?"

Tommy frowned, opened his mouth, then closed it.

"What is it? You remember something," Olivia prompted.

"Well, I think he said, 'give' something, I can't figure out what he said, like phew or X?"

Olivia's expression changed. She knew what the guy was trying to say.

"I need to go." She patted Tommy's arm. "Thank you. You did great."

Tommy's brows rose. He glanced at Mia like she would understand what Olivia meant. "Uh, thank you?"

But Olivia already marched toward the elevator. She pivoted back. Her gaze moved between Lily and Dylan, landing on Lily last. "No playing spy. Got it?"

"Yes, ma'am." He answered right away.

"Got it." Lily nodded.

Olivia stepped into the elevator, the polished metal reflecting her image as she hit the button. The doors shut, swallowing her from view.

"Is this a bad time to ask?" Mia crossed her arms. "You guys seem very nonchalant about the whole thing. This happens a lot?"

Tommy raised his hands like putting up a stop sign. "No, no, not me! Them, yes. They're magnets to danger. I'm beginning to think it's contagious."

"It's not like I asked for it," Dylan protested. "Trouble finds me, us."

Lily narrowed her eyes at Mia. "I have a feeling Mia is pretty used to adventures, aren't you?"

"I take the fifth."

CHAPTER 52

MARINO HOTEL

OLIVIA

W hen Olivia exited the elevator, a prickle ran down her spine.

Something wasn't right.

The hotel lobby thrummed—travelers wheeled suitcases, well-dressed patrons lingered near the bar, staff moved with the synchronization of good training. But Olivia's instincts screamed at her.

Her gaze landed on a Chinese woman near a jewelry store, her eyes sharp beneath the pretense of casual browsing. Across the lounge, a Middle Eastern couple sat too still, their attention too measured. Not tourists. Not guests.

Mossad? Quds Force? MOIS operatives? Hezbollah's ESO? If it was Mossad, she could work with them. The others would be bad news. She'd never dealt with any of them before, but she had heard plenty.

Where were Ron's agents? She'd spotted one on the top floor posing as a hotel worker, but she hadn't seen any in the lobby yet.

No matter. She needed to focus on these operatives. The way she figured, the only reason they were here was the list. But why the hotel?

Of course. Tommy and Mia were considered persons of interest, and their photos had been all over the news. But their connection was to the Morrison murder. Unless the operatives had picked up on O'Shea's trail, arrived after the fanfare, and now believed Mia and Tommy had it.

She forced herself to move normally, walking toward the garage. She didn't look back, but she felt them moving, shadowing her.

This didn't make sense. Why would they follow her? Ah, they watched her go up to the top floor and now back down. And if she spotted them, they made her too.

The moment she stepped into the parking garage, the atmosphere shifted.

Quiet. Still.

A whisper of sound—too soft for an untrained ear. But she knew better.

She spun—just in time.

The man lunged first. She barely dodged. His fist grazed her shoulder as she sidestepped. She struck back—fast, precise. An elbow to his ribs, a knee aimed at his midsection. He grunted but didn't go down.

"Where is it?" he demanded.

Quds Force, then. His accent. His fighting style.

They likely thought she was a Chinese operative. She kept her mouth shut.

The woman closed in next. Olivia blocked the first strike, countered with a palm strike, but she was outnumbered. The man recovered and caught her arm, wrenching her off-balance.

"Argh!"

She twisted to break free, but the woman grabbed her other

wrist. Strong. Trained. Olivia's muscles strained as she fought back, but they were too coordinated, too efficient.

She was about to go down—

Then a knife whistled through the air.

A wet thunk.

The man jolted, a blade embedded in his throat. He made a gurgling sound, hands grasping at the hilt, before collapsing in a heap.

The woman reacted before the Chinese operative was on her.

She moved like lightning—graceful, lethal. A sharp kick sent the Quds Force woman staggering back. Before she could recover, the assassin closed the distance, her fists striking with pinpoint precision—ribs, throat, solar plexus.

The woman reeled, gasping for air, her balance broken.

The killer didn't hesitate. She twisted, her leg snapping up in a brutal spinning kick that cracked against the woman's skull. The body dropped to the ground.

Silence.

Olivia inhaled, heart pounding.

The Chinese woman flicked a gaze toward her, assessing. Then she stepped forward, fluid and controlled, as if nothing had happened.

"Let's move." She spoke in rapid Mandarin. "I didn't know they sent another one. Which unit are you from?"

Olivia played along, her expression unreadable.

The woman's grip on her knife loosened slightly.

That was all Olivia needed.

She lunged.

A sharp twist. She caught the woman's wrist, wrenched the blade free, and used her own momentum to slam her against the nearest car. Before the woman could react, Olivia had her pinned, twisting her arms behind her back in a brutal lock.

The assassin gritted her teeth. "What are you doing?"

Olivia leaned in close. "Sorry, sis. I don't play for your team."

In one swift motion, she slammed her gun butt against the woman's temple. Her eyes rolled back, and her body went limp, collapsing to the concrete floor. Olivia crouched and pressed two fingers to the woman's neck—steady pulse. Out cold.

No time to waste. She patted the operative down for hidden weapons or intel. A slim blade strapped to her ankle, and a burner phone tucked into her waistband. Olivia pocketed both.

She snapped zip ties around the woman's wrists and ankles, then dragged her toward a maintenance door. It wasn't hard to find a utility room. These places always had them. She shoved the unconscious operative inside and secured her to a metal pipe with another set of zip ties. No chance of escape.

Now about the two lifeless bodies sprawled on the garage floor... This was a hotel garage. Anyone could stumble upon this scene.

She moved quickly, patting down the corpses. Another burner phone, a wallet with fake IDs, and a tactical knife. No other intel, but she'd let the cleanup team double-check.

She gritted her teeth as she grabbed each body by the shoulders, dragging them to a nearby supply closet. She stacked them behind mops and cleaning supplies, shut the door, and wiped the handle with her sleeve. It wouldn't pass a detailed inspection, but it'd buy her time.

Exhaling, she pulled out her phone and dialed a secure number. It rang twice before a voice answered.

"Command."

"Phoenix. Authorization alpha nine two seven."

A pause. Then, "Authorization confirmed. Proceed."

"Hotel garage. Two deceased. One package for rendition in utility closet. Civilian exposure risk high. Need cleanup supply closet, fast."

"Understood. Cleanup crew and rendition team en route. ETA fifteen minutes."

"Make it ten," Olivia snapped before ending the call.

She tucked the phone back into her pocket, her wrist throbbing from the fight, but she ignored it. She cast one last look at the utility room door. The Chinese operative wouldn't be waking anytime soon. And when she did, she'd be in a black site far from rescue or mercy.

Next, Olivia had to ditch her bloody clothes transferred from the dead operatives. She went back to the supply closet and swapped tops with the Quds Force woman. Making sure no one was in the garage, she strode toward the exit, vanishing before the first curious bystander could wander in.

Whoosh-click.

CHAPTER 53

SENTINEL VAULT & LOCKERS

PHIL

The metal door swung open with a soft creak, revealing the single item inside.

A book.

Phil's breath stalled.

The overhead lighting glowed on the leather-bound cover, its deep brown worn smooth with age. His fingers hovered over it before he lifted it from the steel-lined compartment, his pulse drumming in his ears.

It couldn't be.

The weight was familiar. The texture, the embossed insignia on the cover—all the same.

The last time he had seen this book, *The Papal Prophecy Codex*, it had been locked away in the Vatican Archives, buried under layers of secrecy and restricted access.

And now, here it was, sealed inside a private deposit box in an unmarked security facility, hidden in plain sight.

O'Shea had retrieved the book, but Phil doubted this had been his mission. By now, it was clear O'Shea was more than an informant—he was an asset, maybe even an operative. Otherwise, Olivia wouldn't have gotten involved.

So why had O'Shea left a message for him to retrieve this codex?

Whatever the reason, it hadn't fallen into the wrong hands.

His gaze flicked toward the security monitor. The attendant in the navy blazer remained at the reception desk, barely sparing him a glance as he scanned another client's ID. The entire Sentinel Vault facility operated on discretion—no questions, no prying eyes.

Still, his gut told him he had seconds, not minutes.

He slid the book back inside. The lock clicked louder than it should have in the hushed vault chamber.

He strode toward the secured exit, his movements calm, measured, nothing out of place.

The biometric scanner blinked green, releasing the heavy door.

As he stepped into the lobby, the shift in air pressure felt jarring. As if he had crossed from one world into another.

Outside, the cool air met his face. He didn't look back.

Late morning traffic bustled past on the street, the Florida winter sun bright but gentle, a pleasant warmth in the crisp air. He scanned the parking lot, checking the rows of cars, the sidewalk, the reflection in the shop windows. No one waiting. No one watching.

At least, not that he could see.

Phil reached his car, yanked open the door, and slid into the driver's seat. He sat there, hands in his lap, forcing his breathing to slow.

Jean-Claude's voice whispered in his mind.

"Don't assume you're safe just because you don't see the threat."

He could still picture the older man's sharp gaze, the way he drilled that lesson into him over and over again.

"Never take the obvious route. If something feels too easy, it probably is."

Phil leaned back in his seat, rubbing a hand over his face. That wasn't the book with the secrets. He knew that much. He could call Novak. Report his findings. Hand it over.

But the thought made his chest tighten.

Jean-Claude had taught him to be careful, to be paranoid, even.

"Don't trust blindly, Phil. Even inside the Church. Maybe especially inside the Church."

Novak had sent him to find the book. Phil had taken that to mean the history book. The codex wasn't it.

His fingers drummed against the wheel as he stared at the store.

Novak wanted an update. But was Novak the person to trust?

The answer wasn't clear. And Novak never gave him a straight answer on why he assigned him, one who hadn't been active for years, when he could have Vatican investigators do that.

No, Phil wasn't ready to make that call.

Yet.

He sat there, gripping the wheel, his thoughts a storm beneath his calm exterior.

Loyalty. Obedience.

These were the foundations of his life—the foundations of the Church, of Vatican Intelligence. He had lived by them for decades. Trusted them. Followed them.

But Jean-Claude had taught him something else—caution.

"Don't assume the man giving you orders has your best interests in mind. Assume he has the mission's best interests in mind. And you may never know what the real mission is."

He exhaled, pulled out his phone, and connected to a secure line. Layers of encryption flickered across the screen as the call dialed.

No answer.

Phil waited through four rings before Novak's voicemail picked up.

"It's me." He kept his voice level. "Call me back when you get this."

He ended the call, gripping the phone a second longer before tucking it away. Novak not answering wasn't a good sign. Phil expected efficiency from the man, not silence.

A bad feeling pressed at the edges of his mind, but he pushed it aside. Right now, he needed to get back to the chapel.

He started the car and eased out of the parking lot, his speed steady. The drive to Marian wasn't too far, but he took the long route, doubling back twice, keeping an eye on his mirrors.

Nothing.

Until there was.

The sedan came out of nowhere.

Phil had just taken the exit toward Marian, the small town where Mirror Estate and the chapel were located, when a black sedan cut in from his right, moving just fast enough to force him to stop.

He slammed the brakes, his heart rate spiking.

And then—

A dark SUV slid in behind him.

His fingers clenched around the wheel.

Boxed in.

Old buildings and dormant streetlights lined the narrow road. Few cars passed through this area. No pedestrians. No easy exits.

The sedan in front of him didn't move. The SUV behind him blocked the only way out. Both had tinted windows, no visible plates.

Deliberate. Coordinated.

Phil's breathing remained steady, but his pulse hammered.

Reverse? Not happening. There was barely enough room to squeeze through on foot, let alone in a car.

Ram the sedan? Possible, but reckless. And it wouldn't guarantee he'd get through.

I need a miracle, Lord!

A bulky man came out of the SUV. Phil tracked him from the rearview mirror. His body type screamed former military, Special Forces, maybe. The man opened the back passenger door, and a well-dressed middle-aged man stepped out.

The middle-aged man approached Phil. "Padre, you are a hard man to find. I'm Victor Marlowe."

CHAPTER 54

MARIAN

MARLOWE

The midday sun cast harsh shadows along the quiet street, the heat clinging to the pavement like a second skin. Marlowe stepped out of the SUV as soon as Luca gave the all clear, the smell of gasoline and asphalt thick in the air. It was noon, the kind of hour when people were too busy with their lives to pay attention to anything happening in Marian's backstreets.

Good. Less witnesses.

He adjusted the cuffs of his suit and approached the sedan where the priest sat behind the wheel. The driver's side window was up, but that didn't matter. His voice carried.

"Padre, you're a hard man to find."

The window rolled down halfway, revealing Fr. Phil's composed face and steady gaze. "What do you want?"

Marlowe stopped just short of the car door, studying the priest, appraising the gamble.

"Just a chat. I understand you were a friend of Adam O'Shea."

No reaction. Not a flicker.

"Not a friend. Never met him."

"That so?" Marlowe cocked his head, considering.

"It is. O'Shea called me for a meeting."

Now that was interesting. "And what was the meeting about?"

Fr. Phil didn't even blink. "It never happened. He got killed."

Marlowe let silence settle between them, testing for cracks. He found none. The priest was good. Too good.

O'Shea had the book. And now, the book was missing. Marlowe didn't buy for a second that the priest wasn't involved.

He exhaled through his nose, tilting toward Luca, who stood a few feet away, phone pressed to his ear.

The second Marlowe scowled, Luca muttered something into the receiver and cut the call. He shoved the phone into his pocket. "That was Ringo. He figured out where the girl is."

Marlowe's attention sharpened. "We already know. Marino Hotel. He figured out which room?"

"Penthouse. That's why there was no registration, no room number."

A slow burn of satisfaction warmed him. That explained a lot. Confirmed why tracking them had been a problem. No record. No trail. The penthouse.

Luca hesitated before adding, "Thing is… the Marino Hotel has ties to the Ghost."

Marlowe inhaled sharply. That gave him pause. The Ghost. A name that carried weight. A name that most people knew better than to cross. A risk.

Still, the book was bigger than one risk.

"Doesn't matter. It's necessary."

Luca nodded once, understanding unspoken. Then he jerked his head toward Fr. Phil. "What about him?"

Marlowe glanced back at the priest, still sitting in the car, still unreadable. "Take him. Encourage him to talk."

Luca didn't need more than that. He signaled to one of the hired hands—a local thug, eager for his cut. The gangbanger stepped toward the car, already reaching for the door handle.

And then—

A shot rang out.

The violent crack cut through the afternoon stillness.

The gangbanger jerked, a startled grunt escaping before his knees buckled. Blood pooled fast on the hot pavement.

Luca cursed and spun to grab Marlowe by the arm, shoving him toward the SUV.

Another shot.

Marlowe's driver's head snapped forward against the wheel, blood splattering the dashboard.

Marlowe barely had time to process before Luca forced him down and yanked the SUV door open. He shoved Marlowe inside, shielding him with his own body as he reached for his weapon.

"Stay down!"

A third shot rang out. The windshield cracked, webbing outward in a violent burst.

The gangbanger's crew scattered like roaches, diving for cover. Another shot. Another bullet whizzing past.

Luca didn't wait. He shoved the dead driver aside, muscles coiled as he threw the SUV into reverse. The tires screeched against the pavement.

CHAPTER 55

MARINO HOTEL

TOMMY

The shower's warm spray had done little to wash the unease from Tommy's gut. He had scrubbed his face, let the heat loosen his muscles, but nothing could erase the tension thrumming beneath his skin. Even in the safe penthouse, dread coiled like a hand on his throat.

He dressed in another set of Dylan's clothes and fingered through his damp hair before stepping back into the main living area. The others were already deep in conversation.

Lily sat cross-legged on the couch, phone in hand, her gaze flicking between the screen and Mia, who stood near the fireplace, arms crossed. Dylan leaned against the window, but his casual stance didn't match the sharp edge in his expression.

Dylan glanced up. "Feel human again?"

"More or less." Tommy dropped onto the couch beside Lily. "What's the latest?"

Lily tilted her head toward Mia. "We're trying to figure out what's on that intel and how it connects to O'Shea's murder."

Dylan raised his hand. "We should leave all that to the professionals. Let's order lunch."

"'Leave all that to the professionals'?" Tommy eyed him. "Since when did you shy away from speculations and danger?"

"Since Olivia ordered." Dylan deadpanned, then took Lily's other side, and handed her a menu. "So, what do you all want?"

Lily opened the room service menu and perused the offerings. She wanted a chopped salad with chicken, Mia picked an avocado melt, Tommy stuck to his usual BLT, and Dylan got himself a cheeseburger. They also selected a variety of beverages.

Shortly after Dylan ordered, his phone chimed.

One alert.

"That was fast." He swiped his phone, and his expression shifted. The easy grin vanished.

Lily moved closer. Her eyes widened.

"What?" Tommy's stomach twisted.

Mia straightened and stepped away from the fireplace. "What's going on?"

Dylan didn't answer. His fingers flew over his screen. "No, no, no… This isn't working."

Lily grabbed her own phone, dialing. "Mom, pick up."

Pulse spiking, Tommy stood and stepped in front of them. "Would someone tell me what is happening?"

Dylan's head snapped up. "Move."

The sharp word sliced like a knife.

Tommy barely had time to react before Dylan pushed them up to the loft.

"Panic room. Now."

Mia stiffened. "What?"

Dylan yanked open the concealed wall panel, revealing the reinforced door. "No questions. Get in."

Tommy didn't argue. He grasped Mia's wrist and hauled her inside.

Next, Dylan tried to push Lily in.

But she didn't budge. "You're not going in, then I'm staying out. Besides, they're probably looking for Tommy and Mia, not us."

He tried to argue, but…

A chime echoed from downstairs.

The elevator.

They froze.

Dylan hesitated, looking between the panic room and the entrance. He tightened his grip on her wrist. "Come on."

But Lily wrenched free as the elevator doors slid open.

Tommy reached for her. "Lily!"

But she slammed the panic room door shut.

The lock engaged.

His stomach dropped.

Dylan was outside. Lily was outside.

CHAPTER 56

TASK FORCE OFFICE

OLIVIA

Olivia had come close to death before, but that was before she reunited with her daughter and Simon. It hit her harder now that she had her family.

Thank you, Lord!

She didn't linger. She hurried to her car and texted Lily to stay vigilant.

The drive to the task force office was uneventful, but she didn't let her guard down.

The unmarked building disguised as a warehouse was tucked beside a strip mall. From the outside, it was just another forgettable unit.

She parked near the side entrance where an inconspicuous For Lease sign hung in one tinted window. She swiped her badge at the secured door and stepped inside, leaving the illusion of a run-down storefront for the hum of controlled chaos.

Agents moved between desks, coffee cups in hand, heads bent over case files. Low conversations overlapped with the occasional ring of a phone, while burnt coffee and printer ink scented the air.

Olivia didn't break stride. She cut straight through the bullpen, past the desks and the briefing room, heading for the lab. She found Deanna hunched over a workstation, two monitors casting a soft blue glow over her face.

Typing away, Deanna barely glanced up. "What's the crisis?"

Olivia held up the evidence bag containing the tiny storage chip. "I need to borrow something to read this."

Deanna stopped typing. Finally, she rolled her chair back, arching an eyebrow. "What is it?"

"Not sure yet. That's what I need to find out. Where can I read it?"

Deanna gestured toward the back of the lab. "Use the station over there."

Olivia crossed the room, grabbed a chair, and powered on the station. The machine hummed as she inserted the microchip.

The screen flickered. Two files appeared.

Her eyes narrowed. The first was labeled A History of Mirror Estate. The second, smaller file was titled For Your Eyes Only.

Her stomach tightened. She clicked on the first file, then scrolled through the pages for anything unusual. It looked like a straightforward historical account—old records, significant dates, mentions of the original land purchase. But then…

Several pages were blank. No text, no formatting, just empty white space where words should be.

She leaned back in her chair, crossing her arms. Was this a dead end? Had O'Shea been played, or was the real data hidden inside this file?

Unconvinced, Olivia clicked back and opened the second file.

A single document appeared. A letter.

Her breath caught as she read the first line: "To my handler and whoever else finds this…"

She scanned the text, her pulse quickening.

> *If you're reading this, I'm already dead.*
> *The list you're looking for doesn't exist. It never did. I can't help but wonder if someone started this rumor just to spark a war. I was chased by DOGE agents, Iranians, and maybe even Mossad. If you're reading this, I hope you can end it before it's too late.*
> *The Vatican guard stole something, but it wasn't a list— because there was never a list. What he gave me was a file. A manuscript. I didn't understand its significance, but I transferred it to this chip. Maybe you'll figure out why it matters.*
> *If you're seeing blank pages in the manuscript, don't waste your time trying to decode them. There's no cipher. No hidden message. The blanks were always there.*
> *Adam O'Shea*

Olivia's hands tightened on the chair's armrests. O'Shea had known he was a target. He'd known they were looking for something that didn't exist.

She disengaged the drive and took the chip out. Then she examined the burners she took from the foreign operatives. Nothing stood out. She texted control to report that she would have items stashed in dead drop 25. The geeks would do their magic.

A new text popped up from Raven. Her eyes widened.

Olivia found Deanna. "Please tell Ron to alert the agents."

With that, Olivia hurried out.

CHAPTER 57

MARIAN

PHIL

T he first shot shattered the afternoon stillness.

Phil barely had time to react before the world turned into a war zone. A second shot cracked through the air, then another. Glass splintered. Acrid gunpowder choked his lungs. Instinct took over. He threw himself sideways, flattening his body against the worn leather front seats.

More gunfire. A sharp, pained yelp. Then silence.

He held his breath, pulse thundering in his ears. One moment, his life had been dangling by a thread. The next, the kid was dead. Who pulled the trigger? And why?

He fumbled for his phone. He needed to call Dylan. Or Ron. Someone. He had no clue what happened, but one thing stuck in his mind—Marino Hotel. Marlowe mentioned it before everything went sideways. Whatever he was planning wasn't good.

The door wrenched open, and a firm hand clamped around his arm.

"Father, let's get you out of here."

A man's voice. Cool. Controlled. British.

Phil twisted enough to get a look. The man crouched low beside the car, eyes sharp, features composed despite the lingering tension.

"I don't mean to be rude, considering you've just saved me, but who are you?" Phil asked, still catching his breath.

"Apologies. Call me Falcon. We've got a mutual friend. Olivia."

Phil's brain caught up. British. Intelligence, no doubt. If he and Olivia were connected, that made them MI6 or something similar.

A woman's voice cut through the tense quiet. "Falcon, all clear. Let's scarper."

Phil twisted toward the sound. A dark-haired woman stood near a sleek black car, gloved hands resting on the roof, eyes scanning the surroundings.

"And that's my partner, Raven." Falcon kept his grip on Phil's arm. "Much as we appreciate your company, Father, we'd rather not be here when the rozzers, uh, cops, show up."

Phil hesitated. His car was useless, its tires shot. He had no illusions about staying put and explaining this mess to the police. Who would believe a priest in a firefight? He'd have to ask Ron for another favor to smooth things out with the local cops.

"All right." He pushed himself out of the car. "But let's make it quick."

Falcon guided him toward the waiting vehicle. Raven slid into the driver's seat, one hand draped over the gearshift. The car smelled of leather and something faintly metallic—gun oil, maybe.

Phil barely had time to shut the door before Raven slammed the accelerator, launching them down the street.

"Is it showing?" she asked Falcon, who had a tablet balanced on his knee.

"Yeah, we've got them," he muttered, fingers dancing over the screen.

She met Phil's gaze in the rearview mirror. "Where to, Father?"

"Holy Angels Chapel, Mirror Estate." He gave directions as they sped through the narrow streets.

His pulse was still steadying, his thoughts racing to catch up. He had questions. A lot of them.

"Did Olivia send you?" he asked. "How did you know I was there?"

Falcon didn't look up from his screen. "No, but we know who you are, and we were tracking Marlowe. Right time, right place."

Phil exhaled. If they were tailing Marlowe, then he was in deeper trouble than he thought.

Falcon cursed under his breath.

Raven shot him a look. "Oh, bollocks."

A prickle crept up Phil's spine. "Something wrong?"

Neither answered. Whatever they saw on that screen rattled them.

The ride was mercifully short. Raven stopped alongside the chapel.

"Here you are, Father." She forced a tight smile. "Say a prayer for us and Olivia, yeah?"

CHAPTER 58

TASK FORCE OFFICE

RON

R on stepped out of his office, rolling his stiff shoulders as he entered the squad room. The overhead fluorescents buzzed, emitting their sterile glow over the desks and monitors. His team was already gathered around the large screen mounted on the wall, their faces illuminated by the images shifting on the display.

Tanner stood to one side, arms crossed, his posture relaxed but his expression sharp. "Left a message for Agent Berrigan. Haven't heard back."

Charlie had a hand on his hip, nodding at something on the screen. Ana leaned forward, fingers tapping her tablet, while Hernandez hovered near the console, flipping through video feeds.

Ron strode up. "What do we have?"

Tanner pointed at the aerial shot of a massive warehouse complex. "Obsidian Rare Works? Too big for a storefront. This place? We're talking *way* more space than a boutique operation needs."

Charlie gestured to another image, a still frame of a chain-link fence with a jagged opening near the base. "Found this behind the building. Cut from the inside. Could be how Tommy and Mia got out."

"I think they mentioned that. Thought I read it in the report." Tanner turned toward his desk and shuffled through papers in a folder. "Ha, here it is. Yup, it was too small for Tommy. They had to work to make it big enough for him."

"So this looks the place, then." Ron slid on his "granny" glasses to inspect the grainy image. "Deserted?"

Charlie nodded. "It's the address on the shipping label. No vehicles in or out since early this morning. No movement in the windows. Security cameras are there, but check this out."

With the remote, he brought up an enhanced frame from the video. The cameras mounted on the building's corners were angled downward, leaving key areas in shadow.

"Whoever set this up didn't want eyes inside. And see these?" He zoomed in on the pavement outside the loading docks. "Fresh tire tracks. Someone moved something big."

Ron breathed out. It wasn't just a warehouse.

"Any way in?"

"Not without probable cause," Charlie muttered. "No chatter about shipments, no official business registered at this address. Place is dark."

"I don't think the shipping label is enough to constitute probable cause," Ana weighed in.

"Got something." Tanner flicked a file onto the screen. A mugshot—Marcus Knox, aka Ringo. Scar along his left jaw. Cold, calculating eyes. "KC came through. She got a print off a security camera near the scene. And guess what? It's a match."

Hernandez brought up a side-by-side comparison—one image showing a blurred figure leaving the warehouse, the other the mugshot. "This is from across the street. Timestamp places him walking out of the building minutes before O'Shea's time of death."

Ron's gaze flicked between the images. "And now we've got his print. That's enough to bring him in."

"Wish we had that kind of luck with Fat Boy." Ana sighed. "He got bailed out before we had a chance to lean on him."

Ron muttered a curse under his breath. "Whoever pulled him out wants him quiet."

Tanner dipped his head. "Or dead."

A tense silence ensued. The pieces were coming together, but the picture still wasn't clear.

"Charlie, Ana, sit on the warehouse. We need to confirm that's Marlowe's hiding place. If he's connected, he could bail Ringo out before we can flip him. That's assuming the locals find him soon."

Then hurried footsteps echoed from the hall.

Deanna burst into the room, lab coat flaring behind her, her voice urgent. "Ron!"

He yanked off his glasses, on alert. "What is it?"

"Olivia said to tell you to alert the agents." Deanna took a deep breath. "She left in a hurry."

"Do you know what happened?"

Tanner was already on his phone, stepping away as he called for a sitrep.

"No."

"What did she have you do?"

"She needed a station to read the microchip. Then she got a text and ran out."

He didn't like this.

CHAPTER 59

MARINO HOTEL

OLIVIA

The drive to Universal CityWalk was uneventful, but Olivia's mind was anything but calm.

She pulled into the parking garage, choosing a spot well away from the designated rideshare pickup zones. The farther from casual foot traffic, the better.

Sliding out of the car, she moved with practiced ease. The weight of the retrieved items pressed against her as she approached the fake utility closet. The air smelled of exhaust fumes and concrete dust, the distant sounds of tourists and honking horns a steady backdrop.

She scanned the area. Empty.

Perfect.

With precision, she entered a code into a discreet panel behind what looked like an electrical access point. A click signaled the panel unlocking. She opened it to a stash of firearms, ammo, and sat phones. She ignored them, deposited the items, then secured it again.

She exhaled. One problem handled. Next stop, Orlando Executive Airport.

Fifteen minutes later, she drove up to the private hangar. A black helicopter warmed up on the tarmac, its rotors already spinning. The logo on the side belonged to a tourist entertainment company, blending it into the background of casual air traffic.

Raven stood near the open door, motioning for Olivia to hurry. As Olivia jogged toward them, Raven tossed her something. A tactical suit.

She caught it, yanked it on over her T-shirt, and secured the zippers as she climbed aboard.

Inside, Falcon was already in the pilot's seat. The engine vibrated through the aircraft.

"We're taking off." His British accent cut over the noise.

She buckled herself in as the helicopter lifted, the ground falling away beneath them.

Raven handed her a tablet. Live feed.

Two operatives stood on the rooftop. One of them adjusted a grappling gun, readying to launch an anchor to the Marino Hotel rooftop, the next building over.

"They're setting up to cross." Raven leaned in. "We've been tracking them, but we were too far out to intercept. And you had your own mess to deal with."

Olivia didn't need the reminder. The Chinese agent. The Quds Force. She scowled at the screen. "Any idea who these guys are?"

Falcon's voice came through the headset. "GRU. Russians."

A fresh spike of adrenaline shot through Olivia. GRU. Russian military intelligence. This just got worse.

If Fr. Phil was right and the list didn't exist, then the rumor had caused a lot of problems. After all, all she had found so far was a history book. If only she had a way to let everyone know the list wasn't real.

Her gaze flicked to the window, scanning the skyline.

"How are we beating them there?" she asked. "They'll see us coming, and they'll move faster than this chopper."

"A risk we have to take," Raven admitted. "We're betting the sightseeing logo buys us extra seconds before they clock us as a threat."

Falcon's voice came through the headset again. "Buckle in. We're about to make this ride interesting."

The helicopter pitched forward, slicing through the air toward the Marino Hotel rooftop.

CHAPTER 60

STAKEOUT

ANA

The afternoon sun hung low, casting long shadows across the quiet street. The air was thick with the scent of warm asphalt and the distant tang of salt from the nearby bay. Ana shifted in the driver's seat, her fingers drumming against the steering wheel. The stakeout was uneventful so far, but most of these things were long hours of waiting, watching, and, if you were lucky, catching something worthwhile.

At least this gave her an excuse to check out her new partner.

Charlie sat beside her, his posture relaxed, but she didn't buy the nonchalance. He had the air of someone always paying attention, always reading the room—or, in this case, the street. He wasn't a rookie. That much was obvious. In his forties, he was more in her age range than the younger agents on the team.

"So, what were you doing overseas?" She crumpled up her snack bar's wrapping.

Charlie didn't look away from the warehouse. "Attached to the Rome Legat."

Ana smirked. "Okay, doing what? Fugitives? Counter-terrorism?"

He exhaled a quiet chuckle. "A bit of everything."

Which meant he wasn't going to elaborate. Fine. She could respect that.

Her gaze drifted to his left hand where a plain gold band caught the sunlight. "You married?"

"Yeah." A small smile touched his lips. "Been eighteen years."

"That's solid. Hard to pull off in this line of work."

He nodded, his expression thoughtful. "My wife makes it work. She's a university lecturer and a freelance interpreter, so her schedule's flexible. Helps a lot with the kids."

"How many?"

"Three. Jamie Beth, our oldest, is seventeen. And the twins, Ryan and Evan, are ten."

Quite a gap, but she wasn't going to mention it.

Ana hummed, letting the conversation settle. He'd answered freely, no hesitation, which meant he wasn't hiding anything there.

Then he reversed their roles. "Have you met Dylan Roche?"

"Sure, I've met him. We all have. Why?"

"Not me."

She rested her palms on her thighs, her slacks hot in the car. "You'll get your chance. You heard about the wedding? Olivia and Simon?"

"Yeah, but I didn't get an invite. I wasn't with the team when they all got the invites." He took a few sips of the water. Smart. Never risk drinking too much on a stakeout. Never know when you needed to run. "That's okay. So, what do you know about Dylan?"

"He's a good guy. Nice."

"That all?"

She shot him a sidelong look. "What are you trying to find out?"

"Nothing in particular. Just getting a sense of him. I only know him as the Ghost's nephew. What about his grandmother, Carol Marino? Have you met her?"

"Yeah, she's been grooming Dylan to take over the empire. I understand she's fading into the background. Why the interest?"

"Just curious." He shrugged. "I mean, it was before my time, but I heard people used to compare the Marino organization to the Gambino crime family and the Lucchese crime family of New York."

"Yeah, but Carol's husband turned away from all that. Now the family business is all legit. Well, there's that bad apple. The Ghost."

"Now that the Ghost lives on the compound, how can you be sure they still walk the straight and narrow?"

She chuckled. "Dylan didn't even know about his heritage until a year or two ago. He's a good kid. And he's dating Lily. He steps one foot out of line, Olivia will have his head."

But something deliberate about the way he asked set off quiet alarms. Why was he interested? Most agents knew not to dig too deep when it came to the Ghost—at least, not without a good reason.

Before she could push back, a dark SUV veered onto the street, its tires rolling over the cracked pavement.

"We got movement." She straightened in her seat.

Charlie shifted, his posture tightening as he tracked the vehicle. It cruised past the front entrance before veering toward the back, disappearing behind the warehouse.

CHAPTER 61

MARINO HOTEL

DYLAN

The steel door slammed shut, locking away any chance of retreat. Dylan clenched his fists.

He was furious—furious she was out here, putting herself in danger. And yet... a twisted sense of satisfaction coursed through him. She wouldn't leave him to face this alone. That was Lily.

No time to dwell on it.

One look at her told him she was ready. Her shoulders squared, her breathing even. Determined. He knew she could fight. She was quick, trained. But bullets were faster.

A ding echoed through the hallway. The elevator doors slid open.

"Let's play dumb," Lily whispered before descending the stairs.

Dylan had no choice but to follow.

Two massive men stepped out, their presence filling the space. The first guy was built like a linebacker—thick neck, wide chest, bulging arms—dressed in an expensive but ill-fitting maintenance outfit that strained at the seams. His shaved head gleamed under the overhead lights, and his hands flexed like he was eager to break something. Or someone.

The second man was leaner but just as menacing. Sharp cheekbones, dark eyes that scanned the hallway like a predator searching for its prey. He had the air of someone who enjoyed the hunt.

Behind them, two goons in the same maintenance outfit followed, hands hovering near their waistbands. Armed. These weren't hotel employees.

Dylan barely breathed as the men stepped farther in, their heavy footfalls echoing in the enclosed space.

Lily gasped, her eyes widening like she was shocked to see them.

Great acting! Dylan took a deep breath and channeled her performance. "May I help you? We don't have any maintenance issues."

Shaved Head's nostrils flared. "Where are they?"

Dylan frowned, cocking his head. "What?" He let out a nervous chuckle. "I didn't call you to pick anything up."

"Don't lie!" Shaved Head hollered. "We know they're here."

Lean Man took a slow step forward. "Mia Granger and her boyfriend. Where are they?"

"Mia who?" Lily blinked bewildered eyes at Dylan. "Babe, do you know a Mia?"

He shook his head. "No clue."

The goons weren't buying it. One of them kicked over a chair, sending it crashing against the wall. "We're here for Mia Granger and her boyfriend. Give them up, and you won't be harmed."

Dylan's heartbeat thundered in his ears. He could feel Lily's breath against his arm—controlled, steady.

Then silence.

And then—movement.

Before Dylan could react, a hand shot out from the side, grabbed Lily's arm, and hauled her into the open.

She twisted, a blur of motion as she elbowed the man in the ribs. The goon grunted, stumbling back, but he was strong—too strong. He recovered and wrenched her back toward him.

Dylan lunged to help, but a crushing force hit him from behind.

Arms locked around his chest, and the solid grip pinned his arms to his sides. The big guy had him.

Dylan threw his weight back, slamming his head into the man's face. The hold loosened just enough. He twisted and drove an elbow into his attacker's ribs, then another.

The guy grunted but didn't let go. Instead, he yanked Dylan sideways, sending them both crashing into the wall.

Pain shot through Dylan's shoulder, but he ignored it, fighting against the grip. He glimpsed Lily grappling with her attacker, shifting her weight to land a sharp kick to his knee.

The guy cursed, but he didn't let go.

Then the shift happened.

The big guy holding Dylan exhaled like he was done playing. His grip tightened for a second—then let go. Dylan barely had time to react before he saw the glint of metal.

A gun.

From the guy's waistband.

Lily saw it too.

Dylan didn't think. He moved.

He stepped in front of her, his body shielding hers.

The gun leveled at him.

And then—

A phone rang.

Dylan's breath hitched. It wasn't his phone. It wasn't Lily's.

The leaner guy cursed and snatched his own phone out of his pocket. His expression twisted as he read the screen, then swiped. "No sign of Mia or the boyfriend, but there's another dude and his girl... Hang on." He raised his phone, and if Dylan wasn't mistaken, the goon took a photo of him and Lily.

The big guy lost his patience and aimed his gun at Dylan.

Then everything happened at once and in slow motion.

The big guy pulled the trigger while the other hollered, "No!"

CHAPTER 62

MARINO HOTEL

TOMMY

A s soon as the lock clicked, Tommy pressed his shoulder against the door, shoving with all his strength. It didn't budge. He swore under his breath, then reached for the keypad, and punched in Dylan's usual code.

The red light blinked. Denied.

"What are you doing?" Mia curled her fingers around his forearm and held him back.

He freed himself, chest rising and falling too fast. "Trying to open the door."

Her sight darted to the crack beneath the door where the faintest glow of emergency lights bled into the dim room they were in. "We should wait until it's clear."

Not happening. "My best friend is out there. And Lily." His gut twisted as he pictured them in the chaos. "I can't just sit here."

"And what, exactly, do you think we can do?" she countered. "From what I've heard, Dylan and Lily have gotten out of jams before. They're resourceful."

"They shouldn't have to." His jaw clenched, frustration thick in his throat. "What if they need backup?"

She squeezed his wrist. "You're an *accountant*, Tommy."

That stung. "So are you."

"Exactly," she said. "And last I checked, we're not armed, we don't know what's out there, and if you go charging in blind, you might make things worse. Besides, you heard Lily. The people coming are looking for *us*, your fake mole or whatever is stored in there. They're not after *them*."

The rational part of him knew she was right. The other part, the part that couldn't stand the idea of his friends being in danger, wanted to keep fighting. He ran a hand through his hair and let out a long breath.

Mia released her cold grip, then stepped away, unfolded a metal chair leaning against the back wall, and sat. He hesitated before taking another chair and settling on it.

She tucked her hair behind her ears, her smile shy. "You know what will help?"

"What?"

"Pray. Let's pray. You can just say what you want from the heart. Don't worry about any prayers."

Looking into her green eyes, he nodded. "Please take care of my friends out there. Please keep us safe. Help us."

She smiled, then closed her eyes, lips moving. After a moment, she made the sign of the cross. He knew that much.

He didn't know if he believed, didn't know if his mumblings would be heard. But a strange sensation hit his shoulders, like a weight lifted. Whatever it was, he was more at peace now.

He swallowed and focused on the door, straining to hear what was happening outside.

Footsteps. Movement. A thud. But no screaming. Not yet.

He counted that as good news.

His fingers tapped his knee. "You mentioned before that your childhood wasn't... great."

Mia stilled.

He almost regretted bringing it up.

But then she exhaled and leaned back against her unfolded chair. "No, it wasn't."

He waited, giving her space to decide how much she wanted to say.

After a beat, she spoke again. "I had a run-in with the law when I was younger. Not my proudest moment."

"What happened?"

She shook her head. "Not something I like talking about."

"I'll bet." He slowed his jittering fingers, not pushing.

"But… a prosecutor saw something in me. Gave me a second chance." Her lips quirked, almost like she couldn't believe it herself. "She made a deal with the judge, got me off the hook, but only if I cleaned up my act. So I graduated high school, enrolled in college. Full ride, all scholarships." She paused. "She became my mentor."

The flickering light from under the door skimmed her face. He couldn't hear anything beyond the door now. "She still in your life?"

"Yeah. She's a judge now. Elaine Hargrove."

"Where did you learn all that… hot-wiring a car, picking a lock, hiding a flash drive in a heel?"

"I wasn't lying. But the Feds gave me a crash course when I said I'd work for them."

Tommy let that sink in. He'd known there was more to Mia than what she let people see, but this? It explained a lot.

"My family's back in Seattle." He offered something in return. "Most of them, anyway."

"You close with your folks?"

"Yeah. I go home twice a year. FaceTime about once a week. We don't always see eye to eye, but they're good people."

"Must be nice."

Did she mean it, or was there something else beneath her words? He opened his mouth to ask—

A strange sound, a muted pop, and then a scream.

CHAPTER 63

MARLOWE'S HOME BASE

MARLOWE

W ho were those people?

The question throbbed in Marlowe's mind as the SUV raced through the darkened streets. The hum of the engine and the blur of buildings did little to quiet the storm in his head. His fingers fisted against his knee. Did the priest know anything? Did he have the list? He should have pressed harder.

Luca repeatedly looked back, his dark eyes scanning the road behind them, a tension in his jaw, a stiffness in his shoulders.

Not until they reached the warehouse compound did Luca relax. Marlowe barely had time to step out before Luca gestured him inside. The others remained outside, silhouettes against the low-slanting sunlight, weapons in hand.

Once inside, Marlowe strode across the concrete floor, the scent of oil and gunpowder thick in the air. He shrugged off his coat and tossed it onto a battered metal chair before turning to Luca.

"Updates on the hotel."

Luca made the call. Marlowe watched him, the way his

fingers drummed once against the table, then stilled. It took only a few rings before Ringo answered.

"Anything?" Luca asked.

Static crackled before Ringo's voice came through, low and clipped. "No sign of Mia or the boyfriend, but there's another dude and his girl."

Luca frowned. "Who?"

A pause. Then Ringo sent the pictures. Luca's phone buzzed. When he glanced at the screen, his entire demeanor shifted, his expression hardened, and his grip on the phone whitened his knuckles.

Marlowe narrowed his eyes. "What?"

Luca hesitated half a second too long. "Uh... this is the Ghost's nephew." He exhaled through his nose. "We can't touch him."

Marlowe's jaw locked. "She's not in charge here. If he doesn't cooperate, get rid of him."

Luca didn't argue. He didn't try to reason with him. He pulled his gun and pressed the barrel against Marlowe's forehead. "I tried to warn you. But you didn't listen."

The cold metal sent a jolt through him. But it wasn't fear that held him still—it was disbelief.

"Call it off." Luca's voice was calm and steady.

Marlowe's breath hitched. "How dare you—"

"The Ghost's nephew is off-limits. So is his girlfriend." Luca's finger rested against the trigger. "Boss's orders. Now. Call it off."

The air thickened, electric with tension. Marlowe's pulse hammered against his throat. Luca wasn't bluffing. The look in his eyes, cool, unreadable, told him this wasn't a plea—it was a demand.

"You're working for the Ghost?"

"Always have. Now, call it off."

A threat.

Marlowe's fingers curled as he reached for the phone. Luca didn't move the gun. Didn't waver.

Marlowe pressed the phone to his ear. "Let them go. Don't touch them."

Ringo's voice crackled back in protest. "No—"

A gunshot. Then another.

The muzzle flash lit up Luca's face.

Marlowe barely had time to register it. No pain. No sound. Just the sharp awareness that this was it.

He knew—death was coming.

Then nothing.

CHAPTER 64

MARINO HOTEL

RON

The tension had been gnawing at Ron since Tanner's report, but when the agent mentioned the maintenance crew, his instincts kicked into overdrive. Too convenient. Too easy to slip past security disguised as maintenance workers. He didn't like it.

Ron needed to go to the hotel to assess the situation. "Tanner, with me." And he strolled out of the office with his senior agent in tow.

Soon, they drove up to the hotel. Spaulding and KC lingered near the entrance. That made Ron's pulse tick up.

"What are you two doing here?" Ron stepped out and approached Spaulding.

"Got a tip that our suspect, Ringo, was seen in the hotel."

"SWAT's ready to move if we confirm," KC added.

Ron exchanged a look with Tanner. The situation was going downhill fast. If Ringo was here, things just got worse.

"We're checking something out," Ron offered.

The four of them didn't need to waste more words. They moved in sync, peeling off in different directions. Ron took the elevator up while Tanner, Spaulding, and KC split to cover exits, the parking garage, and the lobby shops.

The moment Ron stepped onto the top floor, his gut clenched.

Closed for Maintenance. The sign was placed in front of the elevator leading to the penthouse. That wasn't right. His agents hadn't mentioned anything about maintenance work up here. And a bag of what looked like sandwiches, to-go order, was toppled beside the sign.

He turned toward the stairwell. The door was locked from the inside. Blocked.

His jaw tightened. Not a coincidence.

Pulling out his phone, he dialed the lead agent stationed at the hotel. "Report."

"We did a full patrol ten minutes ago. All clear," the agent responded.

Ron's hand curled into a fist. "Well, it's not clear now," he snapped. "Penthouse access is compromised. Get your team to Tanner and follow his lead. Now."

No excuses. No explanations. There'd be time for that later, after he was done tearing them apart for dropping the ball.

Right now, his focus was on Mia and the others.

His phone buzzed again—Tanner.

"Talk to me," Ron said.

"We've got something," Tanner replied. "KC spotted an unmarked utility van in the underground garage. We're going to check it out."

Ron glanced at the blocked stairwell again. "Stay sharp. Someone jammed the stairwell access up here."

Tanner muttered a curse. "You think they're already inside?"

"I don't think. I know."

Another elevator dinged behind him.

He pivoted, hand hovering near his sidearm.

Spaulding stepped out.

They locked eyes, both understanding the unspoken: Something was wrong.

Before either could say a word, footfalls thundered from the stairwell.

Not a casual pace. A hurried escape.

Instinct took over. Ron shifted, pressing himself against the wall beside the stairwell door. Spaulding mirrored him on the other side.

They exchanged a nod.

Whoever was coming down wasn't expecting company.

CHAPTER 65

MARINO HOTEL

DYLAN

The moment stretched and snapped like a rubber band.
Bang.

Lily screamed.

Shaved Head's gun went off, but the shot was muffled. The sound buzzed in Dylan's skull, his ears ringing but not deafeningly so. Not like the last time.

Had he been hit?

He exhaled, but there was no pain, no spreading warmth of blood. Still standing. Still breathing.

Lean Man had shoved Shaved Head's gun arm, sending the shot wide. Now the two were locked in a heated exchange, their voices clipped and tense, but Dylan wasn't about to stick around to hear the argument.

Lily was pale, trembling, her breath coming in short, shallow gasps—but alive.

Dylan pulled her close, one hand gripping the back of her head. "You okay?"

She nodded against his chest, but she wasn't steady.

They had to move.

He scanned the room. The front door was a no-go. Their best chance? Up.

"The balcony," he whispered.

Lily looked up at him, eyes wide, but when she saw his expression, she steadied her stance and eased from his arms. He took her hand, and together, they slipped toward the glass door. The noise behind them covered their movement. The men were still arguing. Shaved Head looked ready to fire again, but Lean Man stepped into his space, chest-to-chest.

Dylan didn't wait for a better opportunity. He opened the door just enough for them to slip through and ushered Lily onto the balcony.

A gust of wind cut through the space, cool against his heated skin. The city stretched out before them, but Dylan barely registered it. He spotted the metal stairway leading up.

Rooftop access.

It was their only shot. His grandfather had built a heliport there for fast escape during his criminal days. He really should have learned more about what else his grandfather had. So, where was the helicopter? And the pilot? No time to think.

He placed a steadying hand on Lily's back. "Go."

She didn't hesitate. Lily climbed swiftly, light on her feet despite the tremor in her hands.

Dylan followed, every muscle in his body on edge. He expected a shout from behind, the sound of pursuit, but none came.

Not yet.

They reached the top, and that's when he heard it—a mechanical whirring.

He frowned and looked up.

A helicopter.

It hovered close—closer than he'd expect for a sightseeing tour. The rhythmic thump of the rotor blades vibrated in his chest. Was this an answer to his unspoken prayers? Someone opened the side door, and his eyes went wide. Did he imagine it?

Now he dared hope they could get out of this. He was about to relay the good news that her mom was in the helicopter when Lily grabbed his sleeve and yanked—hard.

He turned, confused. Her face was urgent, serious. She gestured toward the ladder they had just climbed, then raised her hand, and mimed a gun.

CHAPTER 66

MARLOWE'S HOME BASE

ANA

The SUV slipped behind the warehouse, disappearing for a moment.

Ana's gut clenched. She'd been in this game long enough to recognize when something didn't feel right. A vehicle prowling around the back of a building like this? That wasn't a delivery truck making a late drop-off. And had the windshield been shattered? "We should check it out."

"Agreed." Charlie nodded, his gaze already sweeping the perimeter. "Quietly."

They moved with practiced ease, sticking to the shadows as they approached the rear. Motor oil, damp wood, and rust scented the air. The afternoon sun glowed over the cracked pavement, but beyond that, the warehouse cast deep shadows, the darkness their ally.

Ana spotted them first—two men posted near the back entrance. One was leaning against the metal door, arms crossed, posture loose, but his eyes were sharp, scanning. The other fidgeted, shifting his weight from foot to foot, one hand near his waistband.

She made eye contact with Charlie. This wasn't just some storage facility, this was it. Marlowe's headquarters.

But without clear cause, they couldn't make a move. Not yet.

Then a gunshot cracked from inside the warehouse.

Ana didn't hesitate.

She gave a sharp signal, left. Charlie nodded and peeled right. She crept forward, footsteps silent, nerves coiled but controlled.

The guard on her side turned toward the noise. That was his mistake.

In a single motion, she struck—an elbow to the throat cut his breath short. His cigarette dropped from his fingers, sizzling as it hit the damp ground. She twisted his arm behind his back and slammed him face-first into the warehouse wall. Out cold.

Charlie moved just as fast. His target barely turned before Charlie dropped him with a clean blow to the temple.

Ana grabbed the door handle and yanked it open.

"Federal agents!"

Charlie was already behind her, weapon raised.

Inside, silence stretched too long to be comforting.

Stacked crates lined the walls, arranged haphazardly. It looked ordinary, like nothing more than a forgotten storage space. But something was off.

She exchanged a glance with Charlie. "Where is he?"

Charlie's voice was low. "This doesn't make sense. If Marlowe was here, he'd have more security."

Then—a muffled noise.

Charlie spun toward a far wall.

Ana followed, scanning every detail.

He pressed his knuckles against the surface. Hollow.

She ran her fingers along the seam, feeling a faint draft.

A hidden door.

She pushed against it. And it gave way.

The moment the panel slid open, the sharp, metallic scent of blood hit her.

And then she saw the body.

A man lay sprawled on the floor, a bullet hole square in his forehead. Blood still pooled beneath him, the splatter against the wall fresh.

Her breath caught.

Marlowe.

She had expected a fight. A standoff. Not this.

Charlie cursed. "He's dead."

Ana barely heard him, already scanning for the killer.

Then, a door slammed.

She spun in time to see a shadowed figure bolting through a side exit. Tall. Athletic. Moving fast.

"Suspect's on the run!" she called. "Charlie, call it in!"

She was moving before she finished the sentence, sprinting across the concrete floor.

By the time she reached the alley, the suspect had reached a sleek black motorcycle.

Her heart pounded.

He swung a leg over the bike.

"Stop!" she yelled, raising her weapon.

The engine roared.

Ana hesitated. A shot here was risky.

The bike peeled out, tires screeching as it tore through the alleyway.

She ran, but she already knew—he was gone.

Breathing hard, she yanked out her phone and snapped a picture of the license plate before it disappeared.

Charlie caught up, his breathing steady despite the sprint, his expression unreadable. "You get a good look at him?"

"Not his face." She raised her phone. "But I got the plate."

His jaw tightened. He jerked a thumb back toward the ware-house. "That was Marlowe in there. Who shot him?"

She shook her head. "I'm guessing Luca, his second-in-command."

"Why? A coup?"

CHAPTER 67

THE GHOST'S APARTMENT, MIRROR ESTATE

MARGE

Marge, aka the Ghost, set down her tea, her fingers resting on the plastic cup's white rim. The quiet luxury of her restricted accommodation was a far cry from the stark cell she once occupied. A gilded cage, but a cage nonetheless.

A knock preceded the uniformed guard walking in with a phone in his hand. "You have a call from your caretaker."

She was expecting the call.

"Thank you, Larry." She took the device with precision, like it might vanish if she moved too quickly. Lifting it to her ear, she heard the faintest buzz of the line before the voice came through —calm, impersonal.

"Just wanted to update you that the delivery has been completed as instructed. Package was dropped off at the designated location."

Marge closed her eyes. Just long enough for the words to settle. Her longstanding investment in Luca, positioned as Marlowe's right-hand man for years, had paid off. He'd executed the hit with the precision she'd trained him for, eliminating

Marlowe and securing his escape route before anyone could connect the dots. Another chess piece moved where she needed it, another potential threat to Dylan neutralized before it could materialize.

"I understand. No complications with the delivery process?"

"Everything went according to plan. Clean handoff, no witnesses to the transaction. The paperwork has been handled as discussed."

Aware of the guard's presence, she sipped her tea. "Good. Maintain standard procedures for the next forty-eight hours. Then proceed with the cleanup protocol we established."

"Any special instructions for the follow-up?"

"No changes. Continue monitoring the situation as planned. Use the usual channels if anything develops."

The line went dead.

She disconnected and returned the phone to her keeper. Once he left, she went to sit in the deep armchair by the window. Her fingers brushed over the linen armrest.

The standing instruction was to keep Dylan safe. Eliminate all threats, so Marlowe had to be stupid to threaten her nephew.

Her access to information was still limited, filtered through approved channels. But the last classified ad she checked had been promising. The right whisper, planted in the right place. A carefully timed ripple.

And now, the waters were stirring.

The history book had been smuggled out. No one had paid attention to it.

Who would reach it first? Olivia? Or the priest?

CHAPTER 68

MARINO HOTEL

OLIVIA

The rhythmic *thump-thump-thump* of the helicopter's rotor blades pulsed through Olivia's chest as she focused on the rooftop. The city sprawled beneath them, indifferent to the danger unfolding.

Falcon, the pilot, adjusted the chopper's position, maintaining a steady hover.

"Two operatives on the roof," Raven said over the comms. "They barely glanced at us."

That bought them a few seconds—but not much.

Sure enough, the two men reached the rooftop door, hesitated, then slipped inside.

Olivia's grip tightened on the open side door's frame. From this vantage point, she had a full view of the rooftop and the penthouse balcony.

That was when she saw them. Lily and Dylan.

Her stomach twisted. Why were they climbing up from the balcony? And where were Mia and Tommy?

They had to be in the panic room. But why weren't Lily and Dylan in there too? What forced them out into the open?

No time to figure that out now.

Lily and Dylan had chosen to go up, scaling the metal stairwell toward the rooftop, their movements quick but cautious.

Then—a problem.

One of the operatives who had gone inside hesitated before closing the door. He stepped back out.

Olivia barely breathed.

Did he hear something? See something?

She adjusted her scope, tracking his line of sight. Not toward the helicopter. That was good.

Toward the ladder.

Toward Lily.

Her head was just cresting over the rooftop edge.

The operative took another step forward, his posture shifting —alert. Suspicious.

Olivia's finger hovered over the trigger. One shot could take him down. A clean, quiet solution.

But then what?

A dead Russian intelligence officer on US soil? If this turned into an international incident, it wouldn't matter that she had FBI credentials. Langley would deny her faster than she could reload.

What's my ROE here?

Which rule of engagement applied here? FBI rules? Hold fire unless there's a clear-and-immediate threat. CIA rules? No rules. Just objectives.

Her pulse pounded in her ears. If she fired now, she'd own the consequences. If she waited, she might not have a choice.

Then the decision was made for her.

The operative's focus snapped to Lily. His hand moved—not for his radio. For his gun.

"Falcon," Olivia called into her comm. "Hold position. Raven, I need a distraction. Now."

"On it," Raven replied.

A heartbeat later, the helicopter tilted—just enough to unleash a deafening downdraft.

The gust whipped across the rooftop, kicking up dust and debris. The operative raised an arm to shield his eyes.

That was all the time Lily needed.

She shot up the last few rungs, grabbed the edge of the rooftop, and before the operative could react, lunged low, sweeping his legs out from under him.

The Russian stumbled backward, cursing in his native tongue, but Dylan was already moving. He clutched Lily's arm and yanked her toward the helicopter.

They sprinted across the rooftop, the wind from the rotors slamming into them, their escape within reach—

Until the operative recovered.

He pivoted and raised his pistol—not at them. At the helicopter.

CHAPTER 69

MARINO HOTEL

RON

The air inside the hotel hallway was thick with the scent of carpet cleaner and lingering cologne. Afternoon sunlight streamed through the windows, casting long shadows across the glossy floors.

Ron adjusted his stance, rolling his shoulders once. He and Spaulding had been waiting for this moment—positioned at opposite sides of the suite's door, muscles taut with anticipation. Their surveillance team confirmed the suspects were inside. Given the hotel's occupancy, gunfire was a last resort.

Then—

The click of the stairwell door unlocking sent Ron and Spaulding into motion.

The door slammed open, and a disheveled figure barreled out.

Ringo.

His face was pale, slicked with sweat, his breath coming in ragged, panicked gasps. He wasn't even looking at them—just running.

Ron moved fast, stepped into his path, and hooked his leg, sending Ringo crashing to the floor.

"No! No, no, no! We gotta go! We gotta go!" Ringo thrashed like a wild animal.

"Easy!" Ron's knee pinned him down.

Spaulding grabbed Ringo's wrist and twisted it behind his back as the man kept babbling.

"He's a monster, man! A psycho!" Ringo's voice cracked. "Fat Boy's dead! He snapped his neck like it was nothing! I–I barely got out!"

Ron exchanged a sharp look with Spaulding. Something was very wrong.

No one else came through the stairwell door.

Ringo had been the only one to make it out.

But that meant—

"Who's up there?" Ron tightened his grip.

Ringo kept struggling, but it was mindless panic, not an attempt to fight. "The commando! And the rest of my team—but they ain't coming down! Not after what he did!"

Ron shifted his weight, keeping Ringo in place. "Who is this commando?"

"I don't know, man!" Ringo's gaze darted wildly. "Some freak. He moved fast, too fast. Took down Fat Boy like he was nothing! Just—" He shuddered. "His neck. Just snapped it like a twig. I ran. I ran, man!"

"Who else was up there?" Spaulding demanded.

Ringo's breathing hitched. "A man and a woman. They were there when we got there. They took off while Fat Boy and I were arguing—while we were struggling."

A prickle tingled at the back of Ron's neck.

A man and a woman.

His gut clenched.

"You see where they went?" Ron pressed.

"No, man." Ringo wrenched his head side to side. "I was

busy trying to keep Fat Boy from beating my skull in! But they weren't Mia and her boyfriend. I know that much."

That answer should have relieved Ron, but it didn't.

Because he knew who they were.

Dylan and Lily. The risk-taking duo heading into danger, of course. If they managed to slip away, where were they now?

Before Ron could ask another question—

Ding.

The elevator doors slid open.

KC and Tanner stepped out, guns drawn.

"Everything is under control downstairs." Tanner's gaze flicked to Ringo. "Just him?"

"So far." Spaulding wiped a trickle of blood from his lip. "Yeah, well, you took your time."

KC crossed to Ringo. "What's his deal?"

Spaulding jerked a thumb toward the penthouse. "Says there's a lunatic commando up there."

KC's smirk faded. "And you believe him?"

Ron pushed to his feet. "Apparently, Fat Boy's dead. The others didn't get a chance to fight back. Whoever's up there? They're dangerous."

KC exhaled, rolling her shoulders. "So what's the move?"

Ron's gaze shifted toward the penthouse stairwell.

"Tanner and I will find out what's waiting for us upstairs. You and Detective Spaulding take charge of your suspect."

CHAPTER 70

MARINO HOTEL

OLIVIA

As the operative pivoted and aimed for the helicopter, Olivia's breath caught. No. Before she could react, a shot rang out—Raven's. The man jerked, and his weapon slipped from his fingers as he crumpled onto the rooftop. The tension in Olivia's chest didn't ease. She watched his unmoving form for any sign of life.

The rotor blades whined overhead, the downdraft kicking up loose debris from the rooftop as Dylan and Lily clambered into the helicopter.

Raven gave them a quick once-over before turning to the others. "There's another operative."

Dylan, still catching his breath, yelled over the noise, "Tommy and Mia are still in the panic room!"

Olivia hopped to the rooftop's ledge, her boots thudding the concrete. Raven landed beside her.

Falcon shifted at the helicopter's open door. "Let's move! We're out of time!"

"You stay put," Raven ordered. "We need a pilot alive, and someone has to watch them."

Falcon scowled but nodded, gripping the side of the helicopter.

Olivia was already moving. Her gun up, she sprinted toward the stairwell door where the last operative had vanished. The door was still cracked open. Bad mistake. She pushed through first, Raven covering her six.

The stairwell reeked of gunpowder and sweat, and the tight concrete walls amplified every sound. Olivia barely got two steps down before movement flickered in her peripheral vision.

"Contact!" Raven called.

The operative lunged, a knife flashing in his grip. Olivia pivoted before the blade sliced across the air where her throat had been. She slammed her elbow into his ribs, forcing him back a step, but he recovered fast.

The guy was strong, fast, but reckless.

Raven was already moving, bringing up her weapon, but the angle was bad. Too much risk of hitting Olivia.

The operative went for another strike, knife angling toward Olivia's ribs. She twisted, deflected his wrist, and smashed her knee into his gut. The man grunted but didn't go down. Instead, he lashed out and knocked her gun from her grip.

Not good.

He swung again, this time at her face.

Olivia ducked, the air buzzing as his fist just missed her jaw. She countered, slamming her palm into his throat. The move bought her a fraction of a second.

That was all Raven needed.

The butt of Raven's gun cracked against the operative's temple. His body stiffened, eyes rolling back before he lost his footing. He tumbled backward, colliding with the concrete hard.

Olivia and Raven both stared as the man groaned. His body

armor had taken the brunt of the fall, but he was out cold for now.

"Not dead," Raven muttered, crouching to zip-tie his wrists. "Close enough."

"We'll come back for him." Olivia retrieved her gun. "Let's get to the panic room."

Bodies littered the penthouse. They checked them all, only one was breathing. Raven zip-tied the goon. The one suspect, Fat Boy, she was hoping to flip had his neck broken, likely by the Russian operative.

She recalled the panic room—a reinforced steel door embedded behind a false panel. She led the way up to the loft. She knocked once. "Tommy? Mia? Are you in there?"

A beat. Then Tommy's voice, muffled but clear: "Olivia?"

"Yes, it's me," she confirmed. "Dylan and Lily are safe."

There was a pause. Then Tommy's voice again, lower this time. "I don't have the code. No phone either."

Of course.

She pulled out her phone and called Dylan.

"What's the code?"

Dylan rattled it off, and Olivia relayed the message. A heavy metallic click sounded. Then the door hissed open. Mia and Tommy stepped out, eyes sharp, bodies tense.

"All good?" Olivia asked.

While Mia inclined her head, Tommy raked a hand through his hair. "Better now."

"Would love to stay and get acquainted, but we need to move." Raven had her SIG Sauer at the low ready.

Olivia ushered them toward the stairs, Raven bringing up the rear.

Then—footsteps.

Slow. Deliberate. Coming up the stairwell.

Olivia froze, holding up a fist to signal a halt. She motioned for them to step back, then eased forward. Staying low, she crept toward the edge of the loft and peered down toward the stairwell. Ron and Tanner.

A sharp curse almost slipped out. Instead, she whipped back and hurried to Tommy and Mia. "Listen to me. You never saw us. You have no idea what happened. Just that it was quiet, so you came out."

Mia's brow furrowed, but she nodded. Tommy's mouth opened.

Olivia cut him off. "Raven, put the Russian in the heliport storage room." Raven already headed back while Olivia faced Tommy. "You don't know where Dylan and Lily went. Got it?"

"Yeah." He clawed at his hair again. "Got it."

Olivia cast one last glance toward the stairwell. The footsteps were getting closer.

Without another word, she slipped out onto the balcony, moving fast but quiet. Olivia grabbed the rooftop ladder, hauling herself up in smooth, practiced movements. The metal was cold beneath her fingers, the wind tugging at her as she climbed.

Below—the stairwell door burst open.

She didn't stop.

Raven came out of the storage room and sprinted toward the helicopter. Olivia was close behind. Movement to the side caught her attention. Instinct kicked in. She pivoted toward the sound.

CHAPTER 71

CHAPEL, MIRROR ESTATE

PHIL

After the British agents dropped him off, Phil needed to clear his head. Cold water shocked his senses as he splashed it over his face. He gripped the bathroom sink, staring at his reflection. He looked paler than usual, the lines around his mouth deeper. The exhaustion, the weight of it all, pressed against his chest like an iron slab. He pushed cold fingers to his closed eyelids. *Think.*

Too much had happened too fast. O'Shea's body. Jean-Claude's death. The rental box. The phone with the number. The surveillance footage of the killer. And Marlowe—the man who had already listed the item on the dark-web auction. He didn't have it, but that didn't seem to matter. The flash drive. The girl.

And then there was the codex. Knowing its value, its significance, he left it untouched, locked up in the box.

Unease gnawed at his stomach. He needed clarity, and there was only one place he could find it.

The stillness in the Adoration Chapel—Adoration Room would be a better name—embraced him as he stepped inside.

Candlelight flickered, casting shadows along the walls. The scent of incense lingered in the air, weaving through the silence.

He wasn't alone.

A woman knelt near the back, her head bowed in devotion. Jeremy sat in front. Phil knelt, then slid into a pew, inhaled, and focused on the golden monstrance centered on the altar. The sanctuary lamp illumed the Eucharist.

Seconds passed. Then minutes. His heart rate settled, his thoughts untangled.

Tell Jeremy.

The prompting was quiet but insistent. He frowned, his gaze shifting to the young priest. Jeremy remained still, eyes closed in prayer.

Tell Jeremy.

He hadn't imagined it.

As if on cue, Jeremy stirred. He crossed himself and knelt in front of the altar before turning to leave.

Phil hesitated, then rose, and followed.

"Jeremy."

The young priest pivoted, brows lifting. "Yeah?"

"Do you have a moment?"

Jeremy studied him, clearly noting the gravity in his tone. "Of course."

The office door clicked behind them, sealing them from the world. Phil engaged the lock, not because he feared someone would barge in, but because what he was about to say required absolute secrecy.

Jeremy sat in the chair opposite the desk. "This is serious."

"It is." Phil sat down. "Before I say anything, you need to understand. What I'm about to tell you"—he locked his gaze with Jeremy's—"is confidential. Treat it as if it were the seal of the confessional."

Jeremy's expression darkened. "Understood."

Phil studied him, then dipped his head. "All right."

And so, he began.

He told Jeremy everything—how he had found O'Shea's body, the rental box, the phone with the number inside, the surveillance footage of the killer. He left out the flash drive. The young priest wasn't ready for the girl and the accompanying secrets. Jeremy remained focused, nodding, interrupting to clarify details.

"What's in the box?" Jeremy asked.

"A book that needs to be returned to the Vatican Archives. However, it's not relevant here. It's not the list or the book with secrets."

"That's… still a lot." He pinched the bridge of his nose. Then his brows furrowed. "All right. Let's break this down."

Phil said nothing as the young priest straightened.

"There was a rumor about a book or list containing the names of covert operatives." Jeremy tapped a finger against the desk. "But it doesn't exist."

"Correct."

"Yet there was a book with secrets, a history book, one you know from Vatican Intelligence years ago… but this isn't the book in the rental box. And someone named Marlowe is after this rumored list."

"That's right. The codex is in the rental box."

"Here's what I don't get—if Marlowe doesn't have the list, why put it up for auction?"

Phil shrugged. "He must've had arrangements to buy the list, but someone intercepted it. Can you imagine what the intelligence communities would do to get their hands on it?"

Jeremy whistled low. "But it doesn't exist."

"Someone started the rumor, and no intelligence agency could ignore it. They would at least vet it. No one would risk their operatives' lives over an assumption."

"True." Jeremy rubbed his temples. "Here's what I think—it's a misdirection. Someone wanted something but couldn't get it, either because of security or some other obstacle. So they started this rumor to make everyone who mattered look elsewhere."

"And then they would have a clear path to that something…" Phil rubbed his temples, dread settling in. The tracker. The killer on the golf course.

"Phil, are you okay?"

He gave a firm shake of his head. "I know what they were looking for. Or rather *who*. They knew I would go to Jean-Claude as soon as Novak told me about the book. I found a tracker under my car. And we saw that killer on the golf course. Oh no." He put his head in his hands. He had fallen for it. He had led the killer to Jean-Claude.

"Phil, it's not your fault." Jeremy touched his arm. "You go to the nursing home regularly. That alone shouldn't have raised any red flag."

"Yeah, but I'm sure they would have looked into the residents and found out about our connections. That's what I would have done."

"Anyway, we need to figure out who wanted Jean-Claude dead. And why the lawyer had this other book in a rental box."

Phil lowered his hands. "Right. Jean-Claude's last words were to find the book and the phone."

"So, you found the book. And the phone. He left a number on the phone. If he was killed for what he knew, then that number means something."

Phil leaned back. "You think it's a message?"

"I think it's a lead," Jeremy corrected.

"But what could it be? 66825. Too short to be a phone number."

"Could be that he didn't finish typing?"

A knock on the door startled him.

"Yes?"

"Father, are you in there? Someone is looking for a priest for confession," Leo called.

Jeremy stood up. "I'll go. It's going to be okay. Have faith."

Phil nodded in thanks.

He stared at the numbers: 66825. Then he pulled Jean-Claude's phone from the drawer, willing it to reveal his meaning.

CHAPTER 72

MARINO HOTEL

RON

Ron took the stairs two at a time, his Glock raised, Tanner right behind him. The air was thick with the acrid scent of gunpowder, and the eerie silence pressed in as they reached the penthouse landing.

His gut clenched. Bodies littered the floor.

One slumped against the wall, another sprawled across the marble tile, limbs twisted at unnatural angles. A scan confirmed three down, all of them armed. But no sign of a firefight still in progress. No sign of a commando.

Tommy and Mia stood unharmed amid the carnage.

Mia looked shell-shocked. Her wide-eyed gaze flickering between the bodies as though her brain hadn't caught up with what she was seeing. Tommy, normally quick with words, stood shaken. His lips parted, but no immediate explanation came.

Ron lowered his gun but didn't holster it. "What happened?"

Mia swallowed hard. "We–we don't know."

Tanner grunted and knelt by one body. Ron kept his focus on Tommy and Mia. "Start talking."

Tommy ran a hand through his hair. "We were just chatting. Waiting for our food order. Everything was fine." He glanced at Mia, who nodded weakly. "Then Dylan shoved us into the panic room. Locked the door."

Ron narrowed his eyes. "Why?"

Mia licked her lips, her voice uneven. "Dylan saw some kind of alert on his phone."

"Okay, you were in the panic room. Then what happened?"

Tommy shrugged. "We don't know. We heard a commotion. A lot of shouting. Some gunfire. Then nothing."

Something wasn't adding up. Ron holstered his gun. "And you just stayed put?"

"Until it got quiet." Mia rubbed her arms as if chasing way shivers. "We didn't hear anything for a while, so we came out."

Ron scanned the room again. The placement of the bodies, the precision of it all. This wasn't a random shootout. Someone had taken these guys down efficiently.

Tanner nudged a body with his boot. "The bodies match the descriptions Ringo gave us. Fat Boy's definitely one of them."

Two accountants couldn't have done this. That meant their so-called commando had been here. And now he—or she—was gone.

He turned back to Tommy and Mia. "So where did Dylan and Lily go?"

Mia hesitated a fraction too long. "No idea."

"Why didn't they go into the panic room with you?"

Mia exhaled shakily. "Lily thought whoever was coming up was looking for us. She and Dylan figured they could just play dumb."

Ron's instincts screamed at him. The way Mia said it—too rehearsed. Tommy was sticking to the same script. But it sounded just like Dylan and Lily, the risk-taking duo.

Then a distant whir caught his attention. Helicopter blades.

Tanner moved toward the balcony and hollered. "Just a sight-seeing helicopter."

Ron stayed put, watching Mia and Tommy. They weren't lying outright, but they weren't telling him everything either.

He frowned. A sightseeing helicopter so close to the penthouse?

His gaze swept the room one last time. No commando. No sign of Dylan or Lily.

Just bodies on the floor. And two people sticking to a story that didn't quite add up.

Where did this commando go? Was the helicopter the commando's exfil? But why would he leave without completing his mission, assuming it was to acquire Mia and Tommy?

CHAPTER 73

MARINO HOTEL

DYLAN

Dylan sat in the helicopter, his pulse thrumming in his ears, his focus on the rooftop below. The whirring rotors drowned out most sounds, but he locked his gaze on the stairwell door. Waiting. Watching.

Then—movement.

Raven emerged hefting a body, headed toward the storage room, and went inside.

Dylan exhaled. Almost there.

Then Olivia shimmied up the side ladder, the same one he and Lily had used to escape. She headed straight for the helicopter, but as she reached the open space near the heliport, she turned. Why?

Dylan craned forward. What caught her attention?

A flash from somewhere to the left. Falcon's gun. Then, almost simultaneously, another shot rang out.

The impact was brutal. Olivia's body jerked as if someone slammed a sledgehammer into her chest. The force whipped her backward. Her boots skidded against the pavement before she hit the ground hard, motionless.

Before Dylan could process what happened, the gunman crumpled to the ground, Falcon's precision shot having found its mark. The threat eliminated in an instant of calculated violence that came a heartbeat too late for Olivia.

Lily's scream cut through the chaos.

"Mom!"

CHAPTER 74

CHAPEL, MIRROR ESTATE

PHIL

The rectory office was quiet, save for the laptop fan humming and the wooden floorboards creaking as Phil shifted in his chair. He rubbed his forehead. Data scrolled across the screen. The flash drive's contents were the same files he had seen before. No other files magically appeared.

He had hoped for a breakthrough, but the more he searched, the more elusive the truth became.

Those numbers—66825. What did it mean?

He locked his hands behind his head and leaned back, willing the answer to materialize on-screen.

Then his phone buzzed.

Novak. Finally.

He grabbed it off the desk. "Hello."

"Phil. You found the book?"

"Yes." He didn't say that it wasn't the book of secrets.

"Good. Meet me at the cathedral in two hours."

"Wait—"

But the line went dead.

Phil tossed the phone onto the desk. Novak had asked him to retrieve the book containing secrets. But the book O'Shea put in the rental box wasn't just any book.

It was the *Papal Prophecy Codex*.

He couldn't hand the codex over to the wrong people. Proper protocol was to contact the Vatican and await further instructions.

His gaze drifted back to the piece of paper with 66825 written on it. The numbers mocked him, indifferent and meaningless. Whatever their significance, he wouldn't crack them in the next two hours.

He set his palm atop the worn case on the desk—Jean-Claude's possessions, retrieved from the nursing home. If there were any additional clues, they had to be in there.

Sliding the box closer, he lifted the lid. The scent of aged paper and dust met him, the quiet remnants of a life lived in careful secrecy. A few personal effects: a broken wristwatch, an old leather wallet, a St. Benedict medal, and a well-used wooden rosary. Something about the rosary felt off. The weight wasn't right.

He ran his fingers over the crucifix and pressed along its edges. The wood felt too solid, too heavy, as if something had been built into it. And was that a faint seam near its base?

His pulse ticked up.

With careful precision, he twisted the end of the crucifix.

It unscrewed.

Inside was a wound strip of film—microfilm.

His breath hitched.

He unrolled it under the desk lamp. Instead of the usual, nearly illegible dots and dashes of classified microfilm, this was different. It contained clear text, written in Jean-Claude's meticulous script.

Phil put on his reading glasses and used the phone's camera to magnify the texts. He skimmed the first lines.

The notes chronicled Jean-Claude's exploits. Most were relics of the past, but even now, they held weight. Phil scanned through the pages, absorbing sharp observations about Church affairs, past events, and the quiet removal of certain men. Some had been disgraced, others exiled to obscure parishes—none of it surprising.

Then—

His fingers tightened around the film.

Jean-Claude had been tracking something bigger. Something far more dangerous.

Names jumped out, not just any names. High-ranking clergy, some still in power, others long buried under layers of scandal and secrecy. But it wasn't just about corruption within the Church. Jean-Claude had been following a global thread, one that wove through political upheavals, intelligence agencies, and power struggles far beyond the Vatican walls.

A particular entry made Phil's blood run cold.

"The world believes in convenient narratives. But truth is rarely convenient. The Vatican's hand in the covert nego-tiations between world powers reshaped the course of history, at a cost no one will ever admit. And now, a wolf in sheep's clothing is among us. Alert Guardian. Need to warn Phil."

Phil sat back, the words hammering into him like a fist.

A contingency. Was that what Jean-Claude meant all along? Had he been preparing for this? Preparing him? Was he the contingency?

CHAPTER 75

TASK FORCE OFFICE

RON

R on strode into the task force office, signaling for Tanner to take Mia and Tommy straight to the conference room. They weren't injured, but they were processing everything— eyes wide, movements careful, as if still adjusting. The adrenaline was wearing off, but the situation hadn't settled in.

Ron barely spared them another glance as he approached the squad room. He needed an update before diving into another round of questioning.

Inside, agents worked at their desks, and screens flickered with security footage, facial-recognition results, and live data feeds. He stepped into the center and clapped once. "All right, what do we have?"

Ana and Charlie exchanged a look before Ana stepped forward. "Like I reported, Marlowe is dead. Crime Scene Unit brought back all the evidence. Deanna is downstairs divvying up work."

"So, you just missed the killer?"

"Right." Charlie tapped his keyboard, and the hidden office

inside the warehouse appeared on the screen. The furniture seemed where it belonged except for Marlowe's body, a clean bullet hole through the head.

Ron studied the image, the implications. "Execution?"

Ana looped her hands together. "That's what it looks like. Luca Moretti. Marlowe's second-in-command. Former Italian military, ex-mercenary. Dishonorably discharged. He was running things for Marlowe, but now he's running from us."

Charlie pulled up another screen. A grainy traffic cam still showed a man speeding off on a motorcycle. "Helmet covered his face, but it's him. He ditched the bike near Orlando Studios and disappeared into a black sedan. No plates."

"Was this a power grab?" Ron gestured toward the screen. "If he wanted to take over, he wouldn't be running. Why would his own guy turn on him?"

Ana knocked her thumbs against each other. "That's the question, isn't it?"

"Luca had resources," Charlie added. "This wasn't spur-of-the-moment. He planned it. At least, his exfil."

"Which means a bigger play's happening."

Tanner stepped in, right hand squeezing his stress ball. "Penthouse situation was a mess. When we got there, bodies lying on the floor. Ringo claimed a commando did that. We didn't see him, but we got Mia and Tommy though."

"Now that Marlowe is dead, is the auction still on?" Ron looked to Hernandez.

The tech agent nodded. "Yup, still on."

"You sure?"

Hernandez spun his laptop around, showing an active bidding page. "Still live. Crime Scene Unit brought back Marlowe's system from the warehouse. Once we crack into it, we might shut this thing down from the back end."

"Do it," Ron said. "And loop in Agent Berrigan at Art Crime. This may close her cases."

"Yes, boss."

Ron would have to update Agent Holt with Homeland, but that could wait. Holt's only concern was Mia and her reports. Ron was about to continue when Hernandez frowned at his screen.

"What?" Ron asked.

Hernandez's fingers flew across the keyboard. "Uh... you told me to ping Dylan's and Lily's phones."

Ron's jaw tightened. "Yeah. And?"

"They're just outside."

The door swung open.

CHAPTER 76

ON THE ROAD

PHIL

Time to head to the cathedral to meet Novak.

Phil fumbled with his phone, considering his options. His car was still dead. He could call an Uber, but given the distance, he doubted any driver would pick up his fare. He needed to leave now.

He found Jeremy coming out of the reconciliation room. "Hey, any chance I could borrow your car?"

The young priest locked up the room. "I would, but I have an appointment in fifteen minutes."

"Father, need a ride somewhere?" Leo called from the maintenance closet. He must have overheard the exchange.

"Not a ride, just a car," Phil admitted. "I need to get to the cathedral."

Leo jangled his keys from his pocket and tossed them over. "Take my truck. Just, uh, don't judge the mess."

Phil caught the keys. "Wouldn't dream of it."

During the uneventful drive, the nagging unease remained. In the clergy parking lot, he eased Leo's truck into an empty space.

Sunlight reflected from the cathedral's stone walls, the heat rising in faint ripples from the pavement.

He sat, scanning the area.

Something felt... off.

Shrugging it off, he stepped out and locked the door behind him. The warm air carried a mix of sunbaked brick, motor oil, and a drift of incense from inside the church. He adjusted his collar and started toward the back entrance.

As he walked, he checked the time on his phone. Then a thought struck him. He stared at the keypad.

Then he knew.

He had to call for help.

His thumb moved toward the call button—

A sharp jab against his ribs.

The force knocked the breath from his lungs. A burning sting followed, spreading like liquid fire beneath his skin. His fingers went numb, the phone slipping from his grasp. It landed on the pavement, the screen still glowing.

Dizziness slammed into him. His vision wavered, the world tilting unnaturally.

No.

He tried to turn, to move, but his limbs felt heavy. Voices, distant and warped, echoed in the growing haze.

He barely registered his knees hitting the ground before darkness swallowed him whole.

CHAPTER 77

MARINO HOTEL

DYLAN

Time slowed. Even Dylan's breathing slowed.

The gunshot rang out, cracking like a whip. Olivia crashed onto the pavement, her body going limp on impact.

The shooter's head snapped back, obliterated, as Falcon's precise shot found its mark.

"Mom!"

Lily's scream split the air. Then she bolted toward Olivia. Raven spun, sprinting back. Falcon, already halfway out of the helicopter, cursed and leaped to the ground.

But Dylan—Dylan couldn't move.

No. No. No. This wasn't happening.

Olivia was a ninja, untouchable. She had accomplished impossible stunts, outmaneuvered killers, survived ambushes, and always—*always*—won.

Now she was getting married in less than two weeks. She couldn't die.

And yet, there she was.

Still. Silent. Not moving.

Dylan forced himself to inhale deeply. Forced his feet forward, stumbling after Lily as she dropped to her knees beside her mother.

Then—

His heartbeat hitched.

A twitch.

A wince. An intake of breath.

And then, like her code name Phoenix, she rose.

Falcon hauled her up, while Raven checked the back of her head for injuries from falling.

"Good grief," Falcon muttered. "Thought we'd lost you there, mate."

"You gave us all quite a fright," Raven added, though her grip on Olivia's arm didn't loosen.

Lily was still crying, sobs shaking her, as she wrapped her arms around her mother. "Mom? Oh dear—you—how—?"

Olivia fumbled under her tactical suit, then pulled something free.

A medal.

Dented. Battered.

A bullet lodged dead center.

Dylan's stomach dropped. His brain barely processed what had happened—

Before Olivia crumpled.

His body moved before his mind could catch up. He lunged forward, helping Falcon steady her as she sagged against him.

Her eyes fluttered open. "I'm okay," she rasped. "Just shocked is all."

Then she held it up—the dented, battered medal. Her lips curved into something between a smirk and a prayerful whisper.

"I guess Marie's grandfather was right." Her voice was hoarse but steady. "Thank you, Lord."

Dylan gaped, still trying to catch up.

That medal, the one Lily's godmother, Sister Marie, had

given Olivia. Some story about her grandfather, a Portuguese soldier, surviving a bullet thanks to a specially crafted Miraculous Medal.

Dylan had dismissed it as an urban legend.

Apparently, he'd been wrong.

Falcon let out a gasping chuckle. "Blimey, that's some luck you've got there."

"Or divine intervention." Raven exchanged a knowing glance with Olivia.

"You—" Lily hiccupped through her tears, still hugging Olivia as if she might disappear again. "You scared me."

"I'm okay, sweetheart." Olivia placed a gentle hand on Lily's head. "Just take it easy."

Dylan swallowed hard, shaking off the last of his shock. They needed to get moving. The shooter was dead, but more could be coming.

"Come on." He held a hand out for Lily, voice rougher than he intended. "We should get out of here."

By the time they made it onto the helicopter, he was still trying to make sense of what had happened.

Lily sat close to Olivia, still shaken, while Raven and Falcon worked in practiced silence.

Olivia rolled the bullet-stopped medal between her fingers, her expression unreadable. Then she held it up. "Did Auntie ever tell you about this?"

Lily sniffled. "Auntie said her grandfather had one just like it. It saved his life."

Olivia smiled. "And now it's saved mine."

"Unbelievable." He dragged a hand down his face.

Olivia turned to Falcon. "Take off." While Falcon flipped switches, getting them airborne, she shifted her focus. She pulled out her phone and made a call, her voice cool and controlled. "Cleanup crew needed. One rendition. One pickup. Standard protocol."

A pause.

"Thirty minutes."

Cleanup crew? He exchanged a look with Lily. He might not understand half of what Olivia just arranged, but he knew enough to realize it wasn't normal.

Then she put the phone away. "We need to get our stories straight."

CHAPTER 78

TASK FORCE OFFICE

RON

Ron crossed his arms as the duo entered.

"Agent Peters." Dylan waved as he entered behind Lily who looked like she wanted to be elsewhere. He quickened his steps. "Are Tommy and Mia here?"

Ron didn't answer. Instead, he took in their expressions. Dylan's jaw was tight with restraint, while Lily put on a friendly front, giving a wave to the nearby agents.

"Come with me." Ron led them from the squad room to a smaller conference room and shut the door behind them. Then he faced them, arms crossed. "Sit. Where have you two been?"

They sat at the table. Dylan flicked his gaze at Lily before answering. "We tried playing dumb at first, but they didn't buy it."

"Yeah," Lily joined in. "I figured if we acted like we didn't know Mia, maybe they'd let us go. But they weren't buying it, not for a second."

"Things got physical. We fought back, but then the big one pulled a gun on me."

Ron dropped down onto a chair. "And then?"

"The lean guy got a phone call." Dylan kept his voice steady, but an edge sharpened it. "Right after that, he took a picture of me, then yelled no. At the same time, the big guy pulled the trigger."

Lily scooted forward. "The lean one shoved the big guy's arm, so the shot went wide. Then they started arguing, and before we knew it, they were fighting each other."

"That was our chance." Dylan grasped her hand. "We ran, got up to the rooftop, and hid in the heliport control room until I could check with hotel security. Once I got the all clear, we returned to the panic room, but Tommy and Mia were gone. Figured they had to be with you."

Ron studied them. The timeline made sense. The details added up. But something about the way they told it—the slight hesitation, the glances at each other—felt off.

They weren't lying outright, but they weren't telling him everything, either.

For now, though, it wasn't a crime.

Not yet, anyway.

He let the silence stretch, seeing if either of them would crack. But Dylan met his gaze, and Lily picked at her nails, feigning indifference.

"All right." Ron pushed off the table and gestured for them to follow. "Come on. Let's see Tommy and Mia."

The moment they stepped into the room where Tommy and Mia were waiting, the tension evaporated.

"Hey!" Tommy sprang to his feet.

Lily barely had time to squeak out Mia's name before she was crushed in an embrace.

It was as if none of them had been running for their lives, dodging bullets, hiding in control or safe rooms. They were just relieved to see each other, their laughter and chatter overlapping in a way that made Ron reconsider his suspicions. Maybe they were just four young people who'd been through a lot and were happy to be in one piece.

Still, he watched. He searched for any flicker of hesitation, any unspoken message passed between them. But if they were hiding something, they were good at it.

Before he could observe longer, Deanna burst through the door. "Ron, got something."

He followed her to the squad room where she pulled up an image on the big screen. The black-and-white airport security footage was grainy, but the subject was clear—a man in his late thirties or early forties, moving through the terminal with a group. He had salt-and-pepper stubble, sharp features, and an air of control.

"Facial recognition got a hit." She pushed her ponytail over her shoulder. "Richard Wells aka Spider."

This was likely Jean-Claude's killer.

"What am I looking at? Airport?"

"Spider landed in Orlando five days ago. Came in with Cardinal Bernard and his contingent."

"A cardinal? What for?"

"They're in town for a conference."

Ron frowned. He pointed at the others in the frame. "Who are the rest?"

Deanna gestured to Hernandez.

"Fr. Jacques Benoit, the cardinal's assistant. Fr. Stanislaw Novak, another assistant. And"—Hernandez's voice hitched—"Richard Davenport."

Ron's frown deepened. "Davenport?"

"I'm guessing he used an alias."

He agreed. Same first name, different last name. That sounded off. If this guy was with the cardinal's group, Ron needed to tell Phil.

He scrolled to Phil's name and was about to press dial when

a blocked number called. He tapped Hernandez's shoulder. "Track."

He gave Hernandez a moment. When the agent nodded, Ron swiped to answer. "SAC Ron Peters."

"Cathedral now. Phil in danger." Click. An altered voice.

"I got nada, boss." Hernandez shook his head.

CHAPTER 79

UNKNOWN LOCATION

PHIL

Consciousness crept back through a fog. Phil's head throbbed, his thoughts sluggish from the lingering sedative. A metallic taste coated his mouth, and his muscles ached from prolonged stillness. As his vision cleared, he took in the unfinished basement—the kind tucked beneath old city buildings.

Exposed concrete walls stretched to a low ceiling threaded with pipes and electrical conduits, their shadows forming an irregular lattice under a single overhead bulb. Steel support beams stood like silent sentinels, their bracing sharp against the dim light. Water stains streaked the walls, and the scent of damp earth and old concrete intruded.

Phil was tied to a metal folding chair, the kind churches stacked for parish functions—ironic. The ropes around his wrists and ankles were thick, expertly knotted, biting into his skin with every movement. His Roman collar felt suffocating, his joints aching from the forced position.

A second chair was positioned a few feet away, its emptiness unsettling. The only other features: A rusty floor drain and a heavy metal door, solid enough to smother any sound.

A train rumbled overhead, shaking dust from the ceiling. Near the railroad tracks. Downtown. As the sound faded, silence pressed in, oppressive and absolute.

A door creak shattered the silence.

Phil turned his head, wincing at the stiffness in his neck. His blood ran cold as the man who killed Jean-Claude stepped through the doorway.

But the figure behind him made his heart nearly stop. Novak.

Clarity jolted him. He'd seen the killer before, of course, on the golf course. And then the number 66825 flashed in his mind. The keypad.

Phil's pulse pounded as he registered the numbers on the phone keypad. N (6), O (6), V (8), A (2), K (5).

Novak.

It had all been leading to this.

"So, I see you're awake."

Novak's voice cut through the haze in Phil's mind, sharp and unfamiliar. There was no warmth, no trace of the man he had once trusted. Novak dragged a chair across the floor with an unhurried scrape and settled in front of Phil.

"I must apologize for the circumstances." Novak's tone was almost conversational. "But I needed to ensure we had this discussion without any interruptions."

Phil swallowed against the dryness in his throat. The chair beneath him was hard, and the rope binding his wrists to the armrests bit into his skin. Near the door, a man stood silently— Richard, Novak's enforcer. His presence a looming reminder of how precarious this situation was.

"I don't understand." Phil's voice came out hoarse. "This man killed my uncle."

Novak let out a short humorless laugh. "Spare me the

theatrics. Jean-Claude wasn't your uncle, and we both know it. He was the last keeper of something valuable."

The puzzle pieces shifted in Phil's mind. "There was no order from the Vatican, was there?" The pieces stabilized, cold realization settling in. "You knew if you told me the book was missing, I'd go looking for him. You wanted me to flush him out."

"Bravo." Novak clapped, slow and deliberate. "You were always the sharp one. Your mentor, Fr. Donovan, went to great lengths to hide Jean-Claude, but I knew his precious protégé would know where he was or find a way to track him down. And I was right."

Phil searched him for some flicker of remorse, some trace of the man he once respected. "Why? Did you spread the rumor about the list too?"

Novak tilted his head, feigning innocence. "Perhaps. Or maybe someone else did. Either way, it's been entertaining watching intelligence agencies around the world scramble for a phantom."

"And Victor Marlowe?"

Novak smirked. "Collateral damage."

Phil exhaled, forcing himself to stay calm. "Why betray everything? Your vows, your faith—"

"You still don't get it, do you?" Novak sighed as if disappointed by the question. "It's not about faith. It's about power, and power comes with wealth."

"That's greed. A deadly sin."

"Don't preach to me." Novak glared, his composure almost cracking. Then he leaned forward, his eyes dark with something unrecognizable. "You don't understand the forces involved here. Some people in the Church have plans that go beyond what either of us could imagine. I'm just doing what needs to be done. Now, tell me where the codex is."

Phil didn't answer.

Novak sat back. "O'Shea intercepted the courier. He had the codex." Novak's expression sharpened. "Now, where is it?"

Phil tested the strength of the ropes. The rough fibers dug into his wrists. "You know what amazes me? That you could stand at the altar, consecrate the Eucharist, while orchestrating something like this. You're the kind of man who makes the rest of us look bad."

Novak's eyes flickered with something unreadable before he forced another smile. "Don't be naïve, Phil. The codex is all that matters."

By the door, Richard shifted, arms still folded, his gaze unreadable.

Novak glanced at him, then back at Phil. "Ah, forgive my poor manners. You've met Richard, though not formally. He's been instrumental in all of this."

Richard gave a small nod, an unsettling presence in the basement light.

Phil turned his gaze back to Novak. "You sent Richard to silence Jean-Claude because he knew all the secrets."

The fluorescent bulb overhead flickered as a train rumbled above them, the vibrations making the shadows dance on the walls.

Novak smoothed his sleeve again, his tell for discomfort. "What's done is done. Now, you have a choice. Give us what we need, and this ends well for everyone."

"Everyone except Jean-Claude." Phil flexed his wrists against the restraints. "And me?"

Novak didn't answer. Instead, he spun toward Richard. "Perhaps our guest needs a little encouragement."

CHAPTER 80

EXECUTIVE AIRPORT/BOATHOUSE

OLIVIA

O livia left Falcon and Raven at the airport taking care of the paperwork to return the helicopter. She headed back to her car. Her ribs throbbed with every bump in the road, a deep ache radiating from her side. Just bruised, nothing serious. She'd had worse. No point wasting time at a medical facility when she had more pressing matters. Yes, she'd had injuries before, but this one? This one was different.

She reached into her jacket, fingers brushing against the cool metal medal still hanging around her neck. The bullet was in an evidence bag in her pocket.

She let out a slow breath.

Alive.

Thank you, Lord! I know you guided the bullet.

No time to dwell. There were still things to do.

Instead of heading straight to the boathouse, she detoured toward Orlando Studios. She needed to deposit the bullet and retrieve the flash drive. With that task done, she then drove to the boathouse.

It sat at the edge of the water, weathered and unassuming. Just another forgotten structure to anyone passing by.

Except for the cameras. The reinforced doors. The layers of security measures no one would notice—unless they knew what to look for.

Olivia parked out of sight and stepped out, rolling her shoulders to ease her ribs. The bruising hadn't gotten worse, but it was a constant reminder of how close things had been.

She scanned her surroundings. No one watching. No tails.

Satisfied, she keyed in the access code, let herself in, and shut the door behind her.

The interior smelled faintly of salt and old wood, but beneath that was the sterile hum of high-tech equipment. The SCIF sat at the far end, a reinforced room designed to keep classified conversations classified.

She moved toward it, secured the door behind her, and activated the encrypted terminal.

The screen flickered to life.

Jay appeared a second later, live from Langley.

Dressed in a crisp button-down, sleeves rolled just enough to look relaxed, he was as unreadable as ever. She knew him well enough to recognize that the easy posture was an illusion. Jay never relaxed.

"Any news?"

No reason to waste time. She pulled the microchip from her pocket and held it up to the camera. "All that effort. And this? Worthless."

Jay's expression didn't change. "Explain."

Olivia exhaled. The ache in her ribs flared, but she ignored it.

"The intel is false. There's no list of covert operatives. Just a manuscript of a history book. That's it."

Jay's gaze sharpened. "You saw it yourself?"

"I viewed it myself," she confirmed. "It's a history of Mirror

Estate. There's nothing in that book worth the global panic this caused."

Jay was silent for a beat. Then he leaned back in his chair on the screen, tapping a pen against his desk. "You said a history of Mirror Estate?"

"Yes, nothing special. Land deals. How Dylan's ancestors came here. Things of that nature."

"Send it to me anyway. I'm not sure it's nothing."

"Yeah, of course. The entire intelligence community scrambled for nothing. We need to contain it before it sparks a war. O'Shea warned us as much."

"Let me worry about it. I heard you also captured a couple of packages."

"Right." She braced her arms on the desk. "One Chinese. One Russian. They're being renditioned as we speak."

"Good job. By the way, your Bureau buddies are in the dark, right?"

"Absolutely. Is it all right if I tell Raven and Falcon? I'm sure this is their mission too, even though they told me they were chasing Marlowe."

Jay's pen drummed against his desk. Finally, he inclined his head. "Fine. Tell them. But they'll likely have to wait for confirmation from their own superiors. Any idea who started this?"

"That I don't know. Yet." Fr. Phil might know something about it. But she couldn't give Jay gut-instinct responses.

"Keep me posted." He ended the connection.

Before she deposited the microchip in the drop box for pick up, she made a copy. She'd do a more thorough exam of the manuscript herself. Maybe it contained something useful to Dylan's quest.

CHAPTER 81

CATHEDRAL

RON

The cathedral loomed ahead, its stone façade casting long shadows in the afternoon light. Ron drove the SUV into the lot, his gut tightening as he stepped out. He didn't see the priest's hybrid. A truck parked in one of the clergy spots.

"Tanner, check the plate."

"Yeah, boss." Tanner was thumbing out the text.

They approached the cathedral office. Inside, it was quiet, the faint scent of old books and polished wood lingering. A middle-aged receptionist looked up from her desk, offering a polite smile.

"FBI." Ron held his credentials up. "We're looking for Fr. Phil Shagley from Mirror Estate's chapel."

Her brows furrowed. "I haven't seen any priest come by this afternoon."

Ron exchanged a look with Tanner. "What about Fr. Novak? He's with Cardinal Bernard."

The woman shook her head. "Cardinal Bernard and his assistant left yesterday."

Tanner jutted up his chin. "How many assistants?"

"Just Fr. Benoit."

Ron's frown deepened. "What about Richard Wells?"

The receptionist's face remained blank. "I don't know anyone by that name."

"Er, Richard Davenport?" Tanner corrected, using Wells's current traveling alias. When she shook her head, Tanner waved toward the door. "Do you have security cameras?"

"There's a camera out front. Motion sensor light in the back, but no camera."

Not great. If someone had grabbed Phil from the back, there'd be no footage.

They thanked her and walked out. "Call the office. Deanna and Hernandez need to check street cams and other cams in the area."

Just when they settled back in the SUV, his phone buzzed. "Got something!" Deanna's voice came through the speaker.

"Go."

"The only thing I can find around the cathedral in the time frame is a van exiting the back lot. You're not gonna like it. It's not the best of quality, and the angle is terrible. But it looks like someone was attacked when he walked to the back entrance."

"Attacked?"

"Yeah," Hernandez said. "I'm sending the footage to you now. The person was drugged or knocked unconscious. Or it appears so. Then he was put in the van."

Deanna came back on. "By the way, the truck's license plate came back to Leo Trent, a custodian at the Mirror Estate's Holy Angels Chapel. And this van drove out of the lot about three minutes after the truck went in. A store's camera caught the van's plate. Van is heading west on East Central."

"The van is a rental," Hernandez reported. "Checking with the company now." A brief pause, then, "Rented to Richard Davenport."

"Do we have a location?" Ron asked.

"Sending coordinates now," Deanna replied. "It's an office building. Best I can do."

"Give Ana and Charlie the location," he ordered. Then he took the next turn sharply, checking street numbers.

Up ahead, the shadow of a building partially concealed the van. Meanwhile, Tanner was checking the blueprints Hernandez sent over.

"Delta, Echo, Lima, 3, 4, 7." Ron read off the plate as he keyed his radio. "Hernandez, is this our van?"

The response was immediate. "Yes."

Ron killed the engine, his gaze locked on the vehicle. This was it.

The screech of tires behind him signaled backup. Ana and Charlie's black sedan slid into the lot, stopping beside his SUV. They were already out before the car settled, weapons drawn.

Ron met them halfway, his voice low. "Hernandez confirmed this is the van. Basement office is vacant. Tenant moved out. Space is available for lease."

Ana nodded. "Perfect hiding spot. Isolated, no foot traffic."

When Ron motioned them closer, Tanner whispered, "Two entry points—main stairs and the service entrance. Blueprints show a hallway splitting into three offices."

The basement layout meant limited escape routes—good for containment, bad if Wells had rigged anything. "Ana, take Charlie through the service entrance," Ron ordered. "Tanner, with me. Maintain radio silence unless necessary."

Ana exchanged a glance with Charlie. "Got it."

"Watch for trip wires."

Ana and Charlie peeled away, disappearing around the corner like ghosts. Ron approached the main entrance. The glass doors were unlocked—suspicious.

He inhaled, nodding to himself. Someone had been here recently.

The stairwell stretched below him, fluorescent lights flickering. This felt like a trap. But there was no choice. Phil was inside.

Each step down was slow, deliberate. The basement smelled of dust and disuse, but something else—something recent—lingered. At the bottom, a heavy fire door separated him from the basement proper.

Ron held up three fingers, counting down. On zero, he pushed the door open and swept inside, weapon raised.

The hallway stretched before him, dark except for the emergency exit signs casting an eerie red glow. Three doors, just as planned.

A muffled thump echoed from further down—the middle office.

His pulse jumped.

Through his earpiece, Ana's whispered confirmation came: "In position."

Ron signaled the advance. He edged down the hall, pressing against the wall. Another sound—a voice, too faint to make out words.

His earpiece crackled. "Third office clear," Charlie reported.

Ron stopped outside the middle door. Light seeped through the crack underneath.

He raised his hand, five fingers splayed. The countdown began.

Three. Two. One.

CHAPTER 82

UNKNOWN BASEMENT

PHIL

Phil's jaw ached. The metallic taste of blood filled his mouth as he shifted against the cold steel chair. The single bulb shivered, shaking the shadows across the concrete floor. His wrists burned where the duct tape—the one Richard reapplied after removing the ropes for their last "conversation"—bit into them, securing him to the chair's arms.

Across from him stood Richard. His face appeared carved from stone, emotionless. Except a twitch at the corner of his mouth betrayed something like enjoyment. The gold crucifix pinned to his lapel caught the light, a jarring contradiction to the violence in his eyes.

"I'll ask once more, Father." Novak paced behind Richard, employing the tone he used for confessions. "Where is the codex?"

Phil spat blood onto the floor. "There's still time to end this, Stan. You don't want to add this to your sins."

Richard looked to Novak, who gave a small nod. The enforcer stepped forward, his massive hand fisted.

"You know, priests are supposed to be martyrs. But most of you break pretty quick." His swing connected with Phil's ribs. Shock waves of pain rolled through his body. "By the way, the receptionist at the nursing home was really friendly. 'Oh, he's such a great nephew, always stays after Mass to visit his uncle.'" He mimicked the high-pitched voice.

Phil gasped, struggling to draw breath. The room spun. He felt the tape on his right wrist. Throughout the interrogation, he'd been working at it, further loosening it each passing minute. The adrenaline surging through his system gave him newfound strength.

Richard pivoted toward Novak, granting the opportunity Phil needed. With a surge of desperate strength, he wrenched his right hand free of the loosened tape. In one fluid motion, he grabbed Richard's wrist as the man turned back, using the enforcer's momentum against him. Richard stumbled, off-balance.

"You little—" Richard regained his footing and lunged, face contorted with rage.

Phil braced for the impact, knowing his small victory would be short-lived.

Then he heard it—a faint sound, like the scrape of boots on gravel outside the basement door.

An instant later, the world exploded into noise and motion.

"Federal agents! Everybody down!"

The door burst open with a thunderous crash. Familiar figures poured in, weapons raised, voices overlapping in commanding shouts. Beams from tactical flashlights cut through the dusty air.

"On the ground! Hands where I can see them!"

Richard froze, his fist still raised. Novak stood paralyzed, his composed face slack.

Tanner tackled Richard from behind before he could react. Richard struggled until Tanner pressed a knee between his shoulder blades and secured his wrists with metal handcuffs that glinted beneath the bare light bulb.

"Stanislaw Novak." Ana trained her weapon on Novak's chest. "You are under arrest. Get on your knees and place your hands behind your head."

It seemed Novak might run. His gaze darted to the side exit, calculating. Ron moved to block his path. Whatever fight had been in him drained away. With dignified slowness, he sank to his knees, hands rising to interlock behind his clerical collar.

As Ana secured Novak, Ron approached. "Phil, let's get you out of here."

"How did you find me?" he managed to ask.

Ron frowned. "You know, I don't know. I got a call from an unknown number. A mechanical voice said, 'Cathedral now. Phil in danger.' Hernandez couldn't trace it. Too short."

CHAPTER 83

BOATHOUSE/ORLANDO HOSPITAL

OLIVIA

L ate afternoon light slanted through the boathouse as Olivia updated Raven and Falcon on the false intelligence. The list of covert operatives had been nothing more than a sophisticated hoax, although the auction was real. But the damage was done. Agencies had scrambled, informants had disappeared, and people had died chasing shadows.

"I can't imagine the fallout from this." Falcon shook his head, his feet on the coffee table. "Heads will roll."

"Glad it's above my pay grade." Olivia tossed back her iced coffee.

"Any idea of who started this?" Raven sank deeper into the couch.

"Nope. I'm sure you'll hear from Vauxhall Cross or Whitehall soon enough."

The couple had been MI6, SIS officially, but Raven had been taken off the books after going rogue. Falcon had risked everything to save her, and that kind of loyalty had to have cost him too.

As with many intelligence operatives, the government either wiped your name from the official roster, reassigned you to a dark outfit if you were still useful, or retired you in a way that ensured silence. Since they were still running ops, they must be black-budget operatives, much like herself.

Her cell pinged. Simon. She excused herself and stepped outside.

"Hey." His voice grounded her. "You all right?"

"Yeah, I'm okay. Should wrap up soon."

"Good. Lily's been worried."

Which meant Lily had been calling Simon instead of her. They spoke a bit longer. Then she hung up and called Lily.

Lily picked up instantly. "Mom." Her voice carried an edge.

"What is it?"

"Fr. Phil's in the hospital."

Olivia's pulse ticked up. "What happened?"

"I don't know all the details. We just heard the agents talking."

That was all she needed to hear. She went back inside, told Raven and Falcon she had to go. They walked out with her. She got in her car, and they went their separate ways.

When she arrived at the hospital, it smelled like antiseptic and stale air. She strode toward the front desk, flashing her FBI credentials before the nurse even looked up. "I'm here for Fr. Phil Shagley."

"Room 9A." The nurse barely glanced at the ID.

Olivia strode past. She had prepared herself for the sight of Fr. Phil hooked up to IVs, heavily bandaged, but when she reached the window to his room, she encountered something far less dramatic.

Ron was standing near the bed. Fr. Phil, sitting up against the pillows, had some bruising and cuts, but no broken bones. He looked more annoyed than anything.

Maybe she should just wait outside? But her hand, moving of its own accord, pushed in the door.

Both men looked up.

"Olivia," Ron greeted with a nod.

"Ron." Her gaze drifted to Fr. Phil. "Father."

Fr. Phil released a small chuckle. "Olivia."

No IVs. No casts. Just banged up. Whatever happened, he'd walked away from it.

"How are you holding up?"

"I've been better." Humor edged his dry voice. "Getting old."

She smirked. "You'll never get too old. You need to be well enough to marry us."

That got a laugh and a wince out of the priest. "I will."

Ron checked his watch. "I need to head back to the office soon, but I wanted to let you know Lily and Dylan are fine. Chilling at the task force office."

She already knew that. She'd told them to stick to that story, to play dumb at first.

Ron continued. "They said they played dumb at first, but the bad guys weren't buying it. There was a fight. Then Fat Boy pulled a gun on Dylan."

Olivia made a show of frowning as if processing this. She had walked Dylan and Lily through every detail—what to say, what to leave out.

Ron leaned against the counter. "The weird part? Ringo got a call. He took Dylan's picture, then told Fat Boy no. That's when the shot went wide."

Olivia kept her features schooled. "So, someone higher up overruled the hit?"

She already suspected as much. But Ringo taking a photo before receiving the order was new information. That could mean Dylan was being evaluated in real time.

"That's what I'm thinking." Ron let a yawn slip out. "Tanner confirmed it with Ringo."

The yawn was almost contagious. It had been a long day. Still, she hummed as if considering this conclusion for the first time. Dylan had been important enough for someone to stop the execution. The only person who had the pull was the Ghost.

"Am I hearing this right?" Fr. Phil held up a hand. "Someone pulled a gun on Dylan, and a phone call from someone stopped it?"

Ron nodded. "That's what they said. Tanner got it from Ringo that Marlowe gave the order to stop."

"Marlowe? Victor Marlowe?" The priest frowned. "And where is this Marlowe?"

"At the morgue. Luca, his second-in-command, shot him. He's in wind now."

The priest narrowed his eyes, obviously connecting the dots, so to speak. Luca had to be working for the Ghost. Fr. Phil remained quiet too, though probably thinking, deducing.

"Anyway, got to go."

Olivia waved Ron along. "Glad Marlowe's murder is not my problem."

He studied her, as if debating whether to say more, then shrugged. "I'll keep you posted."

With that, he left.

As the door clicked shut, she stepped closer to Fr. Phil. "All right, Father, tell me about the book."

Fr. Phil exhaled. "Which one?"

Which one? She rocked back off her toes, the motion bringing the ache to her ribs. "There's more than one?"

He rubbed his forehead. "Sorry, must be the head bump. I already told you there was no list."

Olivia reached into her pocket and pulled out a flash drive. She held it up between two fingers. "Right, I know. Here's what I found."

His eyes sharpened. "What's on it?"

"A manuscript. A book." She hesitated. "You were right. There was never a list."

Fr. Phil frowned. "Have you read it?"

"I didn't read the whole thing. I skimmed it. Land deals. Maps. History of the Mirror Estate. Some correspondences."

"In English?"

"No, in Arabic. What do you think? Of course, it's in English."

Fr. Phil pressed his fingers along his brow again. His head must hurt too. "Is it possible for me to have a look?"

She was thinking of showing Dylan. And she had other concerns. "I'm more interested in who started the rumor. I just don't get it."

"I believe Fr. Novak started the rumor. Or at least, he did it on behalf of someone else."

"Who? The Ghost?" It always came back to the Ghost. "Why does she want it?"

His palm lowered to cover his eyes. "I need to think."

She waited.

He sighed. "Olivia, let me seek the Lord's wisdom and rest. Then I'll tell you what I can."

CHAPTER 84

THE GHOST'S APARTMENT, MIRROR ESTATE

MARGE

M arge lounged at the table, fingers drumming against the smooth, weaponless surface. Golden light filtered through the reinforced windows, and the ever-present surveillance hummed, a reminder that she was never truly alone.

When Larry appeared at the doorway, she didn't bother to look up. "Popular today, aren't I?" she quipped.

She settled back in her chair, expression neutral, even as a single thought looped in her mind. Did she get the book?

The steel door clicked open, and Olivia stepped in, her movements controlled, measured. A woman always in command, though tension bracketed her shoulders. She crossed the room and took the seat across from Marge, their gazes meeting over the bare table.

"Marlowe is dead," Olivia announced.

Marge blinked, a slow, deliberate motion. A nonreaction. She had perfected the art of indifference, a skill that had served her well over the years. She couldn't let Olivia know this was old news, so she tilted her head, feigning contemplation. "Is that so?"

Olivia studied her. "Just got word from the task force. They're shutting down the auction and tracking down everyone who placed a bid on the list." A pause. "Art Crime and other agencies are closing their case against Marlowe."

Marge exhaled, masking her interest. Of course, they would shut it all down, wrapping it in a tight bow and filing it away as another successful operation. But the work wouldn't end. Agents would still chase the scattered artwork, dig through provenance records, follow the threads of stolen history back to its rightful owners.

And, sooner or later, they'd call on her.

"Good for them."

Olivia narrowed her eyes, probably debating whether to challenge the casual remark, but she dismissed it. Instead, she rested her forearms on the table. "Did you know what Marlowe put up for auction?"

Marge lifted a brow, waiting. Olivia was pushing. Of course, she was.

When the agent didn't elaborate, Marge asked, "Did you recover it?"

Olivia hesitated, something flickering behind her sharp gaze —annoyance, impatience. "It was a book, a history of the estate."

So the priest didn't find it. Interesting. Marge absorbed Olivia's revelation.

She didn't push, didn't pry. There was no need. Dylan had told Olivia about her quest. They were easy to read, those two. Too easy. Olivia would take the book straight to Dylan, hoping it held the key to whatever mystery he was chasing.

Offering the faintest smirk, Marge tilted her head. "Not my problem."

Olivia's gaze sharpened. "You made it sound like it was valuable intel."

Marge gave a lazy shrug. "I believe I mentioned it was a rumor."

The moment dragged in silence between them. The unspoken things pressed down, thick as the humid evening air would be outside.

Then Marge shifted. "Why don't we talk about Phoenix?"

A flicker. Barely there, but she caught it. Olivia's composure was a fortress, but even the strongest walls had weak spots.

Olivia didn't flinch. Didn't blink. "There's nothing to discuss."

A nonanswer.

Predictable.

But Marge had spent too much time thinking. Watching. Connecting links others ignored.

Olivia's record was impeccable. Too clean. Most of her work was buried under classification, and what little was public read like a curated résumé—impressive, untouchable. At first glance, nobody would question it. But Marge was not anyone else. And she'd had nothing but time to think about it.

Marge's underlings had dug deeper. Supposedly, Olivia had been recruited straight out of college, an untested agent handed sensitive operations far too early. The kind of access no rookie should have.

And then there was the timing.

Olivia and her daughter had resurfaced in the US just as Phoenix went off-grid.

Coincidence?

Marge didn't believe in coincidence.

Again, she held the silence. Olivia didn't fidget, didn't react. But Marge knew better.

"A shame," she said, letting her words drift, casual and nonchalant. "Some people are harder to kill than others."

Olivia remained unflinching. "They are."

CHAPTER 85

TASK FORCE OFFICE

RON

R on stepped into the squad room, balancing a pastry box in one hand and a coffee tray in the other. The scent of warm sugar and fresh-brewed caffeine wafted through the air, catching his team's attention.

Within minutes, the box was nearly empty. Napkins rustled, to-go coffee cups tapped against desks, and the tension of unfinished cases eased.

He let them have five minutes.

Then he cleared his throat. "All right, let's get to it. I want updates. Let's wrap this up."

The chatter faded, and all eyes zeroed in on the big screen at the front of the squad room. The central monitor was already lit up, displaying a web of crime-scene photos, suspect profiles, and evidence logs. Smaller screens at each workstation synced in real time.

Ron addressed Tanner first. "What's the status on the young folks?"

Tanner tossed his napkin into the wastebasket. "Like you

ordered, Charlie and I got them to the estate. Security's locked down tight. Ortiz is handling it personally."

"And what about Art Crime? I thought Agent Berrigan would be here." Ron had already updated Agent Holt from Homeland who was glad Mia wouldn't have to testify and keep looking over her shoulder now.

Tanner smirked. "Oh, as soon as she heard Marlowe was dead, she got so mad. Said after all this time, she was hoping for an arrest. And now, she's got to track down all the stolen and looted artwork."

On the screen, a list of stolen paintings, sculptures, and rare artifacts flickered into view. Some had already been marked as recovered, but many were still missing.

Ron picked up his own almost empty coffee cup. "That'll be a bureaucratic nightmare."

"That's an understatement," Tanner muttered.

Ron shifted his focus to Hernandez. "Auction's officially shut down?"

"Deanna and I made sure of it." Hernandez nodded. "No more bidding, no more shady deals. We've identified most of the buyers, but a few slipped through the cracks. Cyber's still working on it."

"And the item up for sale?" Ron swirled his cup, mixing the dregs back in.

Hernandez hesitated. "That's the thing. We still don't know what it was."

A few heads turned his way.

Ron fortified himself with the last of his liquid energy. On the big screen, a timeline of the auction's key transactions appeared. "What do you mean, you don't know? Crime Scene didn't recover anything?"

Deanna shook her head. "No physical item. But we did find something in the email exchanges."

She tapped a few keys and pulled up a chain of encrypted

messages. Some portions were already decoded, revealing vague references to "the package" and "the list."

"A list of what?" Ron tossed his cup in the recycling.

Deanna exchanged a glance with Hernandez before answering. "Covert operatives."

A beat of silence settled over the room.

"That's false intel," Ana spoke up. "Got it from the DIA."

Charlie held up his phone. "I got the same whispers from my overseas contacts. Fake intel."

So, Marlowe was dead. Art Crime would handle the domestic cleanup, and HSI would take care of the international side. The task force could close this case.

"Oh, I checked in with Marian Station," Ana added. "Let them know their assault suspect is dead."

Tanner shook crumbs from his shirt. "KC told me they booked Ringo, who sang like a bird about all the transactions. Interestingly, all he knows about the item for auction is a book."

"Hmm." Ron sighed. "All right, then. Let's close this. Let's hit the paperwork."

Still, one question nagged at him.

"Good work." He arched a brow Hernandez's way. "Figured out who called me about Phil yesterday?"

"Sorry, boss. No."

Ron's jaw tightened. Who could it be? And why stay anonymous?

Before he could ponder further, Ana signaled for him to follow her. He tailed her to the alcove by the elevator. She stood in the corner, keeping a close watch on anyone passing by. She looked tense, almost wary.

He crossed his arms. "What's on your mind?"

"Just curious. How well do you know Charlie?"

He needed to be careful here. "Not well. He came in to fill in for you and Kyle. So far, I haven't seen anything questionable. Why?"

Ana hesitated, then huffed. "I'm sure he's been vetted thoroughly. It's just…"

"Spill it."

She looked around, then lowered her voice. "When we were staking out the warehouse, he kept asking about Dylan, Ms. Carol, and the Ghost. He was really interested."

Ron almost smiled. Ana was sharp. He'd had his own suspicions about Charlie. Placement in Task Force 629 was by invitation only. In fact, just knowing about the task force required a certain level of clearance. Only a handful of people even knew what it did. So for Charlie to pull whatever strings he had to get his file on Ron's desk?

That was suspect.

"Ever heard the saying, 'Keep your friends close and your enemies closer'?"

CHAPTER 86

CHAPEL, MIRROR ESTATE

PHIL

P hil didn't sleep well last night. Jeremy was kind to drive him back, and Ron had arranged for Leo's truck to be returned. The nurse had given Jeremy the hospital discharge instructions. Jeremy insisted he'd take care of morning Mass. But since Phil was awake, he attended Mass anyway. He needed guidance and sat in the back.

Afterward, he slipped out before any well-meaning parishioners could stop him. He made his way to the Adoration Chapel. Incense lingered in the air, a comforting yet grounding presence. His fingers rested on the back of the pew in front of him, gripping the wood as he tried to focus.

The weekend had been a whirlwind—betrayals, lies, violence. And yet, the answers eluded him, no more tangible than that incense. He had prayed for clarity, for wisdom to piece together the fragments of truth.

He lowered his head to his hands.

What am I missing? How do I proceed?

Fear not, my child. Trust in the Lord.

He pulled out his rosary and prayed. Feeling no closer to an answer, he went back to his office and dove into the recent events.

The whiteboard's glare made his eyes ache. Or maybe it was the lingering effects of whatever had happened to him, the details still fuzzy around the edges. The marker squeaked as he connected another line between his scrawled notes, the sound sharp in the quiet rectory.

He should be in bed. That's what the doctor had said. That's what Jeremy had practically ordered, his younger colleague's face pinched with concern as he'd driven them back from the hospital. "I'll handle everything," Jeremy had insisted. "Just rest."

But rest felt impossible. The pieces were there, swimming before his eyes on the whiteboard, almost forming a picture. Almost. He traced the connections again, willing them to make sense.

Voices in the hallway interrupted. He recognized Jeremy's concerned tone first.

"—should be resting. The doctor was quite clear about—"

"I understand, Jeremy," came Tom's deeper voice. "I won't stay long. But since I'm already here…"

"Five minutes," Jeremy conceded, their footsteps approaching. "That's all I'm allowing. He's had a rough couple of days."

Phil couldn't help but smile at Jeremy's protective stance.

A knock announced them, and both priests stopped in his doorway. Jeremy's arms were crossed, his expression that of a disappointed parent finding their child out of bed past curfew.

"Look who I found wandering our halls." Jeremy aimed a disapproving look at Phil and the whiteboard behind him. "I told him you were supposed to be resting."

"I am resting." Phil gestured to his chair. "Sitting down and everything."

Tom chuckled as his concerned gaze swept over Phil's face.

"You look better than I expected, given what Jeremy was telling me. Something about an abduction?"

"It wasn't as dramatic as I'm sure he made it sound." Phil shot Jeremy a look.

"That's not what the doctor—"

"Five minutes, you said?" Phil interrupted Jeremy. "Why don't you make us all some tea?"

"Oh, no, not for me. I only have a few minutes." Tom sat. "But thank you."

Jeremy hesitated before saying, "All right then, one chamomile tea coming up."

As Jeremy's footsteps faded down the hall, Tom stepped into the office. "Hey, Phil. Jeremy was telling me you had quite the mishap."

"It's nothing." Phil waved away the concern, though the movement made his head throb. "Come, sit." He gestured toward the guest chair, grateful for the distraction. Or was he? Everything felt significant now. "What brought you to our neck of the woods?"

Tom settled into the chair, his hand going into his jacket pocket. "Well, I was in the area for the brunch at St. Matthew's. You know how Sister Agnes gets when you miss her famous egg casserole." He smiled, but it faded. "Though that's not why I'm here."

He withdrew an unremarkable envelope—plain white, standard size—but something about the way Tom held it made Phil's pulse quicken.

"This is for you." Tom examined the envelope in his hands before extending it. "I was at the conference with Cardinal Bernard and his delegation." He frowned. "Fr. Benoit, his assistant, somehow knew I was friends with you. Asked if I would deliver a message."

Phil's fingers twitched toward the envelope, but he forced

himself to remain still. "Seems like an odd request. The cathedral staff—"

"That's what I thought." Tom held up the envelope. "Could have left it with them. But he insisted on hand delivery." He shrugged, but the gesture seemed too deliberate. "I did ask if it was urgent, you know. He said no, but…" Tom placed the envelope on the desk between them. "Something about the whole thing felt off."

Phil stared at the envelope, its blank surface more ominous than any of his scribbled notes on the whiteboard. Another puzzle piece. But would this one show him the whole picture or deepen the mystery?

Jeremy's footsteps echoed in the hall before he stepped through the doorway. "Time's up," he called, balancing a tray with a cup of steaming tea.

Tom stood and smoothed his jacket. "He's right. You should rest. Whatever's in that envelope can wait."

But Phil wasn't so sure about that. As he accepted the chamomile tea from Jeremy, his gaze kept drifting to the innocent-looking envelope.

The door clicked shut behind Tom and Jeremy, and Phil waited until the footsteps faded down the stone corridor. He scooped up the envelope and examined the white paper that bore no external markings.

He reached for his letter opener, a gift from Jean-Claude decades ago, and slit the envelope. He extracted the single sheet and unfolded it.

> *Padre Phil,*
>
> *I became suspicious there's a traitor in our midst. Padre Donovan once told me you were one of the few entrusted with the secret. My contacts at the CIA pointed me to this American, Adam O'Shea, who is here for another reason.*

I'm entrusting him to give you this. Keep the secret safe, my brother.

    Antonio †VX17

Phil read it again, his finger tracing each word as if to confirm their reality. This Antonio had to be in the Vatican Intelligence. The cross and code, Antonio's personal authentication, left no room for doubt. Phil's gaze drifted to the worn spines of books lining his walls.

The traitor had proven to be Novak. Now Phil understood why O'Shea knew of him and called to set up a meeting. Antonio must have handed the flash drive to O'Shea, who'd expressed concern Phil might not believe it came from the authentic source. A note would be needed, but O'Shea couldn't risk another meeting with Antonio. So, Antonio had found another way to get the message to him.

Phil's fingers drummed against his desk. The authentication was genuine. Assuming Antonio was Vatican Intelligence, he wouldn't likely use the cross and VX17 marking unless the situation was dire. Finally, Phil had all the pieces. Now, to fulfill Jean-Claude's last words to find the book, he would need access to it.

That would mean getting Olivia to let him have the book.

CHAPTER 87

CHAPEL, MIRROR ESTATE

OLIVIA

The morning sunlight filtered through the chapel's stained glass windows, and fractured beams of color spilled over the polished wooden pews. The incense lingered, a grounding presence in contrast to the chaos Olivia navigated over the weekend.

She had barely gotten a full night's sleep, but it was enough to recharge. Enough to think clearly. Before coming here, she checked in with Lily. Everyone was safe for now. With Marlowe dead and the truth of the list's fabrication beginning to spread, the immediate danger must've subsided. But intelligence agencies were slow to trust or, in some cases, reluctant to let go of a narrative that suited their interests.

So, she'd given Dylan clear instructions: Keep his security teams at the hotel and the estate on high alert. Just because the list was false didn't mean someone wouldn't come sniffing around for verification.

Now, standing outside Fr. Phil's office, she inhaled deeply to compose herself before knocking.

"Come in," he called.

She pushed the door open and stepped inside. Fr. Phil sat behind his desk, looking better than he had at the hospital but still worn around the edges. A bruise darkened his temple, a reminder of the recent chaos. A cup of tea steamed near his elbow, untouched.

He motioned to the chair opposite him. "Sit, please."

Olivia did, crossing one leg over the other. "How are you feeling?"

He reached for a teacup. "It's chamomile tea. Would you like some? And better than yesterday, thank you. Not quite up for a marathon, but I doubt I'll need to outrun anyone today."

"You never know. And no tea, thank you." She never cared for herbal tea.

Fr. Phil gave her a knowing look, then sipped his tea, and set it aside. "Something tells me this isn't a wellness check."

She softened her posture, elbows resting on the armrests. "You said you needed time to think and seek the Lord's guidance. I'm hoping you have something for me. About the book. And the rumor."

His expression didn't change, but a shift came to his eyes—caution. "I don't have direct knowledge of who started the rumor. Fr. Novak admitted he started it, but he alluded to something more powerful being at play."

"Is that so?"

"And I do believe the Ghost had a hand in it."

She replayed last night's meeting with the Ghost. "Why would she start a rumor about a fake list?"

Fr. Phil folded his hands over the desk. "Misdirection. A distraction. If she was behind it, she wanted something. And my best guess? The book."

Olivia scanned the office. Nothing out of place or moved. "I saw her yesterday. If she wanted it, why not just ask?"

A wry smile quirked his lips. "Did she ever strike you as someone who asks for things directly?"

"No," Olivia admitted. "She doesn't."

"There you have it."

Something about the way he said it... She sensed there was something more. "Are you sure about the Ghost?"

"No, there's a possibility that some other entity started this."

"Entity?"

A beat of silence stretched. Fr. Phil wasn't just any priest. He'd seen and done things most clergy never would. He understood secrets.

He must have sensed her hesitation because he added, "If I could look at the manuscript, I might be able to tell you more."

She studied him. "Why?"

"Because it may be more than a history book."

She pulled a flash drive from her key chain and slid it across the desk.

He plugged it into his laptop, put on his reading glasses, and drew the laptop closer. Then, for the first time since she walked in, his composure wavered. Not much, just a tightening of his jaw, a flicker of something in his gaze.

He frowned, his gaze unfocused, before returning to the text. After a long pause, he rolled back his chair. "Has Dylan mentioned anything about buried treasures?"

Olivia narrowed her eyes. "He has."

Fr. Phil nodded, as if confirming something he'd suspected. He leaned back, removed his glasses, and rubbed the bridge of his nose.

"I believe this book provides clues."

CHAPTER 88

MIRROR ESTATE

DYLAN

Dylan stretched his legs along the stone pathway, hands tucked into his jacket pockets as the cool night air settled around Mirror Estate. The sprawling grounds were silent, wrapped in the hushed tranquility of the late hour. The scent of freshly cut grass and faint traces of orange blossoms drifted in on the breeze, a stark contrast to the chaotic last few days.

His grandmother had been delighted to meet Mia, welcoming her with open arms. Tommy, of course, was already a familiar presence, practically part of the family. But Mia? She had stared in awe at the estate the night before, her wide-eyed wonder a mirror of how everyone reacted when they first stepped onto the Marino grounds.

Dylan had been about to offer her a tour when Lily cut in.

"Oh, Tommy would be happy to show you around." Her fingers tightened around his wrist as if restraining him. She had flashed him that knowing look, the one that meant she had other plans for him. Mia, amused but intrigued, had gone along with it.

Tommy had thrown Lily a betrayed glare before following Mia down one of the long corridors. Dylan had just shaken his head.

That was last night.

Today had been slow, peaceful. Something they all needed.

They had slept in, taken their time over breakfast, then lounged in the garden, soaking up the rare stillness. The exhaustion had even begun to lift.

At some point, Olivia had dropped by, her usual no-nonsense expression in place.

"I got my hands on the history of Mirror Estate." She set a thick folder in front of him.

Dylan had edged forward, intrigued.

"Fr. Phil thinks it might help with your… quest." She'd arched a brow. "If you want, I can make you a copy."

He hadn't hesitated.

But what he hadn't told her—what no one knew—was that he and Tommy had already uncovered pieces of the estate's history long ago. Old documents, faded maps, hidden artifacts tucked away in forgotten corners. But after these recent events, he wasn't ready to dive into the past yet.

Not when Tommy barely made it out alive.

So instead, Dylan focused on something more practical.

By late afternoon, a delivery van brought Tommy and Mia new phones. The moment they unwrapped them, they looked like kids on Christmas morning.

"You got us new phones?" Mia had asked, eyes gleaming.

"Yup. Latest model."

"I swear," Tommy muttered, already scrolling through the settings, "this is the best part of staying at the estate."

Dylan had laughed.

After dinner, the night had cooled, and he now found himself walking the grounds with Lily.

They moved in easy silence, the gravel crunching beneath their feet. The estate glowed under the moonlight, its vast gardens stretching into the distance, shadows flickering against the manicured hedges. It was peaceful. Too peaceful.

Wasn't there a saying, "Things happen in threes"? His first brush with death, then abduction, and another abduction all happened in quick succession. After months of calm waters, now this. At least, it wasn't him at the center. Maybe he was over-thinking the situation.

Lily slipped her arm through his and rested her hand in the crook of his elbow. They weren't in a hurry, weren't trying to get anywhere—just walking, as if the past few days could be left behind for one night.

"It's been a crazy year," she murmured.

He glanced down at her, at the way the garden lights softened her features, highlighting the deep brown of her eyes. "Yeah. Crazy doesn't even begin to cover it."

She hummed in agreement, tilting her head toward the reflecting pool ahead. The water shimmered under the starlit sky, still and undisturbed. Like a mirror.

"You know…" She brushed her fingers against his sleeve. "I used to think we'd never get a moment like this. That it would always be running, chasing, catching our breath before the next thing hit us."

Dylan smirked. "That's kind of our thing."

Lily nudged him with her shoulder. "I don't want that to be our thing forever."

That made him stop.

She took another step before realizing he had frozen. Then she turned back to face him. "What?"

He opened his mouth, then closed it again.

They had been through so much—high-stakes missions, near-death experiences, moments that had nearly torn them apart —but they had never once talked about the future. Not beyond the next problem to solve, the next fight to survive.

But this was different.

This was the first time Lily ever hinted at something more.

Something permanent.

"I just…" He rubbed the back of his neck. "I guess I never thought about it."

Her brows lifted, but she didn't look surprised. If anything, she looked hopeful.

"Well…" She stepped into the space between them. "Maybe it's time we do."

His heart kicked up a notch.

She was so close now he could feel her warmth despite the cool air. Her lavender perfume curled around him, something familiar and grounding. He'd never been the sentimental type, but something about this moment—her, them, here at the Mirror Estate—felt different.

Like a line they were about to cross.

"So…" He tried to keep his voice casual. "What does this future of yours look like?"

Her lips curved into a knowing smile. "Hmm. That depends," she teased. "Are you in it?"

"I don't know." He huffed a small laugh. "Am I?"

Lily reached up, her fingers tracing his jaw. The barely there touch sent a thrill through him. "I'd like you to be."

He swallowed. Hard.

He'd never been afraid of gunfights, of close calls, of putting himself in danger. But this? This was different.

Because this wasn't about survival.

This was about choosing something. Someone.

And for the first time, he realized he wanted to choose her.

Without thinking, he closed the last bit of space between them and rested his forehead against hers. "You know," he murmured, "you're kind of dangerous when you talk like that."

"Oh?" She grinned. "Are you scared?"

His hand slid around her waist, pulling her closer.

"Terrified," he admitted, voice just above a whisper.

She exhaled a soft laugh, and then, as naturally as breathing, he kissed her—slow and deep, the kind of kiss that promised things he hadn't yet put into words.

And in that moment, under the moonlit sky, in the quiet sanctuary of the Mirror Estate, he knew—

This wasn't just a fleeting moment.

This was the beginning of something real.

Something permanent.

Their future.

CHAPTER 89

CHAPEL, MIRROR ESTATE

TOMMY

The scent of roses filled the chapel as Tommy stepped inside with Mia, their fingers intertwined. Mirror Estate's chapel was intimate yet elegant, its stained glass windows casting colorful patterns across the polished wooden pews. Flickering candles along the aisle illuminated the quiet joy on the faces of those gathered.

Mia sighed. "It's beautiful."

He squeezed her hand. "Olivia wouldn't have settled for anything less."

The guests were a close-knit group, an interwoven blend of family, friends, and colleagues. There was no strict division between the bride's and groom's sides, just people who had been through enough together that their lives were entangled.

In the front pew, Dylan sat between his grandmother and Lily, looking far more relaxed than Tommy had ever seen him. Lily, radiant with happiness, whispered something to Dylan, and he smiled before elbowing her.

On the chapel's other side, Sister Marie, Lily's godmother

and Olivia's best friend, dabbed at her eyes with a lace-edged handkerchief. She had flown in from Hong Kong for this, and the moment clearly meant as much to her as it did to Olivia.

Fr. Phil, standing before the altar in his vestments, lifted his hands to begin the Nuptial Mass.

The words rolled over Tommy, the priest's deep baritone filling the chapel. Something was sacred about the moment— not just because of the vows, but because Olivia and the senator had fought for this. They each lived through trials that could have left them broken, but instead, they found strength in one another.

When the vows were exchanged and Olivia and the senator sealed their union with a kiss, the chapel erupted in applause, a ripple of warmth that spread through the gathered guests.

Mia moved closer to Tommy. "Now that's a love story."

"Yeah." He looped her arm through his. "And now we party."

After an hour of pictures, they trooped to the Mirror Estate. The grand room had been transformed into a reception hall fit for royalty. String lights twinkled above, gleaming over the space. Round tables draped in white linen ringed the dance floor, and a live band played smooth jazz.

Lorraine's Kitchen had catered the event, ensuring the food was nothing short of spectacular. But tonight, Lorraine herself was here as a guest, sitting with her husband, Connor, and their young son, Sean. The catering team, made up of her trusted staff and a few temp workers, had taken over, allowing her to enjoy the evening.

Tommy led Mia through the crowd, making introductions as they went. They said hi to Fr. Jeremy and Ms. Carol.

"All right." Tommy grinned. "Time to meet the VIPs of our strange and tangled circle."

First, he introduced her to Clara and Dr. Khoury, who stood with their children, Faith and Jason.

Clara clasped Mia's hand in both of hers, her face aglow. "I'm so glad to meet you. Olivia speaks highly of you."

After sliding her hand free, Mia tucked her hair behind her ears. "I'm starting to think Olivia's been talking about me more than I realized."

Dr. Khoury winked. "That's how you know you're in."

Next, Tommy guided her to Kyle, Ron's son, and his girl-friend, Grace.

Kyle gave Mia a once-over before raising his glass to her. "Heard about your escapade."

"I wish it hadn't happened."

They moved on to Eva and Alex, who stood near Max, the majordomo, and his wife, Kate.

"Finally, we meet." Eva hugged her.

Flushed, Mia stepped back. "You say that like I'm some urban legend."

Alex took a sip of wine before saying, "You'll learn there's no secret in this community."

Nearby, Max and Kate stood together, observing everything with the attentiveness they were known for.

"I'm sure you remember Max from last week, and this is Kate, his wife," Tommy introduced.

"Welcome to the chaos." Kate, who had a softer demeanor, patted Mia's arm.

Mia snatched a cocktail from a server's tray. "I think I like it already."

And then—an unexpected sight.

The cool and composed Kyle froze mid-conversation, his eyes widening as his father, Ron, walked in with none other than Kyle's mother, Sheila. The two had been divorced for ages.

Ron had stood as the senator's best man. Sheila had been the wedding coordinator, hadn't she? They had to be here before everyone, but they must've wanted to make an entrance.

"Watch this." Tommy nudged Mia.

Kyle's jaw practically hit the floor. He gasped. "What is happening?"

"Looks like your folks are playing nice." Tommy grinned. "Isn't that sweet?"

"Close your mouth." Grace nudged Kyle. "You'll catch flies."

He groaned. "This wedding just got a whole lot more complicated."

The evening flowed into the first dance. Olivia, elegant in her gown, glided along in the senator's arms, the two lost in their own world.

Mia nestled against Tommy's side. "They look happy."

"They are." His chest swelled.

After the applause and cheers, guests joined the bride and groom on the dance floor, the band picking up a more upbeat tempo. Lorraine and Connor swayed together, while their son, Sean, tried to convince Lily to dance with him.

Max and Kate, ever composed, danced in a quiet corner.

Tommy spun toward Mia to ask her to dance. But his gaze caught something else.

Near the terrace doors, Fr. Phil slipped out, his vestments long since traded for a simple black suit. His shoulders were relaxed, but a thoughtful weight slowed his steps.

During the first dance, Phil noticed a shadow outside.

Over the past week, he'd taken the time to think, review all the intel files, and listen to the audio recordings again. And now, he believed he had identified the fourth person, the guardian, the disguised voice. His certainty had only grown after Jeremy confirmed how he had known to come to his rescue that night near the rectory. And, of course, there was Ron's cryptic call, warning him of his abduction.

In seeking the Lord's guidance, Phil had asked, "Is it possible?"

The answer had come: *"Seek, and you will find."*

Now, slipping out after the first dance, he followed the shadow.

Then—

There he was.

His back was to him.

The height was right. The age was right. The gait—almost familiar, yet different. But it was something else—the way he carried himself, the way he stilled the moment he sensed Phil's presence.

The shadow pivoted.

The face wasn't as he remembered.

A beat of silence stretched between them.

Then Phil spoke. "Are you ever going to tell Dylan?"

In case you missed it, you can download book 1, *Buried Secrets - Where It All Begins,* or any previous books you've missed.

THANK YOU!

Thank you for diving into *Shadowed Secret*! Writing this story has been such a wild ride and knowing that you've spent time with the cast means the world to me.

I hope you loved reading it as much as I loved writing it. If you'd be so kind as to leave a review on Amazon and/or Goodreads to share your impressions with others, I would greatly appreciate it. Your insights will help other readers find the book.

BONUS SCENES

BONUS SCENE 1

EDMONDS, WASHINGTON

MARGE

The late afternoon sun cast long shadows over the field, stretching the silhouettes of running children across the crisp green grass. A whistle blew through the mix of cheers and scattered conversation among the parents gathered along the sidelines.

To avoid recognition, Marge Beaumont chose a seat at the next field over, where another game was taking place. From there, she could watch the boy while blending into the crowd. Sunglasses shielded her eyes, but she kept her head lowered enough to avoid drawing attention. Her shoulder-length hair moved with the occasional breeze, free and untamed, a contrast to the restrained emotions swirling beneath the surface.

She wasn't supposed to be here.

And yet, here she was.

Her gaze followed the boy—Number 5—as he darted across the field, his dark hair flopping with each hurried step. He was fast. She had to give him that. His limbs were lanky, his movements eager but lacking the coordination that would come with time. He was smaller than some of the other boys, though he didn't seem to notice or care. He ran hard, fought for the ball, and, surprisingly, managed to score two goals.

Not bad.

But when he was in the net as goalie, he was all instinct and no strategy. Twice, the other team found the gaps and slipped the ball past him before he could react. Both times, his shoulders dropped a little, but he never stopped moving, never gave up.

Resilient.

Marge adjusted her sunglasses, scanning the crowd again. No mirrored reflection stared back at her. No sign of the woman she had been trained to hate.

She had known that. She had ensured it.

The boy's mother was at work—Marge had checked, double-checked, and confirmed it herself before stepping foot on the field. Instead, the boy had arrived in a minivan with his best friend's parents, the kind of wholesome setup that should've felt foreign to her. But as he laughed with his buddy, adjusting his too-big jersey and wiping sweat from his forehead, she found herself... studying him.

Was this what it was like to have a child?

She had no frame of reference for it.

Love was never something she'd been taught, not the way normal people understood it. Her childhood had been about conditioning, about allegiance, about proving her worth through obedient precision. Emotions—real, unfiltered emotions—were weaknesses.

And yet...

There was no anger when she looked at him.

She was supposed to hate this boy. She was supposed to hate his mother.

Instead, an odd, hollow curiosity intruded. A strange, detached awareness that this child had come from the same bloodline.

Her bloodline.

The game continued, the rhythm of the match fading into the background as she sat still, watching him. He didn't know who she was, didn't even know she existed. She was a ghost to him—just as she was to the rest of the world.

And maybe that was for the best.

The whistle blew again. This time, it was final. The game was over.

Marge blinked. She'd lost track of time, too absorbed in her thoughts. She needed to go.

She stood and adjusted her sunglasses, preparing to turn away when—

"Mommy? Is that you?"

The words shot through her like a bullet.

Her breath hitched.

For a split second, just a fraction of a heartbeat, she froze.

Then she turned.

The boy stood near the field's edge. His dark eyes squinted in her direction, and one hand shielded the sun from his face. His expression held an uncertain hope, the kind only a child could have, the kind that *expected* the world to make sense.

A sharp pivot. A controlled stride toward the parking lot. She was moving before she processed it.

Her heart pounded, her muscles tensed, but she didn't run. That would draw attention. She just walked—fast, precise, as if she had somewhere important to be.

Her car was parked two blocks away—another precaution, another layer of distance. She reached it in record time, yanked open the door, and slid in before forcing herself breathe.

Her hands clutched the wheel.

That had been too close.

Too careless.

She shouldn't have come.

She exhaled, long and slow, pressing her head back against the seat.

What had she been thinking?

That odd, unfamiliar sense of protection curled around her like an unwanted ghost.

No.

She couldn't afford to feel that.

Her fingers tightened on the wheel as she forced the thought away and jammed the key in the ignition.

The engine rumbled to life, masking the echoes of the boy's voice still ringing in her ears.

She drove away without looking back.

BONUS SCENE 2

WEDDING RECEPTION

OLIVIA

R umbling laughter and clinking glasses blended with the
string quartet as the wedding reception wound down.
Candles flickered in the grand room, casting a warm glow over
the clustered guests, savoring the final moments of the night.
Olivia took a breath, soaking it all in—the love, the joy, the sheer
amazement that she was finally—*finally*—married to the man
she had loved for over two decades.

Simon stood a few feet away, engaged in conversation with
Ron, his dark suit still crisp despite the long night. Every now
and then, he glanced her way, that knowing smile curving his
lips, as if reminding her this moment was real.

She barely had time to register the rush of footsteps before
Lorraine appeared beside her, holding up a sleek champagne
bottle. "A British couple left specific instructions to give this to
you on your wedding night."

A British couple? Had to be Raven and Falcon.

"Thank you." Olivia took the bottle, fingers trailing over the elegant label. Tied to the neck was an ivory card with a hand-written message:

"Congratulations, mate!"

No signature. Not that she expected one. The life of an intelligence operative rarely allowed for sentimental gestures beyond the cryptic. This was them, down to the last detail.

Simon stepped up beside her. "Should we open it?"

She shrugged. "Sure, if you want." Then, noticing his expression, she tilted her head. "I saw you talking to Marie earlier. Looked serious."

"Hmm…" He slid an arm around her waist and scooped her closer. "I'll let her tell you. It's sort of my wedding gift to my lovely wife."

Ah, the suspense. Olivia narrowed her eyes at him, but he merely took the champagne bottle and began working on the cork.

Fine. If he wanted to play mysterious, she'd bite.

She strode toward Sr. Marie, who was standing near a dessert table peeling the wrapper off a truffle.

"Marie." Olivia folded her arms. "Care to tell me what my husband is up to?"

Sr. Marie startled, nearly dropping the chocolate. "Oh. Um." A pinkness tinted her cheeks as she glanced toward Simon. "He told you to ask me?"

"Yes. And judging by your face, it's something big." Olivia leaned in and nudged her dear friend. "Come on. Out with it."

Marie sighed, then straightened her posture. "Simon has been working behind the scenes for months. He's already started the paperwork and process to have me reassigned to the orphanage school when it opens."

"Wait." Olivia gasped. "You mean you'll be moving *here*?"

Marie beamed, a shy smile curving her lips. "He arranged everything. I'll be the school principal. Two other sisters from my order are joining me. They're based in Florida. I'll be arriving earlier as there's a lot to do, hiring staff, setting up the curriculum, and everything else."

Before Olivia could process words, a high-pitched yelp pierced the air.

"Hurray!"

Lily.

Her daughter had overheard everything and was now bouncing in place, practically vibrating with excitement. "You're moving *here*? For real?"

"Yes, for real." Marie laughed, nodding.

A second later, another squeal joined the first.

"Did I just hear that right?"

Clara.

She had been nearby and now rushed over, eyes wide. "Marie, you're really coming here?" When Marie inclined her head, Clara threw her arms around her childhood best friend, hugging her tight. "This is the best news ever!"

Olivia's chest swelled as she watched them, watched the pure, unfiltered happiness lighting up their faces. It was a moment she hadn't even known she needed—one more piece of her past coming home, finding its place in the life she was building.

She turned away from the commotion and searched for Simon pouring two flutes of champagne at their table. She hurried to him, her heart nearly bursting. As she reached him, she didn't stop. She threw her arms around him and smacked a grateful kiss to his lips.

He chuckled against her mouth. Then, steadying them both, he pulled back enough to look into her eyes. "I guess you liked my gift."

"Like it?" She tightened her grip around him. "I love it. Thank you, Simon. Thank you."

BURIED SECRETS –
WHERE IT ALL BEGINS

A SUSPENSE THRILLER

BOOK 1 OF
MIRROR ESTATE SERIES

SNEAK PEEK

32 YEARS AGO

"Took care of the cop."

"Good. Found the evidence?"

There was a pause. "Not yet. Not anywhere in his house."

"Find it!"

No more needed to be said. They knew what was at stake.

CHAPTER 1

FINAL GOODBYE

SEATTLE

Dylan Roche didn't recognize half the people shaking his hand, and the ones he did spoke in hushed voices, careful not to say too much. He nodded, numb, as water dripped from the cemetery's oaks onto the mourners below. His black suit—borrowed from Tommy—fit well enough, though the sleeves hung a little too long.

After the final prayer, Fr. Jon approached. "Your mother always made time for Adoration before her shifts, even if it was just fifteen minutes. I believe her faith shone in a special way. You might be surprised how many lives she touched by being there."

"She was a wonderful woman." Mrs. Patterson from the apartment next door shook his hand. "Always so quiet, so polite."

Dylan nodded. "Thank you for coming."

"Dylan." Tommy appeared at his elbow as the last mourners drifted toward their cars. "You holding up okay?"

"Yeah." The word came out hoarse. Dylan cleared his throat. "Thanks for being here."

"Where else would I be?" Tommy straightened his tie. "Listen, my folks wanted me to tell you again, anything you need, just let us know. Mom's already made three casseroles for your freezer."

Dylan managed a smile. "Tell her I appreciate it."

They walked toward the parking area, gravel crunching under their feet. The cemetery was too quiet, like all sound had been muffled under wet wool. Dylan glanced back once at the grave, marked now only by a temporary placard. The headstone would come later.

"You sure you don't want to come back to our place?" Tommy asked. "Dad's grilling. Mom made that potato salad you like."

"I should head home. Sort through some things."

"Okey dokey." Tommy fished his keys from his pocket. "But seriously, don't be a hermit. Call me if you need anything. Even if it's just to talk."

About to respond, Dylan stopped when movement caught his eye. A woman stood beside a marble angel statue about fifty yards away, partially hidden by its wing. She wore a dark coat, her hair pulled back. From this distance, in this light...

His heart stopped.

"Mom?" The word slipped out before he could catch it.

Tommy followed his gaze. "What?"

Dylan blinked. The woman shifted a bit, and for one impossible moment, he saw his mother's profile. The same delicate nose, the same way of holding her head when she was thinking. But that was impossible. He'd just buried her.

"Dylan? What is it?"

He looked again. The woman was gone.

"Nothing." He rubbed his eyes with his palm. "Thought I saw... never mind. Just tired."

Tommy studied his face. "You sure you're okay to drive?"

"I'm fine."

But he wasn't. As they reached Tommy's car, Dylan couldn't

shake the feeling someone was watching him. The sensation crawled between his shoulder blades like a cold finger tracing his spine. He turned in a slow circle, scanning the cemetery grounds.

Empty.

"Let's go." Tommy got in his car. "See you at the reception hall."

All Saints' reception hall smelled like coffee and casserole. Dylan sat at a folding table, picking at a paper plate of food while neighbors, coworkers, and church friends shared memories of his mother. He should have been listening, should have been grateful for their kindness. Instead, he kept glancing toward the windows.

One older man approached with a firm handshake and a rough voice that carried unexpected tenderness. "I used to come into the restaurant every day—same booth, same order. Your mom was the only one who ever got it right. I wasn't always… the easiest customer. But she never flinched. Gave it right back when I needed it. In a good way. She had a way of making you feel seen."

"Thank you." Dylan smiled.

The man nodded. "Here's my card with my personal number. Take care now, young man."

After he walked away, Dylan picked up the card from the table. Frank Rogers, Attorney. He put it in his pocket and resumed eating.

The stories painted a recognizable picture of his mother— kind, hardworking, reliable. But they also highlighted how little these people knew her. No one mentioned her late-night sketching, her rearranging the furniture when she was worried, or her humming while doing dishes.

"Dylan?" Tommy dropped into the chair beside him. "You're not eating."

"Not hungry."

"Mrs. Chen brought those little sandwich things you like." Tommy's eyes narrowed, the same look he'd worn in college when Dylan had struggled through calculus. "How much did you have to borrow?"

"What?"

"For all this." Tommy gestured around the room. "Funeral home, burial plot, catering. Your mom didn't have savings."

Dylan set down his fork. "I didn't borrow anything."

Tommy's eyebrows rose. "Come again?"

"Life insurance. I didn't even know she had a policy." Dylan reached into his jacket pocket and pulled out a folded check stub. "Check came in the mail two days ago."

Tommy took the stub and examined it. "Atlantic Mutual. Never heard of them." He frowned. "Did you file a claim?"

"No. It just showed up."

"That's weird, man. Insurance companies don't usually cut checks before you submit a death certificate and fill out their paperwork. Trust me, I've seen enough estate settlements to know."

Dylan shrugged. "Maybe someone at the hospital called it in. I don't know how these things work. The check cleared. And I looked. It's not one of those scams—once you sign here, you agree to this loan or some such nonsense."

"Still strange." Tommy handed back the stub. "You have all the luck, though. Remember that scholarship? The one you didn't even remember applying for?"

"Oh, come on." Dylan put his hands up. "Do you know how many of those applications I filled out? Mom was so worried the federal grant wouldn't cover everything. You can't expect me to remember every single one."

"No, but…" Tommy cuffed Dylan's shoulder. "Both times, money appeared right when you needed it most."

Before Dylan could respond, Mrs. Patterson approached with a covered dish. "Tuna casserole for later." She set it on the table. "And, honey, I wanted you to know your mother was proud of you. She used to brag about your job, how well you were doing."

"Thank you."

She patted his arm and moved away.

Dylan slid the casserole farther away, throat tight. His mother had been proud of a management trainee position that barely covered his living expenses.

"Ready to go?" Tommy pushed back his chair.

Dylan nodded. As they gathered their things, that watched feeling returned. He glanced toward the church entrance and froze.

A woman stood in the doorway, backlit by afternoon sunlight. Dark hair, familiar posture. She raised one hand, a wave of acknowledgment, then stepped back into the light and disappeared.

"Did you see that?"

Tommy looked toward the door. "See what?"

The doorway stood empty.

Dylan's pulse hammered in his ears. "Nothing. Let's go."

But as they walked to the parking lot, one thought rang clear: *Someone's watching. Someone who looks exactly like Mom.*

CHAPTER 2

COMMUNITY CARE

The insurance check stub lay beside Dylan's laptop, crisp and official-looking. Tommy's words from the funeral echoed in his mind: *That's weird, man.*

Everything seemed weird these days.

The numbers on his laptop screen blurred together, three red cells glaring like warning lights. His phone buzzed on the table. He rubbed the bridge of his nose before answering.

"Yes, I know rent is due on the first. I'm just asking for a little more time. My mom passed away a week ago. I'm still trying to get things in order."

"I'm sorry to hear that. I'll note your account and give you a little space. When you're ready, we can talk about next steps."

"Yeah. Thank you." Dylan disconnected the call and sank into his chair. His fingers tightened around the phone. The kitchen wall across from him would make a satisfying target. He could picture the phone shattering against the faded paint, plastic pieces scattering across the linoleum.

"Breathe through it, Dylan." His mother's voice seemed to whisper from the empty kitchen. *"Surrender to the Lord!"*

He crossed himself and prayed. *Lord, I surrender myself to you. Take care of everything!*

The tension in his shoulders began to ease. When he opened his eyes, the crushing weight in his chest had lifted, replaced by a quiet certainty that he wasn't carrying this burden alone.

He opened his laptop again, the red cells still glaring at him. The bills hadn't disappeared, but somehow, they appeared manageable now.

After graduating from college two years ago, he moved back in with his mom to save money and helped her during her cancer treatments. Now, her absence became a physical hollowness in his chest, a constant reminder she was gone.

He glanced toward the refrigerator, half expecting to see her studying the doctor's appointment magnet, lips moving silently as she confirmed the date and time. *"Pick up your socks!" "Put the dishes in the dishwasher!"* She used to yell at him for leaving things all over the place.

Now, the kitchen sink gave its own scolding. He pushed back his chair to clean up. His mom might not have bothered to decorate the apartment, but she'd kept her place neat and tidy.

As he turned on the faucet, running water triggered something deeper. Her final days in the hospital room flashed unbidden through his mind. The antiseptic smell, the beeping machines, the way her small frame seemed to sink further into the bed with each passing day. He'd held her hand as she slipped away, her fingers cold and fragile in his grasp.

"I'll take care of everything, Mom," he'd promised. *"Don't worry about anything."*

Shaking his head, he chuffed out a breath. How would he keep that promise? The medical bills alone were staggering, and her insurance hadn't covered everything. His credit card debt loomed large, and the rent was already late.

It had always been his mom and him. She'd worked hard as a waitress to support them. Time and time again, he remembered her kneeling by her bed at night to pray. They'd had happy days in the apartment, celebrating his significant events such as confirmation and graduation. She had been thrilled when he snagged one of the few coveted management trainee spots in the two-year program of a well-known regional property management company.

His phone buzzed, interrupting his reminiscing. Not wanting to answer any more calls from the landlord or loan officers, he checked the screen, expecting to swipe the decline icon. But Tommy's contact flashed. They had been best friends since grade school. They'd gone on to the same college but pursued different career paths.

"Yo," Dylan said.

"Hey, are you still moping around?"

"No, I don't mope around."

"Are you dressed? My guess is you're still in your shorts and T-shirt. It's past noon."

He patted his T-shirt. "So? I have time off until tomorrow. Bereavement leave."

"Yeah, I know. But really, how're you holding up?"

"Meh." The one syllable carried everything he couldn't articulate. How could he explain that he woke up every morning forgetting she was gone, only to remember anew each day? That he'd picked up his phone twice already to call her before realizing she wouldn't answer?

"Tell you what. Why don't you get dressed and come meet me for lunch? I have something for you."

CHRISTMAS MURDERS

A Mystery

PREQUEL TO
KC & ORLANDO PRIME SERIES

SNEAK PEEK

CHAPTER 1

Detective Kylie Cassidy stood on the county courthouse's worn limestone steps and faced Aiden, who had a hand on her arm. "No, I've told you before. I can't help you."

The late afternoon sun cast long shadows across the wide plaza, glinting off the polished brass fixtures at the building's grand entrance. A gentle breeze rustled the old oak trees lining the sidewalk, carrying with it the faint sounds of traffic from the bustling downtown street beyond.

Aiden's fingers tightened around her arm, his eyes flashing. "Come on, KC."

"Let go of me." She tried to pull away without causing a scene.

A deep voice cut through the tension. "Is there a problem?"

KC pivoted. It took a moment to place him—the special agent she'd met at a crime scene months ago. *What was his name again?*

Aiden's grip held strong as he glared at the newcomer a few steps above them. "None of your business. Why don't you keep walking?"

The agent's eyes narrowed, recognition crossing his face. "Detective, is everything all right?"

KC took a deep breath and shook off Aiden's hand. "No problem here. Thanks for your concern, agent." She turned back to Aiden. "Go. We'll talk another time."

Splotches mottled Aiden's face. He lurched toward the agent, spitting out a string of curses. "This doesn't concern you, Fed."

"Aiden!" she snapped. "I said go. Now."

For a tense moment, Aiden loomed there like he might argue further. Then, with a final glare, he stomped off.

KC pasted on an apologetic smile. "I'm sorry about that. Aiden's...Well, he's a family friend. We went to the same school, grew up together. He can be a jerk sometimes."

He smiled. "No need to explain, Detective, uh, Casey, is it?"

"Cassidy. Agent?"

"Nathan Tanner. But you can call me Nate or Tanner."

"Okay, Tanner. My friends call me KC. That's probably why you thought my name was Casey. I hope you found the girl."

She'd responded to an auto accident early in the year only to find the driver killed execution style. Then Tanner and a younger agent showed up, working on an abduction case. She had gotten them a lead. In the end, the sheriff said to close the case when the perp was killed in a shoot-out. Details were murky.

Tanner squinted, then relaxed. "Oh, yes, she's doing well. Thanks for your help."

"Just doing my job. Are you, uh, here on a case?"

He stepped down two more of the courthouse stairs to stand level with her. "Yeah, testifying on a case. You? This is a bit far from your stomping ground, isn't it?"

"I dropped off some paperwork at the sheriff's office." She gestured toward the building down the street. Thinking of the transfer request sent her heart racing. If the transfer didn't go through, she'd be out of a job come New Year. "Then the ASA Sullivan wanted to discuss a case, so..." She shrugged.

"Well, I'd better be going before they send out a search party," he quipped and started back up the stairs. "Good to see you!"

She chuckled. "Same here. I should be going too. You never know. They might find a body in Pine Grove while I'm gone." *As if it would happen, it's more than likely a petty theft.*

An hour later, she drove toward the Pine Grove substation. The Christmas spirit enlivened the town. Retailers blasted Christmas music. A giant Christmas tree with hundreds of ornaments shimmered in the town square. In front of it, a Santa and elf picture station beckoned the kids.

She parked, went inside, and headed to her office and the stack of case files awaiting her. Shoplifting, vandalism, a domestic dispute—the everyday of small-town crime. She reached for the top file. Her gaze drifted to the window overlooking the parking lot. Her hand hovered in midair.

A dark SUV with tinted windows caught her attention. A Tahoe, if she wasn't mistaken. She'd never seen it before, which was unusual in a town where she knew most vehicles by sight. The car idled before pulling away, its movement almost too casual.

She frowned, a slight chill running down her spine. In Pine Grove, unfamiliar faces were rare, and anonymous vehicles even rarer. An out-of-town visitor, maybe? It was the holiday season, after all.

CHAPTER 2

T he next morning, KC's eyes snapped open at precisely 6 a.m., her body attuned to the rhythm of early mornings after years on the force. She swung her legs over the side of the bed, stretched, and padded to the window. The sun, just beginning to peek over the horizon, already painted the sky in soft pink and orange.

"Another day, another dollar." She slipped into her running shoes.

The crisp morning air nipped at her skin as she jogged through Pine Grove's quiet streets. Her mind wandered to the case files waiting on her desk, the interviews scheduled for the day, and the nagging feeling she was missing something important.

As she rounded the corner back onto her street, a flash of red caught her eye. A beat-up Ford Taurus crawled along the curb, keeping pace with her. Cop instincts kicked in, and she slowed, pretending to adjust her shoelace while studying the vehicle.

Aiden's car.

"No, I don't believe this." She straightened up, set her jaw, and marched toward her rented house. Just before reaching her front door, she spun on her heel, ready to confront him.

"Aiden!"

The Taurus was already speeding away, leaving only a trail of exhaust in its wake.

KC shook her head and blew out a breath. *Coward.* She unlocked her front door.

The hot shower did little to wash away her unease. As she toweled off, she caught her reflection in the mirror. Dark hair, hazel eyes, and a face that seemed to carry the weight of generations of law enforcement.

Her aunt's voice echoed in her mind: "You just turned thirty, still single. When are you going to settle down?"

She could almost see her disapproving frown, hear the litany of eligible bachelors from the church. KC had always wanted a family of her own, but she hadn't met Mr. Right yet. And she had a legacy to uphold, a calling to answer. Her father had died in the line of duty. Since his death, her mom struggled and finally succumbed to her drug addiction.

"Sorry, Aunt Mae," KC said to her reflection. For a woman who had never had children, Aunt Mae did a wonderful job as her substitute parent.

Thirty minutes later, KC strode into the Pine Grove Sheriff's substation, a paper cup of coffee in one hand and a case file in the other.

Deputy Johnson nodded a greeting as she passed. "Morning, Detective Cassidy. Your suspect's waiting in Interrogation Room 2."

"Thanks, Johnson. Any movement on the Hendrick case?"

"Nothing yet. But forensics should have something for us by this afternoon."

KC nodded, shifting gears as she approached the interrogation room. She took a deep breath, set down her coffee, and pushed open the door.

Gray Thompson sat at the metal table, his fingers drumming an impatient rhythm on its surface. He was younger than KC had expected, barely out of his teens, with a mop of unruly brown hair, and his gaze flickered around the room.

"Mr. Thompson." She slid into the chair across from him. "I'm Detective Cassidy. Thank you for coming in to speak with us today."

Thompson's leg bounced under the table. "Like I had a choice."

KC opened the file in front of her, taking her time as she flipped through the pages. She could feel Thompson's anxiety ratcheting up.

"Can you tell me about your relationship with Evergreen Financial Services?"

Thompson swallowed hard. "They're just some company I took out a loan with. What's this all about?"

She leaned forward. "We have evidence that suggests you've been less than truthful on your loan applications. Multiple applications, in fact, all with inflated income statements and falsified employment records."

"That's... that's not true," Thompson stammered, but his eyes couldn't quite meet hers.

"No?" She raised an eyebrow. "Because we have copies of the applications right here, along with statements from the employers you claimed to work for. Employers who have never heard of Gray Thompson."

"Come on." He rolled his eyes. "Everybody does that. It's no big deal."

People might inflate their earnings a bit, but they seldom made up employment. "It is a big deal. It's fraud. And it's illegal to lie on financial documents."

His face paled. "It is?"

"I'm afraid so."

He ran a hand through his hair, his composure crumbling. "I

didn't know what to do. I just needed the money, you know? My mom's sick, and the medical bills..."

Everyone had a sob story! She softened her tone. "I understand you might have been in a difficult situation, Mr. Thompson. But what you did is still a crime. However, if you're willing to cooperate, to tell us what happened and who, if anyone, helped you with this scheme, we might be able to work out a deal."

His eyes widened. "A deal? You mean, like, I wouldn't go to jail?"

"I can't promise anything." She spoke with caution. "But if you work with us, plead to a lesser charge, the judge might be more lenient. It's your best option right now."

He went quiet, his internal struggle playing out across his face. Finally, he slumped in his chair.

"Okay," he murmured. "Okay, I'll tell you everything."

A half hour later, she emerged, a full confession in hand. She nodded to Johnson. "Book him."

As she settled back behind her desk, her phone buzzed. A text flashed on the screen.

AIDEN

Need to talk. It's important.

She stared at the message. Her earlier encounter with his car stiffened her spine. She should ignore it, delete the message, and focus on her current cases. But curiosity got the better of her.

With a frustrated groan, she typed out a reply.

KC

One chance. Tonight, 8PM, Riverside Park. 10 minutes.

She hit send. Just what trouble had Aiden gotten himself in?

ABOUT THE AUTHOR

S.F. Baumgartner writes fast-paced Christian suspense thrillers. Book 1 of her Mirror Estate series, Living Secrets, was selected as one of the Top Picks in the thriller category at Killer Nashville, 2024. Her love for writing comes second only to her love of reading.

When she's not busy writing about complex characters, secretive operatives, and relentless agents, she spends her time binge-watching crime TV shows, such as NCIS, or playing with her cats. If you enjoy James Patterson's style—specifically short chapters—you'll love her Mirror Estate series.

To be the first to know about any sales, promotions, and new releases, sign up for our monthly newsletter. By subscribing, you'll stay informed about all the latest happenings and never miss an opportunity to explore this captivating world.

ALSO BY
S.F. BAUMGARTNER

Mirror Estates series

Buried Secrets, book 1

Living Secrets, book 2

Forgotten Secret, book 3

Tangled Secrets, book 4

Hidden Secrets, book 5

Shadowed Secret, book 6

Stolen Secrets, book 7

Box Set (Books 1-4)

KC & Orlando Prime series

Christmas Murders, a prequel

Fatal Invitation, book 1

ACKNOWLEDGMENTS

Publishing a novel is not a solo endeavor, and I'm deeply grateful to those who made this book possible.

A heartfelt thanks to Deirdre Lockhart at Brilliant Cut Editing, Kelsey Darling and Chelsea Lauren from Represent Publishing for their invaluable guidance and support. To the team at 100Covers.com, your stunning cover design perfectly captured the heart of this story.

I also want to thank the amazing beta and ARC readers—your feedback and enthusiasm were crucial in refining this novel.

To my family, your unwavering support has been my greatest strength. And finally, to you, dear readers—this book is for you. Enjoy the journey!

www.ingramcontent.com/pod-product-compliance
Lightning Source LLC
Chambersburg PA
CBHW020653110726
47901CB00001B/166